The Garden of Eloise Loon

Edna Alford

The Garden of Eloise Loon

OOLICHAN BOOKS
Lantzville, British Columbia
1986

Canadian Cataloguing in Publication Data

Alford, Edna, 1947-
  The garden of Eloise Loon

  ISBN 0-88982-082-1 (bound).
  ISBN 0-88982-080-5 (pbk)

  I. Title.
PS8551.L36G37 1986   C813'.54   C86-091303-1
PR9199.3.A43G37 1986

59,070

Publication of this book has been
financially assisted by the Canada Council and the
♪ Saskatchewan Arts Board.

Published by
OOLICHAN BOOKS
Box 10, Lantzville, British Columbia V0R 2H0

Printed in Canada by
MORRISS PRINTING COMPANY LTD.
Victoria, British Columbia

for Beth

"'*Sirs*,' said Tirian. 'The ladies do well to weep. See, I do so myself. I have seen my mother's death. What world but Narnia have I ever known? It were no virtue, but great discourtesy, if we did not mourn.'"

C. S. LEWIS

Grateful acknowledgement is made to the following
where stories from this collection have previously appeared:

Sundogs, Coteau Books, "Barbed Wire and Balloons," 1980.

Ambience, "The Lineman," 1982, CBC; "The Garden of Eloise Loon," 1983, CBC; "At Mrs. Warder's House," 1985, CBC.

Dandelion, "Five to a Hand," 1981; "Transfer," 1981; "Head," 1982.

NeWest Review, "The Garden of Eloise Loon," 1981.

Saskatchewan Gold, Coteau Books (Anthology), "The Garden of Eloise Loon," 1982.

Anthology, "The Garden of Eloise Loon," 1983, CBC.

Descant, "At Mrs. Warder's House," 1984.

Branching Out, "The Birthmark," 1979.

Anthology, "Head," 1985. CBC.

Dandelion, Tenth Anniversary Issue, "The Fathers of her Friends," 1985.

More Saskatchewan Gold, Coteau Books (Anthology), "The Children's Bin," 1984.

Glass Canyons, NeWest Press (Anthology), "Transfer," 1985.

Best Canadian Stories 85, Oberon Press (Anthology), "At Mrs. Warder's House," 1985.

I would like to thank the ♪ Saskatchewan Arts Board
and the Canada Council for their assistance and support
during the writing of this book. I would especially
like to thank Joan Clark and Nik Burton whose personal
support and confidence were invaluable to me throughout.

The author wishes to express her gratitude to Ian Garrioch
for use of his fine painting, "Choice," on the cover.

Contents

Head

Coming home I discovered there was no home left nor would there ever be again. Spruce and poplar and scrub were all in place along the way exactly as I had left them but my head was not where I had left it. I left it on a rock in the sun at the corner of the home quarter, the part not yet broke although I see there's been some breaking done on the next quarter to it. I left it on the big rock because I had never in all the years of my growing up seen the snow cover that rock. I don't know why. Maybe it had something to do with the wind.

At first I thought I might nestle it between some of the smaller rocks in the stone pile but then I remembered the snow even though it was very hot that day I left the head out in the field. And the head could smell the buffalo beans and the mustard and the stubby growth of wolf willow barely poking up out of the tall slough grass.

I wouldn't be so upset if I had thought about it before, about the chance the head might not be there when I got back. But I always kind of banked on its being there all that time looking out over the fields toward the sky, clear and cold most of the time. The clarity is what I mostly thought about. That there still was a place somewhere in the world where I could see things clear and from a long way off, like stars, I guess, or trees along the coulee hill, things like that and maybe more.

For it always seemed to me that if you could see one kind of thing clear and from far off—real things, natural things, trees and stars and such—then you could probably see the other kinds of things too, things you couldn't touch, ideas and feelings and who knows what, clear and from a long way off. I thought about that for years after I left the prairie, right up to now in fact. And I wasn't the only one who had that notion. Most of us did.

I met a fellow once in a Vancouver bar and he was reading a paper and he read me a story about city dwellers, how after a long time living in the city, they lose what they call their long-distance vision. These experts had figured it out. It's apparently because city people don't have to look so far, because they've always got something in the way of their looking, like brick buildings or glass skyscrapers or things like that. They get used to looking close; some of them, it seemed to me when I was there, got so bad they pretty well looked at their shoes most of the time or maybe it was the cracks in the sidewalk they were looking at and some of them in fact didn't seem to be looking out at anything at all. They seemed to be looking at themselves, as if their eyes had kind of revolved inside their heads and faced the wrong way altogether— toward their own insides—which is about as far away from long-distance vision as a person can get.

I was pretty smug in those days, knowing all the time I had my head back there on the bald-headed prairie—looking out at the sky and the fields any time I felt like it. Never anything to get in its way, maybe a storm some days, snow or rain or something, but always afterward the sun came back and all the clear clear sky lit up fine and green or even better, white and clean and fiercely clear. And all the time in the city when I'd see folks on their way to work looking at the grey pavement or the cracks in the concrete sidewalks or the buildings made of marble or cement like headstones, or maybe even at windows that gave them back a likeness of themselves, flat, without flesh, and sometimes wavy like the mermaids in the sea might look to a drowning man, I'd think to myself: *Now if only you could see the world the way I see it.*

I even told the guy in the bar in Vancouver about it. About the prairie and the way a man could see better there than anywhere and he laughed and picked up his glass and made a toast to the province of Saskatchewan and then he laughed again and emptied his glass, said the whole coast was nothing but a haven for prairie dogs like me and he said if things were so much better back there, how come the coast's full of all you

10

stubble-jumpers. Half the province of British Columbia is from the province of Saskatchewan. Which is why he was toasting it in the first place he says. And he says he doesn't mind having to look at the buildings or the roads, which he hears still aren't so hot back there, much less cedars and mountains and such—anything, he says, has got to beat nothing six different ways. And he says he's from around Swift Current himself and why don't I tell him another one.

I never gave a second thought to him or what he said till now. When the mill shut down this fall, I finally come back to the prairie, to see the folks mostly. Then too, I guess I had it in the back of my mind I'd take a drive out to the home place and poke around some. And also I guess I had it in my mind to just take a quick check on the head while I was out there.

Which was how I come to see they'd burned the home place down and planted rape. And when I come to the stone pile down by the slough, I see the birds have picked my whole head clean as a whistle, like one of those buffalo skulls you see in the museums. And in the holes that used to be the eyes, I see somebody took a couple of little stones from the pile and stuck them in. They'd hung a pair of spectacles with wire frames on it. Only there was no glass in them, no glass at all. Nothing a fellow could see through even if he did have eyes.

In Case of Rapture

I might have been able to prevent it if only I hadn't been too stubborn to go for help. Too stubborn or too proud, like him. Maybe both. They could be right. There may have been a way of stopping it. But there's no sense wasting good salt on old wounds. It's done. Save the salt for the smoker, for the whitefish, the jack, the doing down.

The most Sterling could do now is pick up the pieces and haul them off to the Trestle dump. But Sterling won't come. I'll bet you a dime on a dollar he sends Eli Divine from over on the reserve. He's used to cleaning up after this sort of thing. Happens now and again over there, not the exact same thing, of course, but close enough. Too close. Sterling himself wouldn't touch it—froze or thawed—for no man's money. One thing Sterling likes to do is keep himself real clean.

It isn't as if I couldn't see it coming. I could. And did nothing, absolutely nothing to stop it. Except sit with him day after day in his stinking mess of fish. That much I did.

He was Sterling's cousin so Sterling was the one I called. Likely he'll bury what's left. God only knows what they'll do with the house after what he did with it, I think now, looking at the wall. Anyway, Sterling can take it from here. I wash my hands of the whole thing. I only came back to the house to get the auger and the gaff. My new auger, eight inch, Scan Can. He said there was something wrong with it, figured it might have been sharpened on the wrong edge. I'll have to take it into town.

Over at the post office some said I should have taken him down to Battleford, to the mental, he having no family to do for him what family would have done, except for Sterling who really didn't give a damn when it came right down to it. What could they do for him there we can't do here, I said.

12

He's sick in the head, he has visions and everything, they said. He has reason, I said. That's his problem. Reasons. Nothing whatsoever to do with visions. You don't have to have visions to see what he sees. The ice is on the lake, I said. Tomorrow, I'll take him down to see the fish. Which I did.

The lake was just like glass, never froze that way for years. No snow. No snow at all. Just lace on the lip of the lake, that's all. You could see the jackfish feeding in the shallows, see the weeds, the stones, everything all below.

It's what he *knows* is the problem, I said.

That day we went out on the lake he said to me, "You took me everywhere when I was a kid, to town, all over. Remember?" How could he know it was almost all I ever thought of now. "Jesus, Jim, remember the time you took me up to Ivan's and he showed us the picture made of bones. All from the head of a jack. They call them pike, elsewhere, Jim, nothern pike. No offense," he laughed. "Took all those bones from the head of a bloody fish, if I remember correctly.

"'I heard there was a cross in the head of a jack,' he mimicked Ivan, making his voice low and scratchy like the old man's. Ivan's dead now. Course Lena's dead too. Anyway, Ian went on mugging and miming that time. 'And I waited,' he says, slow like Ivan, 'and-I-waited, and one winter, by the lord harry, I caught the right one. The big mother. Put her in a pail and pretty soon the flesh all fell away and there it was—the cross, by God. Not only that,' he says, 'there was angels and the wings of angels. There was the whip, the crown of thorns, the shroud and a whole host of other things'—there must have been a hundred pieces to it all told, eh Jim? I can't remember exactly. He may have said the number, but I don't remember now. All of them were fixed with glue on black velvet in a mahogany frame he carved himself. He had to special order the wood from Saskatoon, he said. A meticulous arrangement of these tiny tiny bones as if they had been ivory or semi-precious stones or something. And you and me, Jim, who wouldn't have been caught in a church in a million years, dead or otherwise, we stood stalk

13

still and gawked like dumb apes and listened as if our lives depended on it while he bloody well told us the whole thing right up to and including the angel wings and the end of the world. And when he came to the part about Gabriel's horn, a perfect minature horn, I must admit, a perfect horn carved out by God, old Ivan said, I'll bet my eyes were big as saucers. You had the logging permit then and I was just a kid.

"Six, seven years later I brought Axton and Davis up with me for the weekend. We were in pre-med then, and I took them over to Ivan's to see his collection. By that time, he had set himself up a kind of museum. Had all sorts of things, antiques and old machinery, and he was selling the frames, some with mirrors in them. Well, I'd already told Axton about the fish picture on the way up from Saskatoon and Ivan was only too happy to go through the whole thing again. He loved to tell the story of the bones. His face lit up like a Christmas tree when I asked him. The old guy really believed it, you know. He actually believed what he said.

"'Ivan,' I said this time when he got to the end of the story and Gabriel had blown his perfect horn—we'd had a few shots of rye back at the house before we came—'Ivan,' I said, 'you've forgotten something.'

'Nothing,' he said. 'It's all there. It's all in the frame. The way I got it set out there, anyone with eyes can see.'

'Ivan,' I said slowly—oh, I was a smart-assed son-of-a-bitch then with two whole years of university under my belt— 'Ivan, they eat each other. They're cannibals.' At first he didn't understand. 'The jack,' I said, cocky as all hell, 'they eat each other. And furthermore, I gesticulated dramatically —Axton started to laugh and had to turn toward the door but I was just hitting my stride—'they'd eat you, Ivan. Or me,' I said, 'if I went down'—which, quite frankly, I knew I never would, couldn't imagine anything of the sort.''

Dr. Ian Addison. The famous.

Well, he was whistling a different tune, as they say, when he came back to the lake this time and you wouldn't have wished what he brought with him on any man. He hadn't been home in years. In fact, I wouldn't have been surprised if we'd never seen him again. But for what happened to him along the way, I doubt we would have seen him drive up to the post office that first day. Mrs. Harrow, who sorts the mail and minds the wicket, didn't even recognize him. This time he came alone.

He'd gotten to be a busy man with not a whole lot of time left for friends. Still, I'd say you won't see the likes of him from here again for a long, long time, till hell freezes over, probably. The other day when I went in to get the mail, Jack Lune told me Ian had been nominated for a prize. Not the Nobel, he said, but something like that. Jack said Nobel was the one who invented dynamite so it couldn't have been anything to do with that. That wasn't Ian's line. Anyway, it seems this was something pretty big from what they said on the news. Jack heard it on the CBC. He always listens to the livestock report which is on around noontime, after the news, the price of baloney bulls and fleshy heifers trading on the open market and all that. I never had much use for it myself. I'm not a cattle man. Course, neither is Jack.

But for years, we never saw hide nor hair of the good doctor. He hired a man to come in and take care of the house now and again. Old man Addison built it fifty-six years ago. Ian grew up there. A big place for this part of the country. Two-by-twelve rafters, two-by-ten joists, fir. The best lumber money could buy. Most of it brought in from a big mill near Salmon Arm. Cedar so fine it would make a carpenter cry. Old man Addison and the wife travelled around quite a bit as did Ian later, brought back all kinds of things which they said was art—maybe it was. I never saw the real thing myself so you couldn't go by me. Plastered the floors with Persian rugs. I only got the oval one Mrs. Harrow made me out of rags. Plastered the walls with paintings from Paris and New York. Sculptures from Italy, china from Holland and the mother country. Some they said was delft. It was more a showplace than a place to hang your hat. A gallery is what it was, Jack said. I only got the white-tail deer head and the stuffed goose, a great grey.

And Ian as a kid never seemed to care much for the china and pictures and souvenirs and that sort of thing, either. Spent most of his time with me down by the lake. In a little A-frame hut I still have up in the bush. I did some logging in the summer, kept a trap line in the winter. Nothing special. A stove, a table, a loft for sleeping in. Ian liked to climb up in the loft and look out the little window over the well toward the lake. He said he could see the fins from there. Of fish, he meant. He always did have quite the imagination. Later, when he went to the high school in town, he told me fins meant something altogether different for him now—infinities or something, he said. Everlasting on and on. I never did get the gist of it. Some things change and some don't. For me a fin still belongs on a fish.

As a kid he never knew the word "no", which was a problem in some ways because he was altogether too cocky by half. And I guess he needed some of that to get him through all the trouble he had—or made. No, he never lost that. I think he was born talking, at least I never saw him when he couldn't and I saw him pretty small. He had dark curly hair that frizzled up in the rain. It was all grey when he came back. And he had a beard and it was almost all grey too.

He always thought he knew everything. He would listen to you tell him about something and then he'd spout it all back as if he had known it all along and was letting you in on something new. Only he'd change it in some way to make it his own. Ian had a plan, a two-part plan. The first part of his plan was to learn to fix or figure anything he wanted to, he said, up to and including himself, I later learned. The other part of his plan was to go to the moon like any other kid.

Old man Addison bought him a pair of skates and new brown breeches with leather patches on the knees, the kind that smell like cheese in the spring when they're wet. So I took him down to the lake one day. He was about six and the lake had been singing for a week freezing up. It was free and clear, just like the last time we went out. And he could look right through the ice and see the fish. I never saw such a look on the face of a kid. As if the universe had split wide open so he could see the insides of it all. He said he wanted to stay outside till nightfall so he could watch the fish swimming with the stars. He had it all figured out.

He said he could skate but he never had so I dragged out an old kitchen chair he could slide along on the ice in front of him so he wouldn't fall. But he grabbed the chair and threw it as far across the ice as he could, toward the point, and then he followed, ankles in, turning in small jerks, but never falling, not one fall. Before we went back to the house, I took him down to the boat dock and told him he could crawl in through the tunnel of icicles formed at the far end. He liked it at first, giggled for a while, and then I heard this whimpering above the wind. It was him. Ian Addison always was afraid of the dark. Which is maybe why he chose the way he did to make an end. Lots of light and lots of fire.

He loved anything to do with fire. The night his Uncle Harry set up the fireworks at the edge of the lake I had to hang on to the little loon the whole time for fear he'd run right for them, which is what he'd already tried to do. But even I have to admit the fireworks were over too soon. Showers of stars, just like being at the fair late at night, after the grandstand, everyone all around you looking up. Volcanoes, Roman Candles, St. Catherine's Wheel, Pirate's Gold and the lovely Prairie Flowers, green and red and gold and blue, all pasted on a snow white sky, beside the frozen moon. I think Harry bought them in Saskatoon on Twentieth Street, right near Joe's Cycle.

How do the mighty fall. I don't say he was mighty—high and mighty maybe, in his way. A lot of that was show, I've always thought—but then I had occasion to see him as some never have—whimpering and feeling his way through the icicles in the dark under the boat dock. The fact is he's the best we ever had. Straight A's, university, medical school, research, the works. He shot right up through it all and shone. Hearing him on the radio that night all the way from London, England, via the satellite, I never was so proud.

17

The thing about him I couldn't understand was him going in for a doctor in the first place because he was a scrappy little beggar as a kid. A boxer or a soldier, maybe. A doctor, I never would have guessed. Not only that, nobody got more pleasure out of burning bugs than he did. Or teasing cats to the point of torture. The fact is he was a crack shot. I taught him myself. And he was good on the traps. Swore off all that later on. Of course he didn't need the meat is what he said and that was so, I guess. And he wasn't really interested in the hides. I've been told a doctor makes a good dollar—though Ian told me once that as far as he was concerned healing's not really a thing that's bought and sold. I told him they should make good for what they do. We can't pay you enough, I said, there's not enough money in the world to pay you for the kind of work you do. But I still think all the skinning helped him when he picked up the scalpel. It wasn't as if he'd never done anything like it before. He sure as hell wouldn't have been squeamish like some. And even as a kid his cuts were clean, sure.

It's never been easy to figure the way a man ticks. The day I went over and found him cleaning the fish, the first day, that is, because afterward, that was all he ever did—never ate or washed—he started the funny talk. The stink was more than anyone could take. He had pails of rotting jack stuck everywhere and the sink was full of flesh and fish guts and scales. Around the chair where he sat was a pile of little white bones, as if he'd been shucking peas or baby corn.

"It doesn't fit," he said in the half whine tone of a kid who can't find his way home. "It can't fit." He wiped the back of his hand across his eyes. The hand was crusted white with a kind of brine from gutting the fish.

"I hope you're not trying to put them all back together, Ian," I said, trying to make a joke.

"What? The fish? No," he spit and laughed. I'd never seen him spit. Then he pitched the filleting knife across the room toward the stove. "Into one, maybe." Then, "No, Jim," he said sadly, "not even one. None. None at all."

It made no sense, even I could tell that. And I felt a certain tingle like an electric shock. It reminded me of the time I went over to the Gunderson place just after the missus brought the third baby home from the hospital in less than three years. When I pulled into the yard, she was throwing all the pots and pans into the rain barrel. Joe was running up from the barn trailing the oldest boy, Jerome. Same kind of tingle then as with Ian. But just for a moment with him whereas there seemed to be no end to the current with Mrs. Gunderson. Ian just got up and smiled normally, offered me a shot of rum and started talking high and mighty sense. He himself was already three sheets to the wind.

"You know, Jim," he said, "I figure there must be at least as many healers in the world,—taken as a whole. The odds say at least fifty per cent of us want it to stop." I must have looked puzzled—when I don't quite understand what's being said, I have a tendency to gawk. "The stock piling," he said. I was never very quick with him once he got past ten or so. He seemed to jump around a lot in his talk. He was hard to follow. "Nuclear arms, Jim. The military."

"Oh," I said, "oh that, again. Where'd you get the fish?"

"I bought them from an old Indian over on the reserve. He's got a net. Divine. Eli Divine. Some I caught."

After that it was every day the same. I never missed a day. I must have known at the time. But it's not the sort of thing you like to say to a man. For a while he made a lot of silly jokes but I figured there was no real harm in that.

Usually he had some new thing to say each time I came. "What in hell are you doing today?" I'd say.

"Reading entrails, Jim. Nothing of consequence. Why? You coming in for a drink or are you going to stay outside and freeze your ass all day."

The next time he would tell me to go away, he had other fish to fry. Or he would sort of hiss at me, "What the hell are you doing hanging around my place again! You're neither fish, nor flesh, nor good red herring," and he would slam the door in my face. One day I came and found he'd taken a piece of white chalk and wrote on the door "GONE FISSION".

He had a bumper sticker on the back of his station wagon. "IN CASE OF RAPTURE THIS VEHICLE WILL SELF DESTRUCT," it said, only he had stroked out the A in rapture and written a U over top of it with a felt pen. In smaller letters across the bottom, the sticker said "Rejoice! The end is near. Prepare." He said he got it in Edmonton. He saw it on the back of a truck there and tracked the guy down and asked him if he had any extras. The driver said yes he sure did and bless you brother or something like that. That's how far it's got, Ian said. That's how bad it is. I said people have been heading for the hills ever since there have been people and hills to head to. He was not impressed.

One afternoon I was sitting on a stool by the stove watching him fillet away just as if he were whittling a fine fan or the wooden puzzle chains some used to make, removing the tiny bones and placing them in the piles, one by one. He had a bread board on his lap and you know, you could tell he'd held a scalpel, fine quick hands. He had my big gaff lying beside him next to the auger on the floor and an electronic gadget for sounding out fish set up on the cupboard behind his back. He had a brand new Norseman ice-fishing tent still in its plastic sack, maybe a half dozen other small packages from Fisher's Department Store in Lloyd, tackle probably, hooks, maybe Rapala, probably Gang. "You look like you're out to catch the monster, Ian," I said. I wouldn't have put it past him, he was that cocky.

There were some who claimed they'd seen a monster in the lake. Some said it was a big black sturgeon trapped when the river changed course thousands of years ago. Some said it had a huge horse-like head. Others said it was prehistoric, more like a dinosaur, with tentacles like snakes or octopus' arms stuck out all over its head. Then there were those who believed it was only a figment of the fisherman's imagination, a trick of rye on water, they said. As if that somehow meant we shouldn't be so scared of it—because it came from the head, not from the water and didn't really come out of the middle of the lake in the early morning after a storm; didn't really feed on foam in the shallow water where some said they saw it from the shore when they were out walking. Mostly older folk. There were some who even pretended they'd already caught her. Or him. Or it. Or them. It all depended on who was doing the talking.

All of this new-fangled gadgetry was a far cry from the way I taught him to fish with a little willow pole, a piece of string and a bit of wire. He'd have been about four, barely in britches the first time I took him out jigging. I bored a hole in the ice, baited his hook with a smelt and told him to dip his line in the hole and jig. Up. Down. Up. Down. Up. Down. Up. Down. Pretty soon he taps me on the back of the parka. "Jim?"

"Yezzir," I says, "what can I do for you."

"This is too boring, Jim. This is really, really boring," he says. "I don't want to do it no more. Maybe we could go back to your place."

"Well, Ian, you can't just stand there," I says, "you got to call the fish." Which he did.

"Here fish fish fish," he laughed. "Here—"

"In your head," the crazy kid, "not out loud," I said. But it just so happened that time he hit it precisely right. By coincidence one came straight up through the hole. With the possible exception of the fireworks or Ivan's picture made of bones, I don't think I've ever seen his eyes or mouth opened up so wide. When I got back to the A-frame I laughed so hard I almost cried. (He could laugh at you when you were with him, but you couldn't hardly laugh at anything *he* did or he got mad.) Still, I got more kick out of that kid. Though right at the moment, I wasn't getting such a big bang out of him. I tried to reason with him about the fish. "You gonna smoke 'em, Ian?"

I taught him everything he knows about the bush. "It's a pity seeing all them fish go to waste," I said, "when you could smoke." I always use the demerara sugar. Leave the skin on the fillet. Add a little salt to the meat, then the brown sugar till it all sort of melts down in. Then it's ready to smoke. I taught him to find the diamond willow in the bush and make wood chips from it. I always found that was the best for flavour. For the smoke I use the spruce sawdust which I put on the bottom of the pan, the diamond willow chips on top. "We could use the old smoker down at the Lakeview Store," I said. "I could help you take them down." They have a burned out old fridge with a hot plate in it. Only takes about three hours and it's done. The racks are perfect to put the fish on. But he'd have nothing to do with it.

"Jim," he said quietly after a while, "did you know there is increasing evidence of a very high incidence of drug abuse, alcoholism and suicide in the medical profession." Of all people I should have known what he was trying to say. I'd known him almost since the day he was born. But I thought he meant he was into the sauce like his dad. Which he was. There were bottles set here and there all over the kitchen and a half empty case from the Liquor Board Store in the corner by the door. Hudson's Bay rum. With his kind of money, you'd wonder he'd be drinking rot gut like that but I guess by then it didn't matter what it was. He couldn't tell the difference. One night, three sheets to the wind, he said, "The loon, as a bird, is much maligned. The loon, my friend, is a family man. The way it carries the young on its back a little ways out from the shore, delivers them to the lake, as it were—the man loon, I mean," he laughed. "Teaching the little birds how to swim. Of course," he laughed again, "they share that, eh? The mother and the dad. One out, one back. You don't have to look at me as if I were a crackpot, Jim. You've seen it before. You've seen it yourself lots of times. What's more, they call to each other across the lake, that call so cold and clear it makes me ache. And then they come to each other, Ivan, —"

"Jim," I said, "the name's Jim." Lately, he'd taken to calling me by other people's names. Not all the time, but more and more toward the end. He seemed to have them all mixed up in his head.

"Jim, yeah, Jim," he said slowly, "and what was I just

about to—right. The loons. They come. To each other, Jim. They come together from all over the place."

He was just like a talking book. I should have carted him off myself right then, but you always think there might be a way for things to turn out right, especially when they seem to be heading hell bent in the other direction. And then again, you can hardly ever guess what's really going to happen if it's bad. Stays hid. The worst things seem to sneak up at first, I've found.

Actually, that was the first thing he'd said in a week that wasn't about the bomb. So it seemed to me a little on the light side, comparatively speaking. One day he told me there were enough of them in the world right now to kill every man, woman and child alive roughly forty times, maybe more if we really knew, he said.

"There's only the one," I said, "as far as we actually know."

"One what?"

"One time."

"So?" he says.

"So what in hell's the point of worrying about the other thirty-nine times?" I sighed. "I guess you're right. I guess we've got ourselves into a fine kettle of fish this time." That was the last I seen him smile.

"You figure the odds, Jim," and he was off and away again, talking in a trumped-up voice like he was an actor. "You are a man of wisdom, a man of experience," this in a kind of hollow, whiny voice as if he were trying to humour a little kid. He raised his arm, dipped and swept it close to the floor and up again, making an arc. "Actually, Jim, no one's laying bets any more. You only have to hear Caldicott speak once."

I have to admit I was getting pretty fed up with the fish and the stink and the mess and most of all with the crazy talk. "Who in the hell is Caldicott?" I said. A man can only take so much of it. "I know you give lectures all over the place, Ian, but you don't need to lecture me. It don't take a goddamn degree to see what you seen. And by the way, if you're having visions—which is what they say—keep them to yourself. Mrs. Harrow over at the post office has told every Tom Dick and Harry within fifty miles of the lake." His face turned almost sheet white and he took off his glasses which were smeared and spattered from the fish. His lower lip began to twitch a little, I'd go so far as to say quiver, even though he was a man.

He dropped his knife and reached down under the chair and pulled up a book, the cover mucked up with the slime of the fish like everything else around the chair, including him. He had two books; the one he'd left on the floor was a new one, *Fishing in the West*. Now I wouldn't mind taking a look at that one, but I'd seen this other book before. One time he even tried to get me to read it. He knew damn well I only ever read one book and that was *A Tree Grows in Brooklyn* and that was in 1945, just after the war. This one was called—I'm pretty sure it wasn't *First Aid*, which is more what you'd expect from a bunch of doctors—no, it was *Last Aid*. I'm almost certain though I wouldn't want to bet my last dollar on it. He just sat for a while stroking the cover of the book the way you see some stroking the Bible. Though he stroked the book, he looked at the ceiling, head back, breathing heavy. His eyes looked like the Greenfield municipal road map.

"Jesus, Jim, I got to the point where I'd tell them almost anything to spare the pain of telling them the truth. What the hell good to them was I then? What the hell good was I to anybody? I'm a doctor, Jim. That's what I am. And the worst thing was I was actually starting to meet people who could hardly wait. They were absolutely ecstatic we were so close to the end of the line.

"I walked out of a church in Calgary just before I came home for fear of what I'd do or wind up saying if I stayed." He paused. "Oh what the hell," he said, "that's a bald-faced lie, my good friend. The fact is I was run out on a rail. They called the police, if you want to know the truth. I don't know what happened to me. Nothing like that has ever happened before. I knew better. I'd already given my speech. I had my turn to speak and I took it and, I think, acquitted myself well—in my usual calm, professional manner, if I may say so. I have always had an excellent bedside manner, I might add.

"Anyway, when the pastor began to call up those who had been saved, I got this idea. I remember him starting to talk about General Jesus, if you can believe it, and all hell just broke loose in my head. I know it wasn't really his fault. He probably picked it up on the tube. But that's when I blew. Before I knew it I was up there beside him ranting and raving, too. 'Now! Now is the time! Will the real salvation please stand up. The man was right. It is in us. Will all the risen please rise!' I hollered. At first the pastor just stood there, mid-sentence, mid-word, mute.

" 'Are you now,' I cried, 'or have you ever been under the care of a physician. Will all those who have ever had a blood transfusion, surgery or medication of any kind please stand up.' Roughly two-thirds rose as one, but I wasn't satisfied. Clearly I had momentarily lost my mind. 'Now, all those,' I went on, 'whose sons, daughters, mothers, fathers, friends of all kinds.' More stood and I thought I could hear the first ones begin to hum. There was a kind of buzzing growing in my head, a humming like a hive, and a smell like lead and zinc, like the smell I remembered from when I was a kid and made the molten soldiers upstairs in my bedroom, home here, at the lake. Tin. It smelled like hot tin. It drove me crazy. Finally, waving my arms like some kind of lunatic, I yelled, 'Now all those who are not sure—innoculates—those of you who do not know if you would by now be dead or maimed or mutilate—tuberculosis, smallpox, malaria, diptheria, polio, tetanus, influenza—need I go on?'

The remaining rose. They all stood. Swaying before me. A steady hum. All but one. The pastor who had been standing beside me all that time sat down. 'You,' I yelled at him, 'it's your turn!' And then inexplicably I did it, for there was no excuse, really, when I look back—they do this business of calling up the saved all the time, Jim, it's part of their religion. We have freedom of religion in this country, for God's sake. I had no right to mock them. None. They know

25

too. They must be as frightened as I. Anyway, I did it. I lunged at him, knocked him down backward on the platform and I remember very clearly now—is there no mercy here, Jim? Amnesia? Morphine? More rum?"

Ian grabbed the bottle and tipped it toward me and I drank some. Then he took it back and tipped her up.

"I scrambled after him," he went on, "and jumped on him and started pounding and yelling at the top of my lungs. I don't even remember what I said. And the humming, that dreadful hum grew louder, to a deafening din. Finally some men from the front row came and pulled me off of him. I'll never forget the look on his face, that fear, the plaster bastard face, like a cast. And sometime after that, the police came. I confess by then I'd completely lost track. I don't remember how long it took." He tipped the bottle again. And I drank with him until he was almost calm.

"They called my friend," he said, "I asked them to. He flew in from Detroit. Another doctor. I'd worked across the States with him last year, did nine, maybe ten colleges with him. Before I came back home." He paused. "Believe it or not, Jim, there are a fair number of people praying in the opposite direction and making money at it to boot, in the name, incredible as it might seem, of a healer, no less. A humanitarian. Indifference, yes. Psychic numbing, yes. But this, this pulling for the horsemen—" He pitched the empty bottle against the wall and it broke clean with a crack.

I have to admit I was shocked. I was no expert on the subject of the horsemen or on Ian, either, I realize now. And as Ian said, I wouldn't be caught dead in a church if I could help it, but I always thought that's why the Man come in the first place, to stop all that—I mean if you were to go by what he actually said. And it seemed to me from what Ian said that the horsemen more or less threw a monkey wrench into the whole thing. You have to wonder who dreamed them up in the first place. Whoever it was, I don't think he was in much better shape than Ian and Ian was in enough pain already without me putting in my two cents worth. From the look of his face which was all white and tightened up, his eyes like small black beads, I could see I'd said too much already. Evidently he was winding up again. "Why don't we go out for a walk on the ice while she's still free," I said. "Do you good to get out." I said this very quiet as if he were one of his mother's trinkets brought over from the old country, something made of glass that I could maybe break if I spoke too loud.

Thing is sometimes he was this way and you could at least reason with him a bit; he'd talk some sense, not good sense maybe some would say, but sense. And sometimes he'd take off the other way. For one thing, I know he stayed up all night long. Some seen his light burning when they passed by his road just before dawn on their way to work in town or hauling grain. And what he was doing was anybody's guess. Except that it had to do with the fish. By the second week the piles of bones had grown and spread all over the kitchen floor and into the parlor.

One day I come in and seen he took all the pictures off the wall. What he'd done with them I wouldn't want to testify but there was still fire in the burning barrel out back when I came by. When I got near enough to the house that day, I could hear him singing at the top of his lungs. "Oh you can't get to heaven/ with Superman/ For the Lord he is a Batman fan/ Oh you can't get to heaven/ with Superman/ the Lord he is a Batman fan/ Ain't a gonna grieve my Lord no more—" and so on. I remember he used to sing it as a kid sometimes when he got off the school bus. Funny how sometimes when a man gets into enough trouble, he goes back to being a kind of kid.

I don't think I ever seen him so happy. Singing and laughing. The fact is he'd taken to pasting the fish bones on the parlor wall, in all sorts of ways, patterns, he says, but to me they didn't make any sense at all. "You see, Jim," he says, pointing at the wall like a kindergarten kid, his finger wagging, shaking his head from side to side and laughing, "they fit. They all fit!"

"*Nothing* fits, Ian," I hollered. "Nothing fits for you any

27

more. Not one goddamned thing. I see sweet bugger all in a bunch of bones. I'm not Ivan and you're not God and it's about high time you tried to snap out of it." He started to cry. It's the only time I ever really lost my temper with him though the good Lord knows he tried my patience lots of times. And the fact was I knew as soon as I said it that it was just as crazy to say nothing fit as it was to say everything did, like Ivan. Who knows? Who can say what another man sees?

All I do know is I couldn't stand to look at him any more the way he was. He had all the windows in the house wide open, the flesh of a thousand jackfish frozen in the pails and sink but still a stink that would knock a grown man down. He'd taken to wearing a skiddo suit over a filthy Irish knit sweater and a blue mackinaw. And he had on a red toque with a yellow stripe around the crown and a yellow tassel on the top. And the muck on his glasses. The glasses so thick. It seemed to me the more that boy read, the blinder he got. He wore brown rubber workboots with the yellow laces and eyelets and trim. They were open and packed with black felt, trailing bits of fish gut on the flaps. It wasn't the clothes themselves. I wear the same kind of thing myself except for the toque. I never liked a toque. I got a muskrat with the flannel flaps. It was the filth I found so bad.

Totally different from Jean Louis MacIntosh, though it's the same stink of the fish that reminds me one man of the other. Jean Louis was a young Cree guide I met one time up at Stanley Mission, north of Beyond LaRonge. I went up there with a wildlife painter once, Jake Wheat, a fellow who used to do the animals and birds around the lake. Especially birds—the snow and the great greys, loons and the red-wing, pelicans, herons, owls, Canada Jay and Blue. He'd have nothing to do with painting people. More and more I see his point.

We picked Jean Louis up every morning bright and early at this camp at the end of the lake. Piles of garbage and fish guts, filth the likes of which you never seen or smelled. Yet that boy, I swear, wore a clean, white, *pressed* long-sleeved shirt every day I worked with him. Immaculate. I never did figure out how he done it. Neither did Jake. And you could see yourself in the high shine of his shoes. Jean Louis wore black boots, army surplus. I remember he wanted a 22. I always wished I could have bought him his 22. Bannock and fishhead soup. I can still smell it. Jake called it jackfish stew.

One time Ian came back from school all in a heat about some doctor he met, a Dr. Johns, Howard Johns. Ian said he was the man who developed the cobalt bomb for the treatment of cancer at the University Hospital there in Saskatoon, back in the fifties. "That's what it's for," he told me, even then. "It's supposed to be for things like that." This is a long time ago now. The whole business works like nothing so much as a cock and bull story. A whopper if I ever heard one. You can see way back and all of it coming on and coming on.

Thing is with doctors, you expect them to be able to cure anything, even themselves. Once Ian brought Jerry and a South American fellow, Juan, I think it was, up to the lake. This was after they had graduated from medicine and they met up here to hunt in the fall. Geese. The great greys. One of them was in internal medicine, one in neurology and Ian, in the family practice, every one a specialist. They were proud of that. So was I.

I happened to have a hell of a bout of the grip when they came, but I figured never was there a better time to have it. When would I ever be among the likes again, I said to myself. Treatment fit for a king. They told me to take two aspirins and get lots of rest. Can't do a thing for you, they said. No cure for the common cold. And laugh. They hooted almost as hard as the time I told them about the allergy, about the fact that I'm allergic to humans,—not all of them, by a long way, only a certain percentage—and not all the time, either. I didn't really find it so funny, judging by what the blessed disease did to me, animal danders or whatever, but they got the biggest bang out of it.

The last time Ian and I went out on the lake there was more snow and we had to go on past the point for a clear patch. He seemed to be in a kind of daze that day though he was making pretty good sense. Too much travel, I thought. Too much pressure. Pretty soon he'll mend. It all takes time. It's too much for any one man. Anyway, we found a clear patch and we were both looking down, watching the big jack moving around and around past our boots. The ice was very smooth, as clear as a mirror, and I could see his face as if it were a photograph, shiny with a crooked smile. You could even see the yellow tassel on his toque. "It's you!" he said, just like that, whatever in hell he meant. The reflection, I guess.

"Swimming with the jack!" he starts again, the loony bastard. "It's you and me, Jim, swimming with the stars!" and he slaps me on the back and laughs. Midday. The sun so bright on the snow you could hardly see the shore. "Instead of an albatross, a cross!" he bellers to the sky. Crazy talk. High time to go back, I thought.

Thing is, later I was outside splitting wood for the stove and there were stars. Even if I'd been inside, I would have heard. As it was I had the best seat in the house, the whole show to myself. At first it was only a glow, like the end of a lit fuse on the edge of the lake. Then the explosion in waves, echoing through the air. And then the fire. Hardly moved the ice at all—and as for the sky, the northern lights held centre stage this particular night. Them and his precious stars.

That's what I said over at the post office yesterday. "Just like a kid," I said. "Something a kid would do. Sterling better damn well get up here and do something about it," though I knew Sterling would never come. Too bad. He hardly knew Ian at all. He'd be a good man for the job. He couldn't care less. "Well," I said, heading for the door, "I guess that's the end of that. But there's no doubt about it, he sure was smart as a kid, I'll testify to that. How'd you think he made it to the moon?"

"What the devil's come over you, Jim Gilchrist?" Joe said. "Ian Addison never went to the moon. It's all in your head. Don't tell me visions are contagious too," he laughed. "He was a M.D., for chrissake. Everybody knows that. I heard him myself on the CBC. They heard him all over the world. Top brass. Nothing but the best. Talking about the nuclear war and all that clap trap. Talking about friends of his who wrote this book.

"Said they wouldn't be here if the time come. No doctors, no nurses, no hospitals, drugs, nothing. He said he was doing preventative medicine, whatever that is in this case. Said that's all there was left for him to do. No cure for it, he said. Him and these other doctors don't believe there's any cure, if you can imagine that. Sounded like some new kind of disease, the way Ian put it. Another new disease, if you please. You can almost bank on it, same as every year they come up with a new insecticide or a new breed of wheat. As if we never saw a war before, as if we never went overseas. You really have to watch yourself nowadays. You can't swallow everything you hear hook, line and sinker. You have to think for yourself. And you have to wonder if there wasn't some percentage in it for the guys that wrote the book."

"It don't mean nothing to me one way or the other," I said, "none of it now. I got no use for history."

"Mounties up?"

"They come up with a man from the Department of Natural Resources and a doctor from Battleford in the DNR van. Took a look, pictures and all. Said they'd be sending another guy along, some big-wig from Saskatoon, this afternoon maybe."

"I heard he strapped it to his back. Where the hell'd he get enough for that? He should have used prima cord. He'd only need a little bit. Could have held it in the palm of his hand."

"No," I said, "they got the cord locked up in magazines. The RCMP keep a very close eye on that. No," I said, "he probably just bought a few sticks of dynamite off a seismic crew. Sometimes they'll sell it to a guy who wants to blow a beaver dam or rearrange the land. On the side. There was a crew working up on the reserve. Just before freeze-up. Figure there's oil up there. They already hit natural gas."

"Byjesus, they own the mineral rights on that land. Before

31

you know it, they'll be coming for the mail in Cadillacs."

"I sure as hell hope so," I said. "Maybe even get a post office of their own."

"Yes, they say old Ian was sharp as a tack."

"Too sharp," I said. "Sometimes I wished he never knew a thing."

"Come again?"

"I said I wished to God he never knew a thing. Or maybe the problem was he didn't know enough. Or not the right things, whatever they are."

Maybe I shouldn't have said it. You shouldn't really say the first thing that springs into your head. Sometimes you should stop and think, because you can't really take a thing back once it's said. But when you see a man you knew as a boy go up like a firecracker in front of your very eyes, you should be able to do something, or at least try. I just sat and watched, when it came right down to it, and for the life of me, I can't remember why. Too stubborn to go for help, like him. Too stubborn or too proud. The doctor who came up from Battleford told me they got ways of helping people like Ian if he could have just held on, if we could only have gotten him down into town, although they couldn't seem to do a whole lot for Mrs. Gunderson, now that I recall.

What's the point of standing here staring at a wall, I think, looking at what he done. I could stay here till the cows come home and it wouldn't change a thing. Save the salt for the smoker, the whitefish, the doing down. Still, I don't suppose I'll ever again see a picture wall made all of jackfish bones. I sure as hell hope not. Once is enough as far as I'm concerned. I must be getting old, for I feel as if I've already seen more than my share. One thing I do know for sure is you can't eat bones. I only come back to the house to get my auger and the gaff. Then I'm gone.

Transfer

He is there. In the shelter. Opposite the Chinook Shopping Centre. Simon is sitting on a bench in the shelter and when the bus pulls up and belches, he rises, moves toward the door unfolding. I watch the back of his head pass by me on the other side of the window. The hair is very dark, still with some brown, but very dark, a crooked oval edge around his ears, his nape. Why he has chosen me this time is a mystery. I am far from attractive.

When I see him come through the door of the bus I lower my head, look out the window at the empty shelter. But he has seen me. I know he has seen me and my face begins to burn. When I worked within the safety of the institution I wasn't afraid of this sort of encounter. In fact I would have "reached out" as they say. I would have said hello, asked how things were going and had he found a job. But what could I do now? To whom could I go for protection if need be, and what would I say? I saw him on the street? So what. He is entitled to walk the streets, ride the bus, the same as I. Yet I am afraid of him, more afraid than I ever was when I worked with him.

Things had gone badly for him last spring in group therapy and, consequently, for me. He was in the Young Adult Group, Monday, Wednesday, Friday, 2:30 to 4 p.m. But he couldn't tolerate any female in the group—even her very presence, no matter how discreetly she dressed, no matter how unintimidating her manner. He fidgeted, wriggled, began to rock his shoulders forward as if he were about to rise, his dark eyes wilder with every rock, his hands first gripping the arms of the chair, then fisted, then pounding, then back to gripping. Then he began to sweat, the water solid in spheres across his brow, along the sides of his nose, on his neck. His face turned very red and he began to smile—not noticeably at first, just a slight twist upward at one corner of his mouth. Just the hint of a smile, not to be mistaken for amusement. There was nothing pleasant in the smile or the high-pitched laughter which sometimes accompanied it. The smile seemed somehow separate from his face. And his behavior certainly had no bearing whatsoever on the group discussion at the time. When this process began I knew it would only be a matter of minutes until he bolted, slammed the door and left us with his empty chair again, yet another terrifying gap in the circle.

I wondered at first what he did after he bolted from the group until one of the group leaders told me he ran. She was in her car and had seen him running past the clinic and down the same street she was driving. She said he ran like a wild deer. She was going thirty miles an hour, she said, and she never passed him before she turned the corner, just watched the grey plaid of what turned out to be his only shirt disappear in the shadows cast by branches on the boulevard trees. Old trees, I remember, heavy with leaves. A kind of tunnel for him, I guess, a tunnel out.

For me it would have been a bus. Unsophisticated, dull, foul-smelling vehicles they may be, but I have to go everywhere on them. Buses are my tunnels. Which may be why I was so fascinated with Simon and the wild, cold smell of him, the rhythm of his running—for later I saw him myself, running. I stood by the window and watched until I couldn't see him any longer. Fascinated.

But this was within the confines of the institutional setting. Lately there is a tendency to regard madness as fashionable somehow, in films and books and television programs. And I have always tried to read, not only trade journals but as far as possible, the recent work of some of the better writers. Through the library, now more than ever, of course, because I have so much time on my hands. These days it's not unusual to see even the splintered, undecipherable speech of the full-blown schizophrenic passed off as a desirable form of communication between one human being and another, as if this could somehow help the situation, no matter how bad it's become.

This fractured language is supposed to mirror our fragmented world, I believe—its complexity and diversity. But if anyone were to ask me, I'd say the world's turned absolutely upside-down. These days you're considered crazy if you're sane. The theory being that no sane person could maintain her sanity in a crazy world. That's how far it's gone. On the other hand, I have yet to see words rise up off a page and bludgeon or rape or otherwise mutilate a human being as human beings will sometimes do to each other, more and more frequently, it seems. As Simon has been known to do on occasion. So words are safe—at least in this country—at least for the time being. They're about the only things that are any more.

It seems to me from my own work and from having heard about the work of my colleagues over a period of some years that madness is anything but attractive to anyone who has seen it. And splintered syntax and confabulation and mysterious opaque delusions are fine on a page which you can walk away from and leave whenever you choose—to shop, play tennis or bridge, go to the bar with your friends or whatever.

Right now I have to look back over my shoulder because I can't see Simon in any of the seats ahead of me on the bus. He must have taken a seat behind me. I look back. Apparently he doesn't see me looking back. But I see him. He has taken a seat near the rear exit on the other side of the bus, beside a young woman—a girl really, and very attractive I would say, with long blonde hair parted in the middle and clipped shorter near the ears where she has curled it. His face is red and I can see him shift from side to side, squirm, begin to smile. And I know what comes next. She doesn't, of course. But I do. No wonder I had to leave the clinic.

I worked in psychiatry for twelve years and I don't suppose I'll ever find anything I like better. But it got to be too much for me. Really, I'm not sure what got to be too much for me, the work itself or all my friends saying over and over, "I don't know how you can stand it, Elspeth Gardner! You're a tower, in my opinion you're a tower of strength!" I don't see them any more, of course.

Dr. Oster referred to my problem as rumination when we talked about the extended leave of absence early in July. I knew the word, of course, and I know that too much of it isn't good for you, clinically speaking, but very little seems to be good for you these days and rumination passes time at least. To hear them talk, nothing is exempt from the finger of doom—and no one. Coffee, spinach, maraschino cherries, baby beef liver, even the innocuous wheat germ is now suspect. A person could starve if she listened to everything they said. You're damned if you do and damned if you don't.

In my professional opinion, the rumination isn't serious. I believe it's realistic. I ruminate about one person and one only. Much of it I can chalk up to loneliness, or rather the difficulty I'm having spending so much of my time alone since I left the clinic. Lately I've become a little edgy, starting involuntarily at every sound, almost fainting when I hear the clatter of the mailman opening my mailbox to drop in something as unpernicious as a telephone bill. Yesterday I was almost turned to stone when a blast of hot air from the furnace lifted my living room drapes.

I'm justifiably edgy. I've been the victim of a series of telephone calls from this patient. Simon has been convicted more than once of rape and assault. I, being a woman, am naturally unnerved by these calls. I'm not overly endowed in any of the physical facets by which women are often judged. I'm not a young woman but not old either—thirty-seven to be precise. I am tall but thin, almost gaunt. I have good legs but a plain flat face and small eyes. My hair is brown. I have taken to streaking it with a brush-on peroxide concoction but it doesn't look professional. I'm one of those people who try out all the commercially heralded miracles and find afterward that I look worse than my former self and bear no resemblance whatsoever to the mythical "Cover Girl" or those among us who so indiscreetly advertise Cross-Your-Heart brassieres.

The disappointment of the hair, I have to admit, was a major one for me, which is clearly an indication of the kind of life I lead—"deadly dull and sedentary" as we used to say about the lives of some of the patients at work. I had hoped that by sprucing myself up a bit I might attract some attention.

Not that I do nothing. I'm out almost every day and night of the week. I belong to the Argyle Book Club. I do volunteer work for the mental health association. I even joined a mixed fitness class at the YMCA in the hope of meeting someone but, and I should have guessed, everyone there came in couples except for me and the plump woman who left her husband at home in front of the television set every Wednesday evening.

I'm not all that particular when it comes to men. My standards are not, as we used to say at work, unrealistic. Not too high at all. I just want some man, unmarried preferably, to take some interest in me as a woman. I'm willing to accept some warts. I don't expect miracles. I just don't want to be alone all the time. To put it simply, I'm empty in this department. And I say this in both the literal and figurative sense of the word. Pride isn't something I can easily afford these days.

I can't afford much of anything these days, emotional or otherwise, not on the salary they're paying me to lead that one godforsaken group at the association office. Mrs. Aimsley said my group would be starting at 3 p.m. this afternoon. I should be there with time to spare. I know it's tokenism—that they let me lead a group at all. I'm very closely supervised even though the rest of the staff pretend I'm one of them. The whole thing isn't particularly exciting but it's out and it's good to get out, we always used to tell our patients, even if it's only one hour a week.

I had to take the bus, of course, since I sold my car, and I hate riding buses on a day as hot as today. I don't mind so much when it's raining. You don't seem to see as far or as much when it's raining. And I had some trouble getting myself organized. I'd still be sitting there in my apartment, ratty housecoat and sloppy slippers, if it weren't for the call

37

from Mrs. Aimsley, which I resented. It's even less likely I'll meet anyone interesting at the mental health association than at the Y. Since Peter left to take the job at the General in August, I haven't seen a single man in the building. Mrs. Aimsley probably thought I'd sit there until the sun went down again, worrying, ruminating, if it weren't for her salvation call.

Nonetheless, I finally managed to roll the "Gentlemen prefer Haines" pantyhose up over my hips, again transform myself into a human ironing board with nylon legs. While performing this distasteful task, I couldn't help wondering what went wrong with Simon. He is a fascinating case, really. Why on earth does he phone me and write those odd odd letters which have been arriving regularly, wrongly addressed, my name misspelled, in pencil, grade school messy—but nevertheless deposited in my mailbox twice weekly (which may account for my fear of the mailman). And why is he sitting behind me on this bus. Coincidence, no doubt. The thing to remember in a situation like this is that you have to remain rational. That's the key.

I never really understood the boy fully. I call him a boy because he is only twenty-one or twenty-two years old although he has already been in enough trouble to last a lifetime. One thing I did understand was that Simon could be described as a "specimen", as the women say. When I saw him for the first time at the clinic last spring, he had just been transferred from one of the large provincial hospitals. He came to us as a day patient for follow-up. Then, I was very much in control of nearly all situations and with my customary efficiency, I took his name, address, no telephone number because he had no telephone (he must make his calls from a booth), medication he was currently taking or supposed to be taking, and his medical insurance number. I told him firmly but, as we used to say, in a friendly manner, that he was to appear at a staff conference the following Thursday at eight a.m. and should at that time be prepared to tell us what he hoped to achieve in the time he spent with us, his goals. What he meant to do with his life from here on in. Meaningful, constructive goals. Everyone had to have them. That was one of the rules.

Yet even while I went through the routine procedure of admitting him to the clinic, I was preoccupied by his appearance. He was very tall and had dark straight hair which had been cut recently, crudely and very short, in the hospital. He wore a grey plaid flannel shirt open at the neck. I remember he had a long neck. The sleeves of the shirt were rolled up three-quarter way, like a lumberman's but the shirt seemed to be too small for him and the cloth stretched tautly over what I remember as an enormous chest. He wore blue jeans which were baggy and which he had also rolled up unfashionably to expose the tops of a pointed pair of cheap black leather shoes.

His face was among the most perfectly formed I have ever seen on a human being and I remember now that I thought of him as a baby then—that is I commented to myself that he must have been a spectacular child. His eyes were evenly dark and almost round, perfectly set below his brow. His nose was aquiline and centred exactly, mathematically, above a full, warm mouth edged on the upper lip with only the hint of a mustache. He had no beard.

I remember too that he didn't seem to be aware of the effect his striking appearance might have upon me or anyone else. It was hard to believe that he had ever found it necessary to rape—to look at him you couldn't help but notice he had more than his share of physical attributes which would normally attract young women. He was restless. He didn't move around a lot, didn't pace as some do, but he kept shifting his weight from one foot to another and looking out the window, at the clock, at the paper on my desk, anywhere but at me. The only other thing I remember is the fear, my almost palpable fear of him right from the minute I met him. And I am certain that the young women he approached, though finding him initially attractive, would have been repelled by this fear as I was.

Contrary to popular opinion, few psychiatric patients generate this fear, at least not the sort of patients we were used to seeing in our clinic. Most of them were lonely, isolated people who needed help but would harm no one except themselves. But I was afraid of Simon, unreasonably, intensely afraid and I couldn't really have explained why if anyone had asked at the time. It was just a feeling I had, but if I had learned nothing else in this business, I had learned to trust my own feelings. And when I read the file which followed him from the provincial hospital—the long history of rape and assault, even in his early teens—I knew my feelings were entirely justified.

For some empirically unfathomable reason and by a process I would rather disregard as verging on the occult, every time I think about him or talk about him to anyone or even write anything about him in letters to friends in other cities, Simon turns up—within days. In letters or by phone, I mean, never in person until today. The thinking seems to draw him in somehow, just when I think I am rid of him.

The bus stop is very close to my apartment, only half a block away. I had timed my arrival exactly. I climbed the black rubber variegated steps, deposited my fare and asked for a transfer. The driver was wearing a cap, one with a shiny black peak which might have served as a mirror if it hadn't been so smudged with fingerprints. His sunglasses would have sufficed if only he had raised his head, but he didn't; they never do, it seems. He just ripped a narrow piece of paper from a pad and handed it to me.

I took it and headed for an empty seat about midway back, one with an open window beside it. I always have such an impossible time opening windows. One of these days I'll die of suffocation and I won't be the least surprised if it's on a bus. Especially on the longer trips through town on a day as hot as today. The middle of September you'd think would be bearable.

I wish the driver had looked up so I could have seen my reflection in his sunglasses. For the first while I was out of work, I hated to face myself in the bathroom mirror in the morning. I even covered it up for a while, taped a sheet over it with masking tape. But lately I spend a lot of time looking in the mirror, and I don't mind going into the bathroom five or even six times a day to put on my makeup and do my hair, even if I'm not going anywhere at all worth going. Not that I'm vain, exactly, but this has become a good time for me. I can fantasize, talk myself into being beautiful and loveable. Imagine me loveable! You'd think this would be a difficult accomplishment before an uncompromising, dispassionate and totally objective mirror, but it isn't at all. In fact every time I do it, it becomes easier. The mirror seems to facilitate the process in some mysterious way. Reminds me of certain patients I've worked with—mirror fascination. Maybe there's something to it. I always thought they were trying to verify their own reality, checking to see if they were really there. But I've discovered their secret. I just disappear altogether if I stare at the mirror long enough. Which is fine with me.

When I put on my dress and shoes this afternoon, the dress looked, I realized sadly, like something someone else's mother would have discarded long ago, and the shoes—the shoes were a painful reminder of my inadequate taste. These articles of clothing were, or seemed to me, fashionable when I bought them. But I don't have an eye for tasteful quality—as one of my colleagues put it not very tactfully. (I brought this remark on myself, to be honest. I was ridiculing myself— scoring points that day by making self-effacing jokes. I should have known better, but then intellectual knowledge and behavior are two different things, I've found with patients.)

It seems to me I've always been this way, through high school, college, professional work—the business about not ever being in step, about never being able to acquire attractive clothes or present myself in a way which is not only acceptable (I was always as far as I know "appropriately" dressed) but attractive to men or other women. In fact, when driven to desperation by time, for instance, or lack of it, I usually manage to buy something absolutely ridiculous which even I, by the time I get home, realize is hopelessly outlandish. The best example of this in my recollection is the time I bought the clear plastic cocktail slippers with the pink plastic flowers on the toes—larger rhinestones for their centres, as I remember, and smaller ones on the tip of each petal. Needless to say, I couldn't even stand up in them. This was closing time, of course, when I was pushed, desperate. (That was the night of the convocation ball and I was, to say the least, desperate.) I am capable of this kind of thing, even now, regardless of all my post graduate work in psychology.

I wish I hadn't thought about the dance. The memory is more than a little painful. I was so afraid of everything—the music, the other girls, the banquet, men, Bruce, my date, a social worker I had met while doing my field practicum. Especially Bruce, I guess, if I am honest. I was so tense I wonder now that rigor mortis hadn't set in prematurely, that something hadn't triggered it before its time.

But in a way I guess it's a good thing I did remember the dance because it brings me back to what I was thinking about Simon. It has to do with love, or the lack of it. That's the crux of the matter. It's quite simple, really. I'm a victim of too much of it (or what has hitherto passed for love with female children) and Simon of too little. And one condition is as lethal as the other. Society would undoubtedly consider my condition benign compared to his—some psychiatrists have even gone so far as to say he is criminally insane and that eventually he will murder to exact adequate revenge. But I think the two conditions are equally dangerous and I am in a position to know.

My capacity for affection is clinically dead. Of suffocation. All the pampering, all the protection—don't walk alone, don't talk to strangers—especially strange men—don't date men older than you, younger than you—don't flaunt yourself, don't wear suggestive clothing—don't come home to this house if—don't expect your father and I to—if you're—be careful—we do this for your own good—because we love you—don't sit with your legs apart—don't wear your dresses

too short, your blouses too thin—don't drink—don't smoke—
don't take rides with strangers—don't neck or pet—don't—
just don't. And all because they loved me, so they said, so
much. So now I don't, or rather can't. The whole thing strikes
me as very amusing just now. An inappropriate reaction, we
used to call it, but I don't work there any more and anyway, I
learned to handle all that years ago. I can handle Simon too.
I've handled far worse situations before. Besides, I don't even
know for sure if he's following me. Small comfort really. If not
me, then surely some other innocent victim who doesn't have
nearly the resources I have in dealing with this sort of thing.
However, if anything does happen, let it never be said that I
was asking for it.

Quite the contrary. I'm actually a walking arsenal. Of
course none of my colleagues knew this when I worked at the
clinic, but I have two cans of mace in my purse at all times
and keys to doors that haven't been opened by me in years nor
will ever be again. And the best collection of nail files Eaton's
has to offer—long ones, short ones, hooked ones—you name
it, if Revlon put it out, I bought it. Hat pins, everything. Even
a compass—the kind from a high school geometry set. In my
case they should say BEWARE OF LADY, not LADY
BEWARE. Never once had occasion to use them but as my
mother always said, you never know. On the other hand, I
would be relieved if Simon weren't after me. I have enough
on my mind already. Maybe he'll get off somewhere downtown and disappear.

Simon is a classic case of maternal rejection in infancy.
Freud would have had a field day with him. His mother hated
him. Freud would have liked that. She literally loathed him
from the moment he was born, perhaps before, and from all
the information available to me in the files, no one could
determine just why—nor could I later, in all the time I
worked with him. Family therapy, group therapy, individual
therapy, primal scream therapy—even with that, no one ever
found adequate reason for the rejection. His mother had
other children and loved them well. Only Simon was the

43

exception. She couldn't have cared less what happened to him, what he did—wished in fact he'd died in the womb. The father did what he could, but he wasn't an educated man. He took Simon hunting and fishing. Simon loved to hunt.

Maternal rejection; mother hate; woman hate; assault and rape. Always other women with Simon. He never attacked his mother, of course. I'd read about this phenomenon before but I had never come across a case which so perfectly illustrated the theory; in its pure form, almost as rare as the classic schizophrenic split—a cliché outside clinical work, but actually very rare indeed. None of the doctors at the clinic had ever seen one, in fact. Most of the time "shatter" was a word more accurately applied than "split". In fact, there is now evidence to support the theory that the classic split is really an extraordinarily sophisticated process of adaptation which the mind may initiate as a defense against the shattering. Multiplicity, I gather, as opposed to chaos. Some of these cases have even been known, through extensive psychoanalysis, to have been reintegrated.

When I think back to when I was a little girl at my aunt's farm near Trestle, I remember feeding lambs from 7-Up bottles full of milk and capped with giant brown nipples. This was in the spring when some of the ewes rejected their offspring. I asked my aunt once why they did it, how they could turn away their own. She said she thought someone or something must have touched the lamb when it was barely born, in a way the mother didn't like, in a way offensive to her somehow. But my aunt said she really didn't know. She didn't seem to think there was anything wrong with the lambs, said they were perfectly all right in God's eye. It seemed unnatural, she said, cruel, but there it was. How could they have done it? Turned away their own?

I'll never understand why they asked me to leave, after all the years I spent, all the work. I know what they said, but I take medication and I see Dr. Severing and I can't understand man as fast as I can no time rhyme. Rhyming again. And now I'm crying. Absolutely ridiculous. Crying over the memory of a lamb, for god's sake, or even Simon for that matter. I'll have to go back home if I'm not careful. A little Kleenex and a touch of Champagne Beige Medicated Make-up—DuBarry, I think it is. I reach into my purse and fish them out. Surreptitious repair.

Moving down Macleod Trail, the bus stops at almost every shelter. Slow and hot, this moving through. I picked the right side of the bus, next to the curb. You can feel the vibrations of the vehicle better next to the curb, and I like the vibrations. Up till now I have occupied my time reading the ads in slots over the heads of the other passengers. No one sat beside me in the seat because I always sit in the middle, now anyway, until someone forces the issue and then I squash myself against the nubbled tin wall of the bus. In order to avoid touching. I know all this but I do it anyway. I read the ads twice (I will do this occasionally), even the Playtex Cross-Your-Heart ones which I hate especially. But I rarely look out the window for the first twenty minutes of this trip. The scenery is hardly conducive to sanity: new and used car lots and fast food take-outs, Denny's, McDonald's, Big Boy, Mr. Submarine. I will not look at them—which is no easy feat travelling down Macleod Trail at a snail's pace. For the last two stops since I finished reading the ads in the slots, I've been forced to watch the people waiting at the stops and getting on. My legs were sticking to the plastic orange seat of the bus by the time we pulled up to the stop opposite the Chinook Shopping Centre.

At 3 p.m. I'm supposed to lead a group in Home Management and Budgeting for chronic out-patients, people who have spent most of their lives in the provincial hospital. Mrs. Aimsley thought I'd be able to do this very nicely—because of my experience, she said, but I knew what she had in the back of her mind. She thought it would be "non-threatening". Mrs. Aimsley is a good friend of one of my former colleagues. I myself have called her on occasion, referrals and the like.

Actually my group in Home Management and Budgeting is far more threatening to me than she will ever know. I'm not doing so well in that department myself lately and it's only a matter of time until my savings are gone what with the price of medication and transportation, that sort of thing. Besides, nutrition is part of the material to be presented to this group and how am I supposed to teach nutrition when practically everything offered for sale is poisonous.

Furthermore, nothing could be much more depressing than trying to teach money mangement to people who have none. I remember going over this sort of thing with Simon. Blithely moving right along through banking, responsible shopping, making lists of necessary goods, et cetera—until I learned he had not so much as a blanket to his name. He had an empty room. The follow-up people were responsible for seeing to that at least. But his room was in the Beveridge Building with all the worst derelicts and drunks in the city barging in at all hours of the night—begging and threatening. That hadn't bothered him so much, he said. After all, he had been in the provincial hospital since he was fifteen—but he had no blanket, he said, and the nights were cold. This was early March and I had lots of blankets, more than my share. So I gave him one of mine. One can't help wondering what Simon would have been like if all this hadn't happened; I mean had he been "normal".

We are up to the Cemetery Hill already. I wonder where he's going, when he will let me know that he has seen me. Because I know he has. It's only a matter of time. And I must prepare for eventualities. Assess the situation realistically. In the letters and phone calls, Simon has consistently spoken of "dropping in", "coming up for a visit". Therefore I must assume he planned to come at some point, wanted to see me. Of course I discouraged any such rendezvous. His potential for violence an obvious factor in my decision as well as the inviolable rule of the profession—NO SOCIALIZATION WITH CLIENTS. Also I was concerned that he might choose to inflict himself on someone else in my neighborhood, be distracted, as it were, and follow some other unsuspecting woman to her door and beyond. Which was his pattern in the past.

I had contacted the police. Not to have done so would have been a significant omission on my part. I may not be functioning as well as I normally would these days, but certainly still well enough to utilize community resources, as it were. Staff Sergeant Detective Nightengale only confirmed what I already knew—nothing could be done until Simon committed another offence. He was legally free to walk the streets unharrassed until he acted again—according to his previous pattern. This is as it should be, I suppose. Lord knows the mentally ill have been abused in the past to such an extent that laws such as the one which protected Simon and left me and other women unprotected and vulnerable represented civilized enlightenment, of a sort. Most psychiatric patients are non-violent, I know. But there are exceptions, and the law has very little truck with exceptions, I'm afraid.

I am afraid. And by the time we reach the bus stop beside the entrance to the Stampede grounds, a fort constructed out of vertical shaved logs sharpened to pencil points along the top and stained the colour of dried blood, I have decided to transfer to a different bus, one which will not take me to the mental health association office but which will divert Simon, confuse him. I will ride that bus (the number as yet undetermined) for a reasonable length of time, then transfer back downtown and from there, catch a bus down Eleventh Avenue, arriving at my destination somewhat later than I had planned—but intact—which seems to me a most important consideration at this time.

This is precisely what I do. When the bus stops across the street from the Bay, I grab my bag, and making sure I have the transfer, exit quickly, hoping he won't notice me leaving. I glance up at the Calgary Tower, then looking back at the bus, I see Simon rising from his seat. He will bolt. This is his pattern. And I run across the street against the light. There are two buses waiting on the other side. Calgary Transit System logo, blue on a silver side. I climb onto the first one, its door already beginning to fold shut. I hand my transfer slip to the driver and say "Transfer please," quickly. The driver looks up at me this time. "Too hot to travel so far today," I say, "especially on the bus. But you people have no choice, I guess." He smiles and rips a transfer from the pad.

I don't even know the name of the route of this bus, much less the number, but I'll find out soon enough. I locate an empty seat near the centre and sit in the middle of the seat. As we pull out, I look back over my shoulder and see a man with short dark hair climb onto the bus behind the one I'm on. Simon has made a mistake. My diversionary tactic has proved rather effective, to my relief. But as I watch, I see the bus behind pull out too and follow us from one intersection to another down Eighth Avenue, heading north, then west, past Mewata Stadium and the Planetarium, onto Bow Trail, then the Crowchild and over the bridge. We are heading for the University. I am afraid I have made the wrong decision again. The first one I made years ago enrolling in the freshman psychology class in the first place.

I am on the wrong bus. I have to get off. I move up closer to the front, find another seat. I am looking out the front window, looking for another bus going the opposite direction. The bus which was behind with Simon on it has moved up beside ours, parallel at the intersection. I think it must be turning left. I can't see him clearly but I know he's there, at the back, his short dark hair giving him away among the younger males who wear theirs longer, below their ears. He seems to be wearing a jacket. It is grey. I don't remember this jacket but perhaps he has a job and has bought himself a jacket for the fall. I myself find it very hot, suffocating, in fact. I am having trouble breathing. My dress is wet around the armpits, my face sticky with sweat. I wipe the sweat away from over my upper lip where it accumulates. Simon is dressed inappropriately, as we say. Wearing a jacket in this heat.

The other bus doesn't turn left at the intersection as I had hoped, but changes lanes again and moves back behind us where it was in the first place. Finally, as we are coming up to Kensington Road, I see another bus approaching on the other side of the street. It is a duplicate of the one I am on. I can't read the destination which I know is printed in large letters behind glass on the top of the bus, but I can't seem to focus on it long enough to make out the words. It will have to do. I reach up and pull the cord, hear the bell and then the flatulent exhaust as we pull up to the stop. I have wrinkled my transfer but I have it in my hand. I must have been folding it or crumpling it during the ride up from town. Calm down, I tell myself. You're a professional.

I step off the bus and race to the intersection waving my transfer so the other driver will see me and wait. I just make it onto the bus. But as soon as I locate an empty seat, I realize I have forgotten to ask for my transfer. On the way back, I look up, checking, a precautionary measure, entirely realistic under the circumstances. And I can't believe my eyes. Simon is sitting in the second seat from the front. How he could have beat me onto the bus baffles me for a moment until I remember his running, the incredible speed. He no doubt crossed in the middle of the street, approaching the bus from the back. I, like a fool, went to the intersection, waving my transfer like a red flag in front of a bull. How stupid of me. I must be losing my faculties. I would never have survived in psychiatry as long as I had if I hadn't been more on the ball than this.

I know it is him though his dark head is turned toward the window. He wears a plaid shirt and he is apparently talking to a rather sultry looking girl with a dark mole on one cheek. She couldn't be a day over sixteen and she wouldn't touch Simon with a ten-foot pole if she only knew what was good for her. But young girls are so foolish these days. She has the top three buttons undone on her blouse. Asking for it. Has the whole world gone absolutely crazy? Where are this girl's parents—that they would let her leave the house dressed like a—well, slut is the word that comes to mind. Talking to a stranger whom she couldn't possibly know a thing about, flaunting herself. Throwing herself at an older man. I check the zipper on my dress. Pull it fully closed. Let it never be said when they find me that I was asking for it.

The bus moves east, back through Hillhurst, onto Memorial Drive. Past the General Hospital which I know is there but would rather not see. I once worked there years ago. My first job out of university.

When we are long past the General, I look at my watch. Twenty-five past four. I've missed the Budgeting and Home Management Group entirely, my carefully prepared lecture on nutrition and poison. I haven't even called Mrs. Aimsley to let her know why I couldn't be there. But she'll understand, I think, when I explain.

I look at my watch again and it is quarter to eleven. It can't be, I think, and check again. Quarter to eleven. I am very tired now. Ever since the sun went down and all the lights came on dividing the darkness into random parts, haphazard splintered patches on my eyes, I have been longing to lie down. I must have covered every square inch of Calgary by now, circled the Tower lit green and red like Christmastime, heard the carillon chime at least a dozen times. But it is not over yet. Simon is still behind me on the bus, though these last two routes we ride alone. There is no one with us but the driver. I hold another transfer in my hand, imagine he does too. My right hand shakes now. I have to hold the wrist with my left hand. I no longer have to check if he is there. He is. Everywhere I go. He waits and watches. Simon is a hunter. He even tans the hides himself, once brought the soft slippery skin of a black bear to the clinic to show us his expertise.

And like the hunter he is, he knows I will eventually make the wrong move—the one that sends me down the street in desperation knocking on dark doors—for help—where there is none to be had—and he knows it. I know it too. But oddly, knowing that and exhausted as I am, I still want to run. To run and run and run until I lose him or whatever it is I am running from.

We pull up to a stop. I look out the window and see we are back at the bus shelter in front of the church, across the street from the Bay.

"Last stop before the barns," the driver says. "This is the last stop. Everybody off the bus." He has removed his hat and his uniform jacket. He wears a grey shirt, gets out from behind the wheel and stands there at the front of the bus holding his hat. "Lady," he says, "it's time to get off the bus. I'm taking it back to the barns in about five minutes."

"I have a transfer," I say and hold it up so he can see.

"That don't make no difference to me now lady. There's nothing left to transfer to. This is the last bus. No buses running out of city centre after 12:20. This is my signal trip."

I am losing my patience. He thinks he is losing his but I am losing mine. "You don't understand," I say calmly, "I am being followed. That young man behind me is following me and has been for a long, long time." Then I whisper, "He used to be a psychiatric patient of mine—he's a convicted rapist. Assault and rape." I am speaking very clearly, though whispering. My enunciation is very clear. I can hear my voice echo in my head. I'm sure he understands my predicament. Why didn't I think of this before, I wonder now. All I had to do was tell the driver, ask for help, as simple as that. But he raises his hand. And I grab my purse and open the clasp. I have my hand inside, in case. But he only runs his fingers through his hair which is dark, I notice now, and straight and closely cropped.

"I hate to tell you this, lady, but there's no man or anybody else behind you. You and me are the only two people on the bus. We're all by our lonesomes."

He has given himself away. I decide against the files and keys. Fumble for the compass just as I fumbled in my purse at my desk all those dreary days at Western High so many years ago. Remembering this makes me sigh, then giggle. But I find the compass by bracing the purse against my thigh. He comes toward me now and I sink low in the seat, cringe against the wall of the bus. It is cold. I whimper at his shadow following the ads for Playtex Cross-Your-Heart and hope to die I start to cry and rhyme TRANSFER I try again TRANSFER TRANSFER TRANSFER but this time there is no time he

51

bends toward me and I am on the floor can not make the doormouse whore and now he reaches out and out I come out comes his eye   I have his eye   I rise   I rise and drive the compass through the grey shirt   spray red spray   and I am over him and down the rubber steps and running on cement and running from the shelter glass past the Bay and the old Herald in the papers they will read that I saved me   I am a river of scream and running toward the tower at the end of the street   the Christmas red and Christmas green of knobs and tower tunnels full of scream I can't live *here* any more it's full of poisoned wheat and maraschino cherries   whores darkness raping darkness   all my dreams   they've emptied me and filled me full of Christmas towers and of time which rhymes with hours and with towers   filled me full of sparkle showers   these carillon chimes

Five to a Hand

Calder moved five packages to the freezer basket, carefully transferred each small solid lump shrouded in pink-brown butcher's wrap and stamped "Ground Beef" in thick blue ink. Then he moved a red fish, like a rock, a whole salmon embedded in ice and wrapped in a plastic bag with a red wire tag, to the left side, piled it on the heap of roasts marked in blue—"Cross Rib", "Blade", "Rump", "Chuck".

The long white box was frosted on the inner walls of three plastic sides only, which he found curious in his digging. Why wasn't the fourth side frosted too? He could hardly keep himself from moving the freezer out from the wall, unscrewing the back panel and tinkering around with the motor. He figured he could have it fixed up in no time flat, given half a chance. Some small thing, no doubt.

If nothing else, he thought, he was a man who knew motors. He'd spent the better part of his life playing with them. Lately, when someone he'd known almost all his life up and died, Calder found himself going over and over his own life in his head, accounting for what he was and why he'd done this or that. Why maybe he should be allowed to go on for just a little longer, might be justified in asking for a few more years. Because Ace hadn't been the first to go. And Calder was no spring chicken himself.

He seemed to have slipped without knowing it into the time of random death among his friends, his family. There had been four deaths in his and Lila's families alone within the last three years, and lately, the odd fellow at work had been biting the dust too. One guy even dropped dead at the curling rink just before the season was over, right on the ice at the end of the eighth. Calder had been there that night skipping for Harold Carson while Harold was in Regina. And here he was again, thinking maybe a man who was good with motors might be entitled to an extension of some kind. His stomach rose and hardened, reminded him, as if he needed reminding, that it didn't make a damn bit of difference what you did or what you were good at. In fact, weren't they always saying the good die young. Maybe he should have veered off the beaten track a few times, kicked up his heels a bit—like Ace. That hadn't been any help to Ace, finally, Calder knew that. But at least he'd had a bit of spice, at least he'd had a little spice in his life.

He sighed. The fact was he didn't have time for the freezer job right now. He had to find the fingers. Connie said she had put them in a little brown paper bag, like the ones corner grocery stores kept under the counter for penny candy for the kids. She said she remembered putting them on the right side but just now she wasn't in too good a shape to remember anything much, Calder thought, what with Ace's dying and all the busywork getting ready for the funeral. Not to mention the bickering about whether or not Ace should be cremated, which is what he had asked for. Calder thought if that's what Ace wanted, that's what they should do. He couldn't for the life of him understand what all the fuss was about.

He went back to rooting, half in the freezer box himself, his short stocky body bent at the middle, his eyes squinting in the small cold light. His hands were nearly frozen, his own fingers numb. But he couldn't seem to find the little bag with Ace's fingers in it. Obviously they weren't on the right side. They must be on the left. So he began to transfer all the cold hard lumps of meat and fish and vegetables and pie fruit Connie had bagged last fall back to the right side. About half way down on the left he finally found the bag of fingers, wedged between a packet of chicken wings and a slab of burgundy liver.

Although Calder had been throwing slabs of meat and fish here and there all over the freezer, when he first felt the slightly damp brown paper of the small bag, he heaved himself out of the box and backed toward the furnace at the far wall of the dark basement where he stood for a few minutes blinking and focusing on the shelves full of tools and the racks of rifles screwed into the concrete, becoming more and more clear as his eyes adjusted. Ace had been a hunter. He was good with guns and good with motors, too, for that matter, which was probably why he and Calder had gotten on so well over the years.

Ace had started out as a blacksmith in Trestle and had worked at that till the trade all but disappeared in the fifties. The image of Ace, bent over the anvil, guiding tongs which held a dull red iron object in its curled jaws, a ploughshare, rectangular, long, with one corner of the metal folded back in a small triangular flap like the page of a book folded back and marked so you could go back and find the part you needed whenever you wanted without having to reread the whole thing. Like Calder's father's Bible full of pages folded back on the right side at the top corner, at all the places which had anything to do with resurrection. Ace, just finished the folding, walking carefully over to the water trough for the tempering. The secret way he had of tempering which, Calder remembered, brought the farmers from all over the district to the Trestle shop. Because Ace's work never cracked. Ace's work was tempered right. Ploughshares and files and horseshoes, harrow discs, and later, machinery parts of all kinds. But he never told a soul his trick except for Calder. He wasn't a man who talked much, but he talked to Calder. And Calder was proud of that.

The last time Calder had seen Ace was in the fall, after he lost the fingers. They knew he had cancer by then and they had already opened him up and sewed him shut. He had just finished a course of chemotherapy when Calder and Lila made the trip out to the coast. The chemotherapy made him pretty sick and he was weak, but Calder thought he wasn't really looking too bad and the doctors had told Connie everything would be all right. But as soon as Calder and Lila had stepped in the front door of the wartime house in Burnaby, Ace had taken Calder downstairs to the shop and showed him exactly where he lost the fingers, showed him the sawblade, the indelible brown stain on the concrete floor and all, and then he held up the hand, his right hand. Calder couldn't even remember the rest of the hand now, looking back, only the spaces, only the missing fingers. He hadn't known if it was the flight out from the prairie that had made him sick or the sawblade or the finger spaces or what, but he had to take the basement stairs two steps at a time and even then he just barely made it to the bathroom.

Now here he was again, on almost the very same spot, only this time it was spring. Calder looked over at the stain on the floor, found himself staring at the Black and Decker power saw hung on a hook in a pegboard full of tools. He blinked, wondered how long he had been standing there and looked over at the freezer, its long white lid still raised, the inner rectangle glowing faintly like winter light at five o'clock on the prairie, a sort of blue yellow light which made him instinctively cross his long arms across his chest, grip his hands on opposing shoulders and rhythmically slap the flesh of his upper arms with his cupped hands to help the circulation along a little bit, he thought, though he knew the cold was as much inside him as out. Digging through the freezer for Ace's fingers was only part of the reason for the chill, probably the smallest part. He turned his left wrist toward his face and squinted at his watch. Later than he thought. It had taken him almost twenty minutes to find the bag of fingers.

"Calder? Calder? It's time to go." It was Connie, her voice high-pitched and sort of formal, Calder thought. But she didn't ask about the fingers.

He cleared his throat. "I'll be right up Connie," he called back, sort of formal too, tight, as if his voice were frozen, couldn't be heard by anybody but himself, like a kid who climbs inside a cardboard box and closes the flaps over his head or crawls into a culvert and then yells and hears his own voice echo back and knows the other kids don't hear, can't hear him on the outside. So really you could say anything you wanted at a time like that, usually corny stuff or dirty stuff, words you wouldn't ever say anywhere else. But right now, at fifty-eight and just before Ace's funeral, the memory made him feel bad and kind of scared, not frisky as it might have even a few years ago. All he said was, "I'll be right up Connie," though he was pretty sure she hadn't heard a word.

He went back to the freezer, leaned over and lifted out the little bag, the top of which was folded over, marked, he saw, with blue felt pen in formal block letters, not Connie's writing. It must have been done at the hospital, Calder thought. ARNOLD FREDERICK DOLLARTON, which was Ace, but nobody who knew him ever called him Arnold. Everybody called him Ace because of the way his hair kind of came to a dark point in the middle of his forehead, this when he was younger, of course. And because of his luck at poker. Calder had never known a man better at bluff than Ace.

He looked down at the bag, drew his hand across his forehead and smiled because the thought that crossed his mind was that Ace must be getting quite a kick out of this whole thing. Then he thought maybe it was a joke. He figured Ace was having one last one on them and there were no fingers at all in the bag, probably sausages or something. That would be like Ace—wanting to kind of liven up the proceedings a little bit. He had always hated weddings and funerals, christenings and confirmations, all that sort of stuff. Nine times out of ten he'd come in roaring drunk and Connie would have to spend the whole service with her fingers on her lips trying to keep him quiet.

Calder unfolded the top of the bag, held it close to his face and peered down into it. The light from the freezer filtered through the brown paper making it glow gold, making it look warm somehow though it had just come from the freezer. But Calder couldn't deny what he saw. You had to at least believe in what you saw with your own eyes and there was no doubt whatsoever about what that was in this case. Lying together toward one corner of the bag were Ace's fingers, the finger-nails clean and white as they never were on Ace. The nurses must have cleaned them up at the hospital. When they were on Ace, they always had a line of grease ringing the quick and the cuticle both, making rough circles around the nails, just like Calder's who now glanced quickly at the nails on his own fingers holding the bag which he then dropped and which fell back to the bottom of the freezer, and he had to lean over and fish it out again.

"Calder?" He heard Connie coming down the basement steps. "Calder?"

Not wanting Connie to actually have to see the bag in her state, and not knowing what else to do, Calder slammed the freezer door shut and shoved the bag into the pants pocket of his light grey suit. He headed for the stairs. He caught Connie about half way down and extended his arm up toward her, patted her on the shoulder. "It's all right Connie," he said quietly, but she wasn't pacified. Standing on the step above him, her eyes were level with his. Her eyes were dark, tired grey and rimmed in red. He hated to have to look at her eyes but he did and nodded and then it seemed to be all right and they went upstairs to get Lila and Connie and Ace's kids who had just come in, one from Winnipeg and the other one up from the States.

Following Connie up the stairs and feeling the cold hard lump in his pocket move up and down his thigh as he took each step more carefully than the last, Calder remembered what Connie had said at breakfast about the fingers. Apparently Ace figured they could put the fingers back on the hand at the hospital, that they'd knit back on. Calder knew they could do that sort of thing nowadays but it wasn't as simple as Ace had thought. Working with the flesh of a man just wasn't the same as working with motors. There were no guarantees when it came to doctors and human beings. Anyway Connie said the fingers wouldn't knit, the nerves and such. It hadn't worked, because of the cancer, maybe, or the chemotherapy or something. Nobody really seemed to know for sure. But they took the fingers off again and threw them into the garbage in surgery, the garbage which Calder had heard somewhere was burned in the hospital incinerator anyway. What difference it would make to Ace where they were burned, at the hospital or at the crematorium, was a mystery to him.

After it was over and Ace woke up, Connie said he was mad as blazes. Roared and swore and carried on something fierce. Told them they better goddamn well get back there and fish those goddamn fingers out of the goddamn garbage can and give them back because he goddamn well wasn't going to leave the hospital without them.

By the time they climbed into Connie's brother-in-law's van, Calder could feel the fingers wet against his thigh. It occurred to him that shortly they would thaw and he thought at first that he would take them out of his wool suit pants pocket and hold them in his lap or better yet, put them on the floor, but he didn't want to get Connie all worked up again and she was sitting right beside him. "How far is it?" he said as if he really didn't care but wanted to say something for the sake of conversation, hoping she wouldn't guess why he'd be in any hurry.

She raised her eyes from where she had been working with her fingers in her lap, making the "Here is the church/ here is the steeple" peak, like a little girl, Calder thought, and felt his throat begin to ache and tighten up. "You mean the funeral home, Calder?" She turned her face away from his the moment their eyes met, turned and looked out the van window. "My guess is it would be about a forty minute drive," she said. "It's way over in North Van. It's the closest place that—well, you know what Ace wanted done, Calder. There aren't too many of those places around, not like the regular ones. They had the chapel and everything so we thought it would be just as good to have it all together, like—" Her voice cracked then and she started to cry again and Calder was sorry he had asked. You didn't hardly seem able to say anything at a time like this that didn't make people feel bad.

As usual on the coast this time of year the weather was hot and humid and Calder was alarmed when after only ten minutes on the road, a small wet stain appeared on his thigh.

He said nothing, but looking out the van window as Burnaby rolled by, he couldn't help wondering why this sort of thing always seemed to happen to him. Not that he harboured any hard feelings toward Ace, but it seemed to Calder as if someone had a pretty peculiar sense of humour. It wasn't that he minded helping out. He didn't. He saw it as his duty. God knows a person could lend a hand at times like these and he had been close to Ace after all.

He had been close to his cousin Bernie too, and he hadn't minded making funeral arrangements when Bernie had died in a trailer fire up in Yellowknife. He hadn't even minded all the complications of trying to help Aunt Myra decide whether to bring Bernie's sealed coffin down for the burial or whether to leave him up in Yellowknife. And God knows Bernie went up and down like a jackhammer in Aunt Myra's head for three days before anything was resolved. Complications were part of life, Calder thought, maybe all of life, especially at such times as these.

He had taken all this in his stride—until he'd walked into Godwin's Funeral Parlour the afternoon of the funeral and seen all his own kids but one, four of them, huddled around the chapel announcement panel cut in the shape of a stained glass window, peaked like the ones in churches. One of the boys looked to Calder as if he were just barely holding himself together, one of the girls was dabbing at her eyes with a Kleenex. The other two kids looked hang-dog, as if they'd lost their best friend. Calder had been surprised, couldn't really understand why they were so worked up since they'd hardly ever set eyes on Bernie. But they had never been to a funeral before and Calder supposed that was the problem. So he walked over to kind of let them know everything would be all right and they shouldn't be scared or anything. He put his arm around Brenda and, scanning the group, his eyes finally fell on the announcement panel. There it was, in small white wooden letters stuck onto a black velvet background.

FUNERAL SERVICES FOR THE LATE
CALDER SAMUEL BARN
CHAPEL OF THE MOUNTAIN ASH
JANUARY 22, 1979
2:30 p.m.

Calder just caught the funeral director as the other mourners were beginning to arrive. "Hey you jokers!" he said in a voice altogether too loud, sharp as a tempered nail; it carried through the door of the chapel and echoed and came back out again, so he whispered the rest. "You fellas got the wrong Joe," he said, trying to lighten things up a bit, which was his way. But he made his point; they had it changed in no time, before the service began.

Afterward, when he thought about it, what bothered him most wasn't so much seeing his name come up like that, though he had been a bit taken aback by it at first. What bothered him was seeing the kids, seeing what it would be like, even though they knew he wasn't the man who was dead. It was sort of like seeing the preview of a picture show or something. Seeing their faces in a way he should never have been made to see, he thought, if things were fair—which they weren't. He knew that much. He wasn't a kid after all. But he still felt that this was a sight he should have been spared by rights, his own kids all worked up over him going. You were supposed to be dead for that, and up until now, Calder believed that being dead meant you couldn't see too much of anything, let alone your own folks worked up at the funeral parlour before your own casket got carried in on the shoulders of your neighbours and nephews and some of the guys from work.

Later that year, when Harvey Wittaker died, Calder had been asked by the widow to take Harvey's clothes to the funeral parlour so they could dress him for the casket. He and Lila were staying at the Wittakers' and bedamned if he no sooner got back from the funeral parlour than the phone rang, the mortician saying the shoes didn't fit, could they bring down another pair. Calder had never heard of putting

61

shoes on the corpse before in the first place, but it turned out he had taken his own shoes down, to dress the dead, no less. Wasn't that what the others had said at the time, and hadn't they all had a good laugh, even Harvey's widow? He finally had to throw out that pair of perfectly good black leather oxfords because every time he went to put them on, all he could see was the mortician trying to shove them onto Harvey's dead white feet. And now Ace's fingers, of all things. A fellow just had to wonder what would happen next.

But till now, he at least still believed that being dead meant you couldn't see too much of anything. After this morning, he even had to think of that in a different light, as if he didn't have enough to handle already. Ace was the sort of man who didn't believe he would ever die, which pretty well took care of the hereafter as far as he was concerned. More than once during the funeral services in Trestle, years back now, after the part the preacher always said about the resurrection and the light and all that, Calder had heard Ace mutter, "Nothing but a crock of bullshit." And Connie shushing and Ace rolling right along with "Why don't he cut the crap and get to the point. All we gotta do is get that poor bastard in the ground. That's what we come for. He ain't listening anyway. Any fool can see that." And Connie's face turning beet red, her eyes smarting water, not from grief but pure embarrassment.

Calder could see her eyes just as if it had happened yesterday, as if they weren't in a van at all, weren't moving through Burnaby toward Ace's crematorium, but up in the north country again, back in the bush where it was so quiet a man could still hear himself think. As if Calder weren't himself carrying the fingers of his own brother-in-law in the pants pocket of his Sunday suit.

Which was what troubled him now as they turned off the freeway into North Van. The fingers, cold and wet and for a long time now not hard, but limp. But he could feel a soft pressure, nonetheless, where the lump was on his thigh and he tried to imagine just how the fingers were lying in the pocket, tips down or up, imagined the fine dizzy circles of the prints, like webs, on each fingertip. The circles moving in and in toward the centres of the soft pads. And suddenly he was sick, desperately trying to swallow waves of heave. Like salt water, like the five-foot swells off the coast the day he went salmon fishing with Ace in the kids' ketch off Gambier Island.

That was the time Ace told him about the salmon people in the Interior. Ace had said the Indians there used to have a kind of ceremony when the first salmon run in the spring. And he said the Indian people actually believed you had to keep every bone of every fish from that supper, every single bone, and then you had to take these bones down to the lake, they said, and throw them in. And if you ate a bone or lost one or even missed in your throw so the bone fell on the sand and didn't get to the lake, then the babies born after that would be missing something, an eye or hand or leg. Apparently these folk believed that's where babies came from, according to Ace. Of course they had a good chuckle out of that, out in the Strait, drinking Lamb's Navy rum on the deck and shooting the breeze. He hadn't thought about the fishing trip in years, and until now Calder had always figured it didn't much matter where you threw the bones, in the lake or on the land. It was all the same. Nothing would come of it anyway. And Ace had thought the same—still would have if it hadn't been for these bloody fingers. Though now when Calder thought about it, that wasn't the way with motors or electricity or anything like that. Something always came of something there, maybe turned into something else, but never into nothing. He wished he could talk to Ace about it but Ace wasn't up to talking much these days.

The whole thing seemed so crazy to Calder, especially when he thought of Ace who had no use at all for the hereafter in the forty or so years Calder had known him. Calder had wondered right away why on earth Ace figured he had to have the fingers along with him when he went to the crematorium when everybody knew Ace believed a man went nowhere at all at the end of the line. But Connie had said he wouldn't leave without the fingers. After the amputation, she'd gone up to see him at the hospital one afternoon and he reached down into his bedside table and pulled out this little brown bag and told her what was in it, told her to take the fingers home and she said what for and he said to put them in the freezer for Christ's sake, that's what for. They weren't goddamn well going any place he wasn't, he said. Ordinarily you would think they'd have given Ace the fingers in a jar of alcohol, Calder thought, like Grandma Spese's gallstones. But they didn't. The fingers had been put in a small brown paper bag, like the lunch bags Lila bought at the Safeway in packs of two hundred, only this was smaller. Anyway, Connie took the fingers home and Calder could see her in his head, bent over in the cold, blue-yellow light, stuffing the little bag down between the chicken wings and a pack of liver the colour of wine.

On the way in from the airport, Calder was driving but he could hear Connie telling Lila how Ace had taken to reading a lot in the last few months, which surprised Calder who never read himself and figured Ace for a man who was good with his hands but not too carried away with words, especially when someone wrote them down. But Connie said a couple of months before he lost the fingers, Ace found this article in a magazine, *Maclean*'s, she thought it was, where they were doing these studies on phantom pains people had after they'd had a leg off or an arm or hand, or any part of them which had been lost. The article reported they'd been taking these pictures with a special camera that used ultraviolet rays. As Calder understood it, they had actually photographed the outline of a guy's leg that had been taken off after an accident of some kind. So they said the man wasn't crazy after all to feel pain in the leg that was gone. It wasn't all in his head, Connie said, the way they used to think. Come to think of it, Calder was in some pain too right now, and Ace was gone wasn't he?

Ace had showed Connie the picture and said wasn't that something what they could do nowadays with a little gadget like a camera. And Calder remembered that he himself had heard how they'd figured out pit vipers could only see in infrared light and somehow bees saw flowers by ultraviolet rays. There seemed to be no end to the ways the different creatures of the earth could see. What would they think of next, he wondered.

Moreover, he had just seen on TV where they put chips into an old lady's head to bring her memory back. Chips. What kind of chips? Microchips, Calder remembered they'd said, but what on earth did it all mean. Calder already had one hundred and thirty-seven pieces of shrapnel floating around in him, one large shaft lodged in the fatty tissue near his heart. And that was enough of that, he thought. Of course this couldn't be the same kind of thing. Otherwise, they wouldn't do it. Besides, his problem these days was the exact opposite. He remembered too much already. Still, the pit vipers and the bees and how they see was, he allowed, a find if you were interested in the facts of light. And now, on top of it all, they'd up and made some light themselves; only a little bit, it was true, out of a particle they'd said was thousands of times smaller than a mite. But homemade light, nevertheless, and there was more where that came from, they said. They'd only just begun to make the light.

So Connie figured that magazine article was where Ace got the idea of taking the fingers with him wherever he went, especially since he had the cancer already and wasn't too optimistic about the outcome, in spite of what the doctors said. She said he told her he wanted those fingers back when the time came and she should see to it for him.

When Connie had come up to Calder after breakfast this morning and asked if she could talk to him in the bedroom, she told him what Ace wanted. She wasn't feeling up to it herself, she said, though she would do it if she had to. So Calder had offered to take it off her hands. What else could he do? Connie was Lila's sister after all, and he had been close to Ace. Wouldn't Ace have done the same for him if the shoe were on the other foot. Yes, Calder thought, he would've. What's more, Ace wouldn't have given a tinker's damn about the stain on his pant leg. Ace would've paraded in here like a veteran, under the circumstances, even supposing his pants were covered with cowshit.

The van pulled into the parking lot of the crematorium. For a long time now, Calder had kept his hand on the cold wet lump on his thigh. He hadn't really thought about what he would do when he had to get out. He was pallbearer, after all, and a man had to have a certain amount of dignity in such service. When he took his hand off his thigh, he was horrified to see the small wet blotch had turned a colour which reminded him of nothing so much as the half-water, half-blood soup at the bottom of a pie plate full of chicken thawing on the kitchen counter. Calder tried to imagine the inside of the paper bag, tried to figure how much blood and ice there could be in two fingers, from any hand, even Ace's. People had always said Ace was full of piss and vinegar anyway. Calder had to smile and turned toward the van window so Connie wouldn't see. But he didn't feel much like smiling anyway when he got up to leave the van, because the stain had crawled in a thin line halfway down his pant leg, making it look as if he'd momentarily lost control of his bladder. He tried to cover it up when he walked by hiding it with the splayed fingers of one hand, but he had to be careful about that too because one of the funeral attendants looked at him in a very peculiar way when he went through the door of the chapel. He realized right away that he must have appeared a little as if he were playing with himself or at least thinking about it. So he took the hand away and found that a small dark matt of blood had appeared where before there had been only the suggestion of a wine stain in the water mark.

For the first time since that morning, Calder began to worry about the mechanics of his actual delivery. How and when would he be able to give the fingers back to Ace? When no one was looking, of course. That much was obvious to him. He didn't want to make a spectacle of himself, and most of all he didn't want to upset Connie any more than she already was. He had left her in an anteroom outside the chapel where she could stay with Lila and collect herself before she had to walk down the aisle before Ace.

Calder thought maybe he could sneak into the room where the casket waited and get his business done before the service began. But that didn't work out. For one thing, he couldn't sneak in early because the funeral attendant gave no sign as to which room Ace's casket was in. And for another, when they finally did get into the room, the casket was closed. So he accepted the fact that he would have to wait. But for what? He began to worry that the ceremony might be closed casket. Then what? He couldn't very well just lay his package on the top like a bagged lunch for the trip. On the other hand, he had promised Connie and more or less promised Ace—who wasn't supposed to be around anymore—but Calder *felt* as if he'd promised Ace, in his head sort of. It felt as if they'd shaken on it and when you shook on a thing, that was it for Calder. He was as good as his word. That was his way. Finally he thought all he could do was wait and see. Wasn't that the way it always seemed to go in this world. Lila, wait and see if you're pregnant first, then we'll figure out something. Wait and see if my unemployment comes in, then we'll know if we can make it through the winter without selling the house. Wait and see if Ace and Connie really do pull up stakes and head for the coast before you get all worked up, Lila. For God's sake, wait and see.

The whole family had missed Connie and Ace and the kids when they left the prairie, missed them something terrible. Not just Lila, but Calder and their kids and Grandma Spese. Grandma Spese especially hated to see Connie move so far away. Right off she got into the habit of thinking every time she saw Connie would be the last because of the distance in miles and time, her visits a kind of repeating death, like Ace's semi-automatic rifle he brought back from the war—just like the sound of that rifle, only slow, the shots coming a long time after each other, echoing, Christmas, Easter, Thanksgiving, Connie's birthday, every year the same. By then all Grandma Spese's kids had moved away from the prairie except for Lila and Calder.

As Calder and five other men carried Ace's casket down the short aisle, Calder made up his mind he would wait and see if they opened the casket or not before he got all worked up. The ridiculous thought of himself asking the guy to open the furnace door for a second so he could chuck in the little bag of Ace's fingers flickered in Calder's mind for a split second. He couldn't keep from smiling. As luck would have it, Lila was staring straight at him and if looks could kill, Calder thought he'd be lying up there beside Ace right now.

It would have been closed casket too if Connie hadn't got so upset toward the end of the service after the organist played "Beyond the Sunset", this song because, as Connie said in the van on the way down, Ace always did love the prairie sunsets. But Connie insisted they open the coffin so she could have a last look and say goodbye, which she did. Then the attendant asked the mourners if there was anybody else who wanted to pay his last respects and a few people stood up in the front pews, Ace's kids and one of his sisters. Calder stood up at the back with another pallbearer, a stooped pale man who looked at least twice as old as Ace even if he was dead, and they moved out toward the aisle. Standing close behind the pale man, Calder reached into his suit pants pocket and carefully locked his fingers around the bag, tucking in the edges as he did so. He withdrew his hand slowly and held it by his side.

Ace's kids were almost finished paying their respects now and the man in front of Calder edged a little closer to the casket. Calder followed him, shuffling. He could feel the fingers through the wet bag now, and they seemed uncomfortably soft and warm, probably from the heat of his thigh in his wool suit, he thought. He had started to sweat as soon as the service had begun, not just from nerves, but because it was genuinely hot and close in the chapel.

He could have seen Ace now if he had looked. But Calder didn't want to look. He had a silly sort of idea in his head that Ace might be smiling, as if he had come up with a pretty good hand, as if he held the king of spades, and queen and jack and ten. But of course, he wouldn't be smiling anyway, Calder corrected himself, even if he'd come up with the best hand in the world. You never could tell with Ace. He was a man with a poker face if ever there was one.

When Calder's turn came to pay his respects, he closed his eyes and bowed his head. He ran his and Ace's fingers over the cold brass handles on the casket, squinted at the edge, then making a slow smooth motion, a kind of passing over the lip of the coffin, he prepared himself for the final delivery. This last operation was tricky. He felt he had to be precise, the way you have to work when you're tinkering with fine wire in small motors. Calder aimed carefully and lodged the package as deep as he could between Ace's neck and chest and when he did it he could feel the smooth sleeve of Ace's dark suit coat, and inside the sleeve, he could feel the arm, stiff as a two-by-four.

Calder thought of the hand, of the gaps on the hand where the fingers used to be, like gaps in the mouth of a six-year-old boy losing his milk teeth. And he thought of the ultraviolet light, and he thought wasn't it something what they could do with a little gadget like a camera nowadays. When he came to the head of the casket, he had to clear his throat. Then he opened his eyes and high-tailed it back to his seat. He knew Lila was trying to catch his eye as he hurried down the aisle but he never let on he noticed. At first he thought she was mad at him for the stain on his pants; she probably thought he'd lost control. But suddenly there was no doubt in his mind whatsoever that she knew about the whole thing. Even supposing he never said a word to her about it, she would have known. He and Lila must have been married too long, Calder thought. There didn't seem to be anything he could put over on her any more. He would fill her in on some of the fine points anyway, on the flight home when he could talk to her alone.

Later that evening, just before Calder and Lila left for the airport, Connie went down to the freezer and came back up with a salmon which she gave to Calder to take back to the prairie, a whole salmon embedded in ice and wrapped in a plastic bag with a red wire tag.

The Late Date

Some stories should be told straight, Marilyn thought. She knew that now. But at the time, she had spoken of her experience as a late date. In the residence, in the dark, whispered stacatto across the tiles between the beds, to Gail, her roommate from Trestle. Since then she had told her tale many times over the years and there was no longer any feeling attached to it other than the concern about the telling itself, the timing, the well-delivered line.

Until today. If it hadn't been for Heather, her hammer and clatter, Marilyn knew she would have been able to perpetuate the lie through middle age and menopause, right into old age. Even now a part of her would have preferred it that way. The altered version had come to feel a lot like truth over the years.

Most of the morning Heather had been on the patio, sawing, of all things, hammering and clattering in a way you would have expected from one of those do-it-yourself women on television who kept trying to persuade Marilyn to identify various basic carpenter tools and put them to use. One of these programs followed "Keep Fit" which Marilyn never missed because her body, of late, had begun to develop folds, the atrophy of the flesh taken hold, she believed, prematurely, like the grey which she had streaked in such a way that it would turn entirely blonde in the sun. Most of the time she spent on the patio these days was for the fresh air and the light, not the tan, which in her case was usually a burn anyway that turned to uneven blotches of brown before nightfall. This process not only disgusted her but gave her something of a fright because of the cancer scare. The push for Vitamin D which was on around the time Heather had been born was gone, replaced with warnings against the danger of taking too much sun. Ultraviolet rays were the culprits, they said. So she had covered up her arms before she took her coffee out to the patio for the ten o'clock break. She didn't have to teach but she had a stack of papers to mark and couldn't really afford to take the whole day off. She had put on her sunglasses, too, before she had come out, carried a wide-brimmed cotton hat, shielded her face from the sun. There were minor side-effects, webs of wrinkles at the corners of the eyes, spawned by the sun, they said now, not by smiles. The sun induced relexive frowns instead.

She chose a green plastic webbed lawn chair in front of Heather's open-air shop, sat down and put on her hat. She had no trouble reading the letters upsidedown on the sign her daughter painted, alternately frowning, perplexed, and faintly smiling, lost in some private thought.

I AM NOT

A VIRGIN—

AND I AM *NOT*

A WHORE—

The letters were painted in chunky black blocks lined on the inner edges with a luminescent red, and, although they were very large, there was room on the sign for more--as if what was already written there were not enough. Shocked, Marilyn dropped the hand with which she shielded her eyes to her lap, leaned over the sign for a reluctant but closer look as if it were a corpse she had been asked to positively identify. It must be for the march, she thought numbly. Heather had said something at breakfast about a march.

Large, unwieldy lilac bushes, purple and French white surrounded the concrete blocks of the patio, leaving only a narrow path to the garden at the back. Their odor was oppressive in the heat, the spears sprung by the sun almost overnight. Early this year. They had never bloomed before until mid-June.

"Where did you get the boards?"

"The bristleboard?"

"No, the lumber."

"At Beaver on the South Side. They're one by two's," she

said, glancing at them over her shoulder. They were stacked neatly on her right. She had placed Ron's heavy-duty automatic stapler beside them. Marilyn had given it to him last year around this time, for Father's Day. When Heather returned to the sign, her auburn hair fell over her eyes. She had begun to wear it long and the sun accentuated the natural red highlights, like Ron's. She had washed it after breakfast and it was, Marilyn had to concede, lovely, wavy, clean. She flicked it back from her forehead, away from her eyes. It swung perfectly to the side, a good cut. Good and thick and clean.

Marilyn set her cup on the cement beside her chair and stood up. She had been the same age as Heather was now, just over eighteen, had just finished her first year at the university. General Arts, the perfect program for a girl who wanted a liberal education, and lots of time to decide what she really wanted to be. As Marilyn had told Heather more than once, an arts degree in itself didn't qualify you for much. Marilyn had later gone on to the college of education, then to teach.

The summer between her first and second year of university, she had applied for a job as a psychiatric aide. In those days they called the position Summer Relief. Every spring the provincial psychiatric hospitals recruited summer replacement staff in a basement room on campus which one reached by means of a network of brightly lit, subterranean tunnels. The applicants were almost all young women. In fact, not one young man could be found among the recruits assigned to the same hospital as she had been, perhaps because the wages were so low, perhaps for other reasons.

Certainly the competition for summer jobs seemed to Marilyn as fierce then as it appeared now. Two hundred fifty dollars per month minus thirty-two dollars a month for room and board in residence was not lucrative by any means, but it would help pay for tuition and books the following year. They were to take their meals in the staff dining room of the main building which one reached in the early hours of the morning and late at night by means of a subterranean tunnel connecting the main building with the residence.

72

For those who had no previous employment experience in the real world and no family connections in business, the possibility of getting a regular job—the ones usually reserved for young women such as clerking, cleaning, typing—was remote and Marilyn had been elated to land any job whatsoever, even this one. Elated, although she had been advised against taking it by a very perceptive professor whose mother had worked in a similar institution and who felt that the price exacted by such employment would likely be far greater than any amount of money could offset. Theoretically, he was quite right, of course. She had, in retrospect, agreed with him a thousand times.

Her mother and father delivered her. The highway was flat and straight, the fields flat and green and all around them so that it seemed as if they were the centre of an enormous green circumference and were moving through a tube, half green, half blue, tilted, suspended at that radial line on the central standard clock which marked the end of her childhood and her protected walk with them. They were silent, apprehensive too. She thought they would never get there, that somehow her father had his foot on the gas pedal and the brake at the same time.

Now, with Heather, Marilyn knew what they must have felt then, on the way down that clear spring day. She and Ron had tried to give their daughter shelter and they had, to nurture her and, at the same time, allow her the freedom she needed to learn to think for herself. Marilyn laughed. And so she has, she thought, peering through her fingers at the sign. So she has. Heather looked up. Now Marilyn wished she could have given her a cocoon, camouflage, to keep her safe from what she knew was in the world, what she had begun to learn when she was barely eighteen.

Recently she had read an article which declared that the decade would be marked by images of dismemberment, mutilation and rare disease. The author of the article was alarmed by the rise of an apparently malignant tendency in the human psyche to derive pleasure from such imagery.

73

Several of Marilyn's friends, women she had met the year of her summer relief, were still in the field and had told her some of the things they had seen over the years, were witness and nurse to the numberless victims rising like wraithes from the pit, men and women and children who preceded the images or followed them—no one seemed to know which.

Certain uncomfortable fragments of that eighteenth summer had resurfaced when Marilyn read the article; but she had put them out of her mind, or rather replaced them very carefully in the deeper recesses on a solid shelf in the hope that they would remain there, not fall off again, reappear behind her eyes. This did not prevent her from hauling out her humorous anecdote about the first "man", correction, "men" she ever saw when it seemed to be socially appropriate, that is whenever certain allowable indiscretions were afoot, too many drinks, an intolerable boredom with broadloom and rare bric-a-brac. On such occasions Marilyn would describe the experience as the highlight of her "liberal education". How I put myself through an insitution of higher learning in a most unusual way. Garnished with her famous one-liners. After all, it was a party, wasn't it. The mandate was entertainment. The story had to be palatable, served, as it were, with dry martinis and fresh paté.

The high sun on the back of her head, like a lamp in a projector, drove the lighted image round inside her dark skull, taste, touch, sight, sound, smell, a better example by far than she had used in her lecture before dismissing her students, before the Friday bell. A spherical film. Dizzy, she stumbled forward, caught her sandal on the corner of a concrete block and almost fell, staggered around and sat down again, alarmed.

"Mom?" Heather said, beginning to rise, reaching up as if to catch her but it would have been impossible, too late. She was too far away. She could never have been there in time.

"I'm all right, Heather. Too much sun. I'll move my chair over to the corner in the shade." Which she did. But the move had the effect of convincing her that the management had only dimmed the lights. The show was not over at all; in fact, had just begun.

Marilyn took off her hat and shook her head from side to side which loosened the pressed hair and cooled the wet scalp beneath but had no effect whatsoever on the film, brought no measurable relief from the dizziness. She had applied so much pressure to her eyes that now she could hardly see outside her head at all. Inside, the intensity of the light increased. She thought it might help if she spoke.

"Married," she declared to the back of Heather's head, then laughed.

"Pardon?"

"I said 'married'. I know what you're going to write next. On the sign. You're going to write 'What am I?' It just struck me. 'I AM NOT A VIRGIN AND I AM NOT A WHORE—' *What am I?* comes next, right? And I say—a married woman." Marilyn laughed. "I'm your mother. That's what I'm supposed to say, isn't it? Do I get a prize?"

"The booby prize maybe. God, Mom, I'm not Bob Hope, you know. I'm not doing this for laughs."

"I know, Heather, for heaven's sake, I know. Just a little old-fashioned joke. Humour your old mother. If I were you I'd never pass up a good laugh, or any laugh for that matter. *It's a long way to Tipperary, it's a long way to go—*" Marilyn sang.

"If that's your idea of another joke, my face cracks—with pleasure, right? Leacock, if I remember my grade ten English. Something to do with celluloid collars. Besides, it hasn't been all that funny for you, correct?" Heather looked up, directly into her eyes.

"Right," Marilyn said. An interlude. The shorts. Coming attractions. No relief in sight.

After she had checked in at the administration office in the main building, her mother and father drove her over to the residence across the grounds which were manicured, the fine lawns interrupted at regular intervals by well-ordered flower beds, circles and diamonds of loam containing perfectly linear rows of geraniums, petunias and marigolds surrounded with alyssum.

And the lilacs. The purple and white garlands of lilacs weaving in and out around the grounds, the suffocating smell of lilacs surrounding the copper-domed shell of the main building. Red. Brick. Red brick. Bricks, thousands and screaming thousands from Medicine Hat. Tons and tons of screaming brick locked in mortar. As if enough of them could keep the madness out—of the rest of the world, that is, Marilyn thought. In, if you looked at it from the point of view of the staff. Nothing was more obvious to her now than the fact that it hadn't worked, the multiplicity of madness being what it is.

In fact, the institution to which she had been assigned was already pioneering in two areas. One, psychopharmacology, including the development of LSD, and two, the dismantling of the enormous reptilean "institution" to which she had come. In its hey-day, it had sheltered or incarcerated, depending on how you wanted to look at it, more than thirty-five hundred patients, a larger city by far than the host community named on the official map distributed throughout the province, the one followed by her father the day they drove down.

The latter development had attracted a great deal of attention throughout North America and, under a hairdryer in the residence, Marilyn herself had read the accounts of the miraculous transformation, (none of which mentioned the mortared dome, the shell), the transfer of all the patients from this institution to half-way houses and nursing homes, back into the community. She read these articles in major American psychiatric journals, was duly impressed by the awesome progress leviathan madness had made since the days of 999 in Toronto and the concept of asylum as sanctuary.

Diminishing patient count was critical. The entire staff knew yesterday's number by the time they hit the floor for the seven o'clock shift. And Marilyn was dismayed by the aged, bespectacled man in an old felt hat who that first day tapped with his cane on the glass doors of 1 C-D, beseeching her to let him back in, as if summer relief could do any such thing. Some of these old boys, she was told in passing, had been in for thirty years, knew more about the place than senior staff, called it home.

"Go way. Get back, old man," she heard one of the staff say. "He wants back in the dorm, the crazy old son-of-a-bitch. Remember the poem he used to say when we put them down to bed. Hit the hay, old man. Hit the hay.

> 'Now I lay me down to sleep
> I pray the Lord my soul to keep
> and if I die before I wake
> I pray the Lord my soul to take
> the goddamn stupid effing little bitch.'

Gordon, get the switch. Jesus, he's completely incontinent, pissing on the rads at the new place. Making himself right at home, I guess. Get the switch. One thing you can say about this place is it sure as hell must look safe to them compared with what's going on outside."

He came back to the hospital every day. Eventually he was readmitted to Marilyn's ward. What she remembered most about working with this particular patient, apart from his shorn head, was his boots. Bending over his boots. Tying the laces on his boots. Big, black, leather-soled boots. All of them had the boots. But this man had, on several occasions, used them on other patients. And once on a female staff. She couldn't remember his name.

That first night in residence had not gone well. After the preliminaries, where are you from and what are you taking at university—Gail from Trestle, Physics, Chemistry and Biology; Marilyn from Saskatoon, English, French and Philosophy—they unpacked, lined the tops of their vanities with tiny ornamental bottles of perfume, lipsticks, alarm clocks and various creams, stuffed the drawers with clothes, nylon stockings, hair rollers, notepaper and envelopes for letters home. Then they went to bed and immediately fell into an uneasy silence, rigid beneath the pristine sheets, abrasive with starch, the silence in the dark broken only once when the housemother entered the room with a flashlight on her rounds, cast a tight shaft of light through the room which ricocheted off the walls. She had come to check if they were there. They were not. In their minds, both she and Gail were on their way north, back home. They slept fitfully. Marilyn had a dream which confirmed all her worst suspicions about the job and the place; and Gail had an asthma attack, the first of many which were to occur with frightening regularity whenever she came off shift. Marilyn listened to her laboured breathing intermittently throughout the night. From their early, tentative talk, Marilyn gathered that Gail had come from a family very much like her own. And that she was just as afraid as Marilyn of the dawn.

The next day they showered, dressed and descended through the residence stairwell to the basement which contained a recreation room, laundry facilities, and at the far end, a large door, gun-metal grey, the small high window reinforced with wire mesh. They read the rectangular silk-screened sign on the door. A red arrow directed them through: TO SEWING ROOM. TO LOCKSMITH. TO MAINTENANCE. TO MAIN BUILDING. Each with a yellow arrow pointing left or right.

"We'd better get a move on," Gail said. "We wouldn't want to miss our fitting, now would we, dear," she mimicked the housemother, an exaggerated high-pitched whisper. "You'd think we were on our way to the mezzanine of Mayfair Fashions for godsakes, something for grad or maybe a bridal gown."

They entered the tunnel which turned out to be surprisingly bright with painted pipes, red and yellow and white, running along the ceiling on either side of the fluorescent lights. There was a continuous mural of large sunflowers along one wall. It looked as if it had been painted by a child or like something you might find in a prehistoric cave. Later Marilyn learned the first year university students had gussied the tunnel up the previous spring during their festival of Van Gogh whom they had crowned the patron saint of madness and of art. Clever, Marilyn thought.

When they reached the sewing room, a Mrs. Clements,

identified so by a badge, black on white, appeared from behind a partition at the back. Marilyn stared at the badge, a primer on the nature of institutional life. Everything and everybody tagged, from head to toe, Marilyn thought, if you tended toward morbid humour. Mrs. Clements called Gail into the fitting room first. She returned transformed. A la Nightingale. All she needed was a lamp. Later, Marilyn would look back on that moment as prophetic. Gail stayed on after the rest of them had fled back to campus in the fall. She was the only one of them who would become a nurse.

There were no uniforms in Marilyn's size, Mrs. Clements said, but she would do the best she could. Marilyn told her she liked the tunnel, which she honestly did. Mrs. Clements eyed her quizzically through the slits of a narrow half-squint, as if she'd just arrived from another planet. Which, in a way, she had. "Yes," Mrs. Clements finally said, "I suppose you would."

"How long have you been here then?" Marilyn asked.

"Long enough to remember finding the old defectives in the tunnel eating salamanders after they'd wriggled out of their jackets over on 2B and gone AWOL. This was before they brought in the drugs. Oh, I remember the salamander snacks all right. You don't forget a thing like that."

"Pardon?"

"Away without leave," she said. "That's the only part of it you wouldn't understand. The rest is plain English." Mrs. Clements stood back and looked at her. "You're nothing but a twig, are you, dear. Wear that one and leave these with me. I'll take them up. Bring the one you have on back with you next time you come."

The uniform Marilyn wore was four sizes too big and four inches from the floor. It was starched as stiff as a board. She looked as if Mrs. Clements had dressed her up for Hallowe'en. If she had had a small red nubbled plastic nurse's kit with the tablets of candy hearts, the outfit would have been complete. The uniform was short-sleeved and, within minutes, Marilyn had begun to develop a collar of red rash at her neck and two smaller bands of itchy lumps around her upper arms. She had them all summer long. The hems of the skirt which met at the front of the uniform clacked as she left the room. Mrs. Clements laughed softly.

By the time they had found the dining room through the labyrinth of walls and halls, had asked directions twice along the way, they were late for breakfast. They hardly had time for the coffee and lukewarm porridge and toast. There were only a few staff left in the dining room when they arrived, lingering over coffee, assigned to another shift, perhaps, Marilyn thought, afternoons, evenings, maybe nights. She was afraid that sooner or later her name would come up and she would be assigned to nights.

When she finished breakfast, she placed her tray in the aluminum rack near the door. Gail followed. They had been told to report to different wards, Gail, 2B, and Marilyn 1C-D Left, which was in another wing. The face of the woman appeared in the doorway before them, out of nowhere it seemed, but she must have been waiting there quietly, perhaps for a long time.

"No and no and no and no," she bellowed toward the open door through which Marilyn and Gail were about to leave. "I will not believe/ that this is so." Her hair was grey, cut straight across and blunt around the ears—a few years later this would become fashionable but then Marilyn and Gail and most other girls wore their hair bouffant, back-combed with a rat tail comb, shellacked, in veritable hives.

The woman had the wildest eyes Marilyn had ever seen, Hollywood's idea of Jane Eyre's eyes. But this was as far as you could get from the silver screen, Marilyn thought. She wore a faded, sagging shirtwaist, short sleeved, a small floral print which used to be pale blue but now was closer to grey. She looked so clean, Marilyn thought, so fiercely clean, scrubbed the way fastidious mothers keep their children when there is no water. Marilyn stood as if stunned. So did Gail. The woman was blocking their way. Arms outstretched, she began to sing and sway.

"Motherhood and apple pie, motherhood and apple pie, apple pie and other lies—"

"Excuse us," Gail finally said from behind Marilyn.

The interruption enraged the woman. She grabbed hold of the door frame with one hand and flung the other arm out toward them. "I will not believe that this is so!" she shrieked and spit into Marilyn's face. "Such a cacophony and such a howl will ring down, ring down millennia—such a howl as has never been heard before—the angels will bow. The voices of those who nurtured and bled and born and began again, suckled you over all this time. WE WILL CRY. WE WILL CRY."

All of this rapid fire. Marilyn was, as she had feared she would be, terrified, paralyzed.

"IF THIS IS DONE," the woman screamed, and then she began to hiss, "you will not hear your various gods or any one alone or none again. My voice will be in all of you—in all your good goodbyes, obstructing all your high and heavenly ways—forever, yea for all of time.

"Dolorum," she chanted, "and Hecuba dragged backward into the gloom with you. The myth of the cloud and the eyes will be *nothing* in the rising tide this time. YOU DO SO KNOW WHAT YOU DO. OH YES YOU DO. Every mother you ever had or dreamt of having, every woman you ever had or dreamt of having, every have you've ever had or dreamt of having, every halving and coming together and halving, halving—"

What had frightened Marilyn most was not the power of the tirade, although she had to confess she had nothing whatsoever in her life with which to compare it and she had been in church nearly every Sunday morning of her life. What petrified her was the fact that the other staff behind them remained inert all that time, engaged in quiet conversation. The incident in memory stopped in time, a jammed projector, and the crazy she raged over the same words again and again while Marilyn and Gail remained passive, silent. For an instant, Marilyn had even felt that she was the one who was out of step, not this woman raving in front of her eyes.

Then the woman began to smile and sing, plaintively this time, like a child, really more of a sigh than a song, the same tuneless song as before, "Motherhood and apple pie, apple pie, apple pie—"

"Wind her up, Gracie, that's the end of the set. Floor show's over till the next shift." A tall, blond young man had come up from behind them and extended his hand toward the woman. She reached out for the hand, then curtsied, her head down; after she had risen, he placed his right hand behind his back in a gesture of gallantry and he bowed. Then he cupped his left hand toward Marilyn and Gail and in a stage-whisper said, "Listen to this." He turned to the woman. "What's your name?" he asked.

She smiled and chanted in the same numb song sigh as before, "Suzie Suzie Rotten-Crotch, Rotten-Crotch, Rotten-Crotch—"

Then to Gail and Marilyn again, "But we call her Amazing Grace. That's what she usually sings. Besides, Grace is her name." He turned back to her. "Right?" he said. She did not respond. "Move along, Gracie," he said, "I gotta go to work." She stepped aside and he walked through the doorway. Marilyn and Gail were right behind him.

Moving along the corridor, the young man glanced over his shoulder at Marilyn and Gail. "You summer relief?" he asked.

"Yes," Gail replied, "first day on the job."

"Great," he said. "We could use a little fresh blood around here. That was Grace. A woman ahead of her time. She was an English teacher, Master's, I'm told. Figures she's cornered the market on false faith and the big bang. My name's Bill Neilson. What wards you been assigned?"

It happened that his ward was the same as Marilyn's. He directed Gail toward her floor. She had been assigned to the defectives, he said. "You and me are with the old geezers down on 1 C-D." They continued down the corridor. For

82

some reason, he did not seem in the least worried about getting there on time. "What's your name?" he asked as he slipped his key into the lock of a door which divided two wards, the movement easy, automatic, as if he'd opened it a million times before.

"Marilyn," she replied.

"As in Monroe?"

"No," she said. Bill Neilson wore bifocals, very thick on one side, almost opaque. She hadn't noticed it right away, but he had practically no vision left in that eye. Later, he told her his vision had never been good and that the one eye had been injured in a schoolyard fight when he was just a kid. Somebody in the eighth grade had hit him with a stick. But the other eye, instead of deteriorating along with it, had progressively improved and would, he hoped, continue to do so.

"Hey, Monroe," one of the staff called from the main bathroom on the ward, "c'mere." They had all begun to call her "Monroe" after they heard Bill use the name at lunch. Marilyn hesitated outside the door.

"I just have to finish cleaning up the games in the day room," she called back.

"Hey! Miss Summer Relief!" another voice yelled, Mr. Zwicky whom she had just met. "We've got a job for you to do in here." Marilyn knew. This was toward the end of the first shift and she knew they were up to something sinister even before they called her. But she couldn't believe it. Initiation of a sort, she thought. She was familiar with the form but not the sport. She folded her arms across the sturdy breast of her new uniform.

"Bet you never saw anything like this," Mr. Zwicky said as she entered the room.

A young, but veteran aide regarded Marilyn with amusement. The aide was leaning against a cupboard on the opposite wall, the frosted gloss of a plum lipstick pressed to her teeth in a ridiculous thin grin, in a let's-see-how-the-varsity-virgin-handles-this, borderline leer. She was humming the tune from the beauty pageants, "Here she comes, Miss America."

"No," Marilyn found herself speaking in a remarkably clear voice, in spite of the flush of embarrassment and resentment on her face. "No I haven't. Never before."

There was a row of open showers at the far end of the room. Porcelain. The white bowels of the old institution worn out, pocked and greying in eroded spots. Inserted in each stall was the alabaster flesh of one old man, all sizes represented, mostly stooped and some protecting, even then, most private parts. But mainly they stood with their arms limp at their sides, legs slightly apart, as if they were in a line-up like the ones Marilyn had seen on the silver screen in crime movies. She was jolted by her response which at first she could not articulate, but which eventually came, rose clearly from her open throat. "At least the bowels of hell are clean." And to herself, in that still, that quiet part of her where no one ever sees—*They do it to each other too. Of course they do.*

She glared at Bill who was standing beside a trolley of white towels with some of the other staff, some she hadn't even seen before; they must be from the afternoon shift, Marilyn thought. Mr. Zwicky and the aide had laughed out loud but Bill did not even smile, had regarded her carefully through his glasses which had slid low on the bridge of his nose.

"We used to use the hoses," Mr. Zwicky said, holding a thick white canvas rope with a chrome nozzle on the end, "before the pills—I believe they refer to it in admin as the psychopharmacological revolt—but now we just turn on the overhead spray. I remember the day they put them in."

"Revolution," Bill said on his way out.

That first shift had almost swallowed her whole. After supper in the staff dining room, they went back to the residence and the girls on summer relief began to gather in the lounge in the basement from their scattered rooms. Everyone eventually spoke—everyone but Marilyn. The stories began to emerge. Perhaps that was where she had learned how to handle her anecdotes. Serena Wainwright had been sent up to the dispensary for fallopian tubes. The worst of it was, she had gone. She was mortified. She was an honours Biology student. She would never live it down, she said. We wouldn't ever tell anyone, would we now. Let's all take a vow—and so the evening went. That bloody vow. There were many such as the summer progressed. They may as well have had their lips sewn shut when they left, they had taken so many vows of silence and discretion. None of them had daughters then—nor had they even thought of them.

Later that week, after the shift had changed, Bill stopped Marilyn in the corridor and asked her to go out with him on the weekend. Saturday night.

All day long the girls in the residence primped and curled their hair, painted their nails, tried on each other's dresses and lipsticks. And, for the first time since she had arrived, Marilyn thought she might make out all right here. She might survive. She was excited, proud, in fact, that she had been asked out so soon, and more than a little eager to get off the hospital grounds.

After supper in the staff dining room, gooey dumplings in string beef stew followed by a bright red cube of India rubber Jello, Marilyn had skipped her way back through the tunnel to the residence and took the stairs two at a time up to her room.

She and Gail giggled in front of their vanity mirrors. They traded eyeshadow. Marilyn was wearing a pale green mohair sweater, popcorn stitch, and Gail had decided to wear a blue seersucker dress. So Marilyn traded her blue shadow for the green. She also backcombed Gail's hair and loaned her a pale blue velvet bow comb. These combs were a particularly popular accessory that spring. Gail posed in front of her mirror with her hand on the back of her neck just as she had seen the starlets do in the pictures in *Screenplay Magazine*. "If only the guys in Trestle could see me now," she said.

Marilyn told her she thought her date, who worked in Maintenance, was cute, and Gail said she thought Bill was too, in his own way, even if he couldn't see his hand in front of his face. He had nice hair. "And ears," Gail said and snickered, "also a good physique." That's what they used to call it then. A good physique.

They agreed they wouldn't be late coming in, at any cost, because if you broke the curfew, you got CB'd, the house-mother said, and could you imagine anything worse, they said, than to be confined to barracks in a dump like this, for days, maybe even weeks. On their way down to the lounge, the voices of other girls echoed in the hall, diminished to whispers when Gail and Marilyn passed the open doors. Secrets sifting through the air. An isolated laugh. Someone softly cursing her wet hair.

Gail's date came first. The girls from the residence had begun to gather, regular staff and summer relief together. They sat in the lounge where they waited, those who had dates. Those who did not stayed in their rooms or wafted periodically past the lounge wearing their pink plastic curlers or towels on their heads and old jeans, making it perfectly clear that they weren't waiting for anything or anyone, and couldn't have cared less.

There were three pay phones in booths just off the lounge. They rang constantly that Saturday evening and finally one of the calls was for Marilyn. Bill. He said he would be a little late, would she wait for him. She said yes, she would. No problem. She had been in town all afternoon, since right after shift, and she wasn't really ready anyway.

Marilyn sat on one of the sofas which lined the walls and watched the other girls make or wait for calls. She had only been away from home one week. On Sunday evening she would phone her family as she had promised. The longer she sat thinking about it, the more she wondered what on earth she would tell them. Last night I went out on a late date. At least they had heard of things like that. Providing, of course, she wasn't stood up. More to the point she wanted to ask why. Why didn't you tell me before? The world is not the way you made it out to be.

An old man, Yacob Cain, had died that morning on her ward. He was impacted, they told her, and they laughed when she hadn't known what that was. And yesterday the barbers came to shave the old men. One of the barbers was

86

short and asked the patients if any of them had had any luck in the bushes lately. It took Marilyn a few moments to figure out what on earth that might mean. Until the barber winked at her and smiled. He told gruesome stories about the hanging tree on the front lawn where many a patient had met his end, or hers, over the years, ever since they had opened the doors, the tall barber said.

And the little Charlie who sat in the barber's chair and roared like a lion every time the barber came near him with the long razor. The little Charlie who saw pillars of animals moving up toward heaven and the stars, up through the ceiling of the patients' dining hall where he sat and ate like a bird, he was so enthralled. And Hershel who spent all of his days rubbing off the arrows painted on the floor, thin trails of yellow arrows leading the old men toward the toilets without doors and the sinks, the stink of incontinence everywhere. And James who sometimes ate his own excrement and sometimes painted his chrome glint-armed chair in the day room. Half a dozen of them, maybe more, pinned to the walls of the corridors on crosses of their own construction, invisible in the air; one of them regular as a cuckoo clock cried out to the empty air, "The Itmosphere, O my God, the Itmosphere." All her old men, showered and shorn. And now Marilyn knew exactly what she would say when she phoned, would say if only she could. Come down and take me home, back to the patio surrounded with honeysuckle and lilac, iris and bleeding heart, back to the small lawn and the lingering of the long summer afternoon with a good novel and a tall cold glass of pale pink lemonade. And a radio and a song. "Hot town, summer in the city", or "The morning sun is shining like a red rubber ball," "Oh, Sweet Pea, come on and dance with me," "Zorba the Greek". How could she make it through one more day let alone the rest of the summer.

On Tuesday afternoon, she had been sent to 3K to pick up some special medication and there she had met a woman who never stopped talking. As soon as Marilyn set foot on the floor, the woman began to follow her. "My name is Cheryl. I was raped when I was seventeen. I was walking across the railroad tracks under the overhead bridge by Early's Seed and Feed in Saskatoon you know and a man jumped out of the dark and grabbed my arm and it broke and that was twenty-three years ago and they brought me here and they didn't know what happened to me I never spoke since then not a single word and now they give me some new pills and I spoke they're pink and white and pretty soon I'll be all better don't you think and then they'll let me go and I'll go home my name is Cheryl I was raped when I was seventeen I was walking across the railroad tracks under the overhead bridge by Early's Seed and Feed in Saskatoon you know and a man jumped out of the dark and grabbed my arm and it broke and that was twenty-three years ago—"

Which is a far cry, Dad, Marilyn said to him in her head, from the joke Mr. Archibald told you when you were raking the lawn just before we drove down. The one about the prostitute walking across the overhead bridge with no underpants on, headed for 20th Street, and an Englishman walking along underneath at the same time looks up and sees what you know he sees. "Pretty airy up there, ain't it, sweetie?" he says in his Cockney, and she hollers down, "What'd ya expect? Feathers?"

Go away, she told Cheryl, told all the pictures reeling in her head. Just go away. And don't for God's sake tell me this is real, this place. She began to understand old Grace, Amazing Grace, and for the first time, she became aware of the lethal danger here. It was possible that by the time she got home, Marilyn Marie Dufreysne, whoever she used to be, could have disappeared without a trace.

Mr. Amien, the supervisor of her ward, found her on her coffee break sitting beside the billiard table in the day room with a branch of lilac she had picked when they were out for the afternoon walk. She had removed the small purple flowers from a blossom on the stem, one by one, dropped them on the floor in front of her. She was in the process of gathering them all up, cupping her hand to hold the delicate debris when Mr. Amien walked in. "You better get the broom, Marilyn, you'll drive yourself round the bend trying to get them all that way." He sat down beside her, a large man with big hands, a strong thick neck. "While I'm here," he added, "I'm going to give you a little free advice. Let them go. Let some things go. You can't keep them all. It's not up to you to do the accounts. You come from a good home. I could tell that about you right away. You're green. You've had more than your share of love, too many safe nights." He lit a cigarette. "You're walking around without a skin. You're packing all of this in and you can't. Toughen up. Let some things fall by the way.

"When you leave this place, just go. The staff here, a lot of us are getting on. We grew old here. We're just like the chronics," he laughed, "we've got no place to go." He stood, walked toward the tall bright windows of the day room, windows wavy with the heat, and looked out. "No," he said, "that's not true." He stood quietly for a few moments while Marilyn regarded his back, the seam down the centre of his long white coat. "But you," he said slowly, "as long as you leave it where it lies, who knows. You could do anything you want. If you don't it will drag you down with it, so help me God. And no matter where you are, no matter who you're with, it will eat you from the inside out. It will swallow you whole. I know your type." At coffee that morning, Marilyn remembered Mr. Zwicky whispering to the aide that Mrs. Amien's divorce papers had finally come through.

Bill appeared at the residence door just as Marilyn was about to go back to her room. Never again, she had made up her mind, I don't care what excuse he comes up with. Hell will freeze over before I go out with him.

"Put your shoes on Nellie, we're a goin' to the city," he said, smiling.

"Not this time," Marilyn replied. "I'm not going. I don't think you're my type."

"I called," he said, his smile fading, "but I guess I didn't actually tell you what was going on. I'm sorry about that.

89

Really." He paused. She said nothing. "I was with Wally Salt and Grant McKay. We had to take Grant into the Psyche Centre. He went up the pole, crossed over to the other side. I could tell he was headed in that direction, was well on his way when I met him yesterday morning in the hall over on the garden wing. He wanted us to stay with him awhile. Just sit. Dope and booze. Even a litle glue, if you can believe it, the stupid son-of-a-bitch. So we did that and then Wally and I went over to the hotel for a beer."

"It's already ten o'clock," Marilyn said. "The curfew's midnight."

"I'll get you back all right. Sign out." She hesitated as if she were thinking it over twice. "Come on, Monroe," he said, "we're wasting valuable time."

"My name is Marilyn Dufreysne. Marilyn Marie Dufreysne. If you can't say that, don't say anything." The housemother looked up from her book and appeared to smirk. While Marilyn signed out, the woman never spoke, just glanced from Bill to her, then back to Bill. Something told Marilyn she knew more about him than she should, more than she would say. On the way down the residence steps, Bill told her the housemother was his aunt. His whole extended family had worked at the hospital at one time or another, he said. "A family tradition, maybe some sort of quirky genetic trait. Too bad it wasn't law, eh? Anyway, lots of the families in this town went the same way," he said.

They walked slowly through the grounds along a paved path which wound around the side of the hospital to the main parking lot. There was only half a moon but it shone on the bank of lilacs at the back of the lot dividing the hospital from the rest of the world. There were two cars parked near the wall of the building although the lot was usually full during the day. Bill stopped at a side door lodged in a wall of solid brick. There were no windows on this side on the ground floor. He pulled a cluster of rattling keys from his pocket. "Just a sec," he said, "I have to check on something here before we go. You staying or coming with me?"

Marilyn followed him in through a narrow hall lit dimly with a small yellow light bulb. Another door. Another key, and the hall opened into a wider hall, a long hall which looked as if it had no end, just intermittent yellow bulbs and a receding, unreachable point in the dim distance where the walls appeared to intersect. They passed what seemed like a hundred doors, some with silk-screened labels, new and faded. Some doors remained unmarked. All she could hear was the sound of their walking and the monotonous hum of a large fan, the occasional gurgle in a hidden pipe, sewage stalking out or fresh water moving in, fluids moving back and forth from floor to floor in the deep institutional night.

Finally Bill stopped and unlocked a door clearly marked PATHOLOGY/MORGUE. They hesitated there. The top of Marilyn's head barely reached his shoulder. He looked over it and she looked up at him.

"Do you come here often?" Marilyn asked in a thin voice, mocking. He looked away.

"No," she heard him say softly to the black and white tiles on the checkerboard floor, "no," to the disinfectant air. "Only when one of my friends checks in. Overnight."

They passed through an anteroom banked with large, unlabelled drawers and entered a small, cool room. No windows. Only the one door. A single extended tube of soft fluorescent light was suspended beneath a row of cupboards on the wall to the right. Everything was made of stainless steel, the sinks, the cupboards full of narrow drawers labelled in type or fine black ink. In the centre of the room there was a long steel table surrounded by a gradually sloping trough, like a lip, which ran around it and into a small steel sink which Marilyn supposed was at the foot end. The table was very clean, a shaft of dull gleam fell across it through the doorway from the yellow bulb of the anteroom.

Bill flicked a switch and filled the room with a funnel of blue-white light which descended from the stem of a surgical lamp centred directly above the table and, for a moment, obliterated everything. Marilyn felt nothing at first except the fright. Yet the fear moved quickly on, she had no idea why.

And then she was calm, a cool colloidal calm. Now, she realized she hadn't felt that way for years. When Heather was a baby and she nursed her in the night, sometimes then she felt it coming on.

When she looked around the room again, she found Bill standing in front of a shelf which held several large clear jars. All of them marked. Patient: Yacob Cain. Liver, Stomach, Right Lung, Brain. Heart. These organs were preserved in some kind of brine. Marilyn thought of pickled eggs. Then, for a moment, the organs looked like continents to her, mapped, as if someone had taken a globe and carved all of the continents out, then carefully placed them separately in jars and set them, evenly spaced, upon this shelf. But this image, too, was instantly replaced by her old friend, Frankenstein, which, after all, made more sense, she thought. She'd seen the movie at the Broadway Theatre with her brother when she was eight. Dr. Frankenstein bottling brains. She had run out through the lobby onto the sidewalk, raced all the way down Broadway to Ruth, up Landsdowne, home, all the way home. She had run all the way away, but it was too late. She knew as soon as she was through the kitchen door. He was there. And over the days and weeks and months, she gradually got used to having him in her head, and by and by came to know that she would always carry him with her, regardless of her age.

They walked out the way they came in, took the same route back to the parking lot, Bill stopping at every door he had to lock, turning his back to Marilyn, rattling keys, then moving toward her once more. Near the end of the corridor, he traced with his hand up the length of her spine, under her sweater, beginning at the small. And she was the first out the door into the lilac air, the first one in the car, the first one on the blanket by the river, the first with her face to the stars.

Marilyn started and began to tremble when she remembered their coming together. She had felt as if she were coming apart, pieces of her flying through the dark, lying on the table, on the floor, on the counter, in the sink, in the corners, clinging to the ceiling, and some part of her tapping on the door, wanting, not out but back in again, in to that other girl she had left back there before the small, cool room and the wet dark, the girl who saw the world as whole, all the blossoms back on the stem, everything and everybody mended.

It couldn't be done, of course. And she knew. But, at the same time, (and this was still a mystery to her), she also knew that it could. That they could make another one, out of the flesh of the past, out of the spent parts. The legacy of all the people on earth who had ever lived, who had cradled the singular universe.

"I know why you took me there," she said on the way back to the residence. "I knew it all along. I didn't do it because of that."

"Really," he smiled over at her, the fine stubble of a faint beard along his jaw visible in the soft light from the dash. His glasses low and heavy on the bridge of his nose. "The fact of the matter is I never took you anywhere. I was under the impression that I asked you and that you went down there of your own free will. You could have stayed back at the car."

"Besides," she went on, "you didn't seem all that close to him if you want my opinion. On the ward. As far as I could see."

"Yacob and I go back a long way."

"You teased him unmercifully."

"We had an understanding, Yacob and me. He was the first patient I ever saw. He was planting flowers on the grounds the day my dad first took me up to the hospital on his day off to pick up his check. Yacob and I have been looking after each other off and on now for the past three and a half years, although tonight, I have to admit, if feels like three and a half hundred."

"I didn't do it for Yacob Cain," she said. "I want you to know that. I did it for you and me." She paused. "Or maybe both. I don't know. Who knows. Does everybody always have to know? All I can say is they must be a hell of a lot smarter than I am if they always know."

He smiled again. "You're all right Marilyn Marie Du-freysne," he said quietly. "You got a good head. I think you're going to make out all right in this life."

"I'm never going to go to bed with you again," she said, "if that's what you think. You know that, don't you. You played your ace."

"We didn't go to bed, if you'll remember right. We did it on the river bank. Unless you're the kind who calls it a river bed. I suppose that'd be more refined. Incorrect—but more refined."

"Well, the consequences of this evening could very likely be more serious for me than for you, if you know what I mean—and I'm sure you do."

"Look, I'm not perfect and neither are you. If you don't learn anything else while you're here, you'll learn that. That much at least I can safely guarantee."

"It doesn't necessarily make things right," she said. Then quietly, "It doesn't necessarily mean I'm sorry either." He looked at her curiously, surprised.

The next night in residence, after lights out, Marilyn told Gail about the showers and the morgue and the various parts of Yacob Cain who had died on her ward the day before yesterday; and she told her about her late date. Bill Neilson was horrible to have taken her down there in the first place, she said. She wouldn't be in the least surprised if the shower trick that first day hadn't been his brain wave. She had been confined to barracks for two weeks because of him. And she had decided she would never ever in this life go out with Bill Neilson again.

Yet here she had spent the whole afternoon with him, she thought now. Four hundred miles away and twenty-seven years later. She wondered what had become of him. Was he married? Did he have kids? Had he moved to Montreal or Winnipeg? Had he stayed?

Heather was finished with the first sign. Marilyn looked at it for a long time. The morning after feeling come again, she thought, the moment gone and no way of knowing when or even if it would come again. Even now, after all these years with Ron, when it was over and the bedding was all rumpled on the floor and the space extended between them forever over the cold wet sheets, it always seemed to her that this could never really happen in the first place. The swollen flesh on her and in her at the same time. Maybe there was such a thing as restoration, she thought. Why not?

She removed her sunglasses, smiled, and rubbed her eyes. Then she leaned over and tousled Heather's hair. Her head fell sideways, swayed a little under Marilyn's hand. The hair was long and smooth and clean. "You got an extra brush?" she asked.

"Sure," Heather replied, looking up, "why not."

"Only I'm moving my sign to the picnic table," Marilyn said. "I'm not leaning down on the cement. It may be spring but the concrete is still cold and it is still hard and I, as you know, have been having a lot of trouble with my knees lately."

Heather looked up again and Marilyn could see it in her eyes this time. She knows, Marilyn thought, already she knows too much.

"What is it," Heather asked quietly.

"Oh nothing. I was just thinking about something that happened a long time ago, long ago and far away as they say in the fairy tales."

"What happened to you, Mom?" Heather was examining her face.

"But before I start to paint I have to go inside," Marilyn said, rising from her chair. She felt as if she needed to have a damn good cry is what it was, which seemed absolutely ridiculous to her now in the warm June sunlight and after such a long time.

The Birthmark

"The things that happened to me meant something, I realized, more than I had known when they were happening, and I meant something too. Stories were told about me; therefore I existed."—MERNA SUMMERS, *Calling Home*

Ingrid was on the porch zipping up her high black leather boots, Italian, the best she could find in the city, $235 a pair. She could hear Uncle Frank's voice through gaps in the weather stripping around the door leading from the kitchen to the porch.

"She's on her way to Templeton's. To see her grandma." That was how he put it when he told the others where she was going. Ironic, the way he said it. What was there left to see?

Ingrid straightened. Then she pulled the kid leather gloves out of her Gucci bag, pulled them carefully over the finely manicured nails, unpainted today because of the funeral. She pulled each glove over the slender fingers, pushing the leather tightly to the joints between the fingers and hands, caressing the soft leather smooth over the backs of the hands, over the wrists. Then she pulled the cuffs of her sable coat down over the tops of the gloves.

She had done well—at school, at the university, with the oil company. She had finished her doctorate in engineering and now she worked in Calgary. In fact, she held a most significant position in her field, even if she did say so herself, and her salary was commensurate. She could afford to dress exactly as she wanted, fly anywhere she pleased. She had flown here, had chartered a plane to the funeral. As usual, the relatives had raised their eyebrows when they heard, letting her know what they thought of this latest extravagance. It was flagrant, they thought, disrespectful.

"It saves time," Ingrid had told them. She remembered saying the same thing to her superiors. She had to go to this funeral, she had said, but she would fly. She would be back as quickly as possible. And she would. But she had to go.

Now she was ready for the drive to Templeton's Funeral Home to view the body. At least she was dressed properly. She would be warm, was glad she had brought the sable cap as well as the new coat. The weather had changed dramatically since her arrival and even now she doubted whether she would be able to leave for Calgary on schedule. The fear lay exposed on the surface of her mind. She could be trapped. Here. Among them.

There had been blizzard warnings on the radio. Ingrid peered through the tiny square of the porch window. Already you could scarcely see the houses across the alley. The vindictive wind had whipped the drifts blind white against the back fence, lifted the lids off the metal garbage cans, clanged them against one another like cymbals, scattered the tins in the alley, rolling them to and fro whimsically, like paper cups; shaken their guts out, exposed all the refuse of the house, so carefully packed and sealed and hidden. The wind had decorated the white ruts with streamers of tin cans, used Kotex pads and little mounds of curled and frozen potato peelings. It had sprinkled wet black coffee grounds, like dark confetti, over the fresh downfall, completely different from the molded drifts closer to the house and the fields of satin slipper snow you would normally see after a mid-winter melt, glossy, pearl-white. This new snow swirled like a poltergeist, sweeping and stirring the garbage, aimlessly lifting and whipping and scattering.

Watching it made her dizzy. She tried not to panic, tried to swallow her confusion. Loss of control. She feared this above all. Still, the dizziness reminded her of a seizure. The beginning of a seizure, though she hadn't had one in years. She no longer took medication, hadn't given a thought to the little tablets of dilantin and phenobarbital since her final checkup with the neurologist. But she knew it was possible. The doctor

97

had told her the seizures could recur, later, under stress. Another electroencephalogram, electrodes stuck into her Medusa head, brilliant complex patterns between her eyelids and her eyes. Confusion. Loss of control.

They had cut off her hair. She had been allowed to grow her hair long for the first time. She had been eight years old. And her hair was good. Long and thick and for the first time since she was born, straight. No cold wave. She was allowed to have no cold wave. But the paste they used at the base of the electrodes where they were attached to the scalp hadn't washed out. It stuck fast in small white lumps and her mother had said it would be better if they cut it off. It would be easier to manage just for now. It would grow out again, she said. She hadn't been harsh, Ingrid remembered. Her voice had been so soft, so soft, the way she spoke to Dad's friend Arnold who had polio in the fifties and still limped. Ingrid wasn't like him, of course. She had felt perfectly fine, if the truth be known, except for the lapses, which she couldn't really remember—only the spinning before. Only the slight tilt of walls. Tipsy walls, she had called them then, altered angles now. She had worn her hair short ever since that time, cropped close. She had chosen so.

Her mind ferreted, feverish. Hadn't she proven she could handle stress, to everyone, to herself? Hadn't she done what none of the others had, taken on more and more and more until even her colleagues marvelled at her stamina? All of it true; nonetheless, she became aware of herself staring without sight. Symptomatic. The quiet frozen stare before the storm. The nauseating hiatus.

She couldn't leave until she knew. It would be criminal to drive now, before she knew for sure. And she wouldn't ask one of them to take her. So she stood and waited. Peered through the window, squinting as if she had to protect her eyes from the wind, though she was indoors. Squinting as if she could allow in only a little bit of light at a time. Squinting to ward off staring.

She began to notice her breathing, shallow, erratic, fright-

98

ened. Then saw the frost of her own breath against the window. She stood back from the window and breathed deeply. She exhaled. There it was, visible in the air, like a Hollywood ghost, frosty, ethereal, there and gone. You could see through it, but it was there. Proof. The pitiful, delicate, opaque breath. A kind of whimsical consolation prize for living in the north, she supposed, but proof nonetheless.

Memory whipped her from behind, caught her unaware— Grandma standing on the stoop, wearing a red toque and red mitts, sucking in her breath, then blowing out a silver cloud, throwing her head back, unrolling a hefty bolt of laughter. And a little girl standing beside her in a yellow plaid parka with a hood trimmed in white rabbit fur, her miniature lips gaping up at the miracle, at the magical rotund grandma who had pulled the proof out of her body like a rabbit out of a hat. The little girl took a breath, then blew.

There it was. Her own breath. Just like Grandma's. Magical. Mysterious. As inexplicable as that first sickening reel toward the floor, that first derailment of her thought.

Ingrid turned from the window. She felt chilled, felt her skin begin to shrivel, shrink away from the silk lining of the sable coat. Her legs felt as if they were made of raffia, unable to support her sudden weight. She leaned against the kitchen door, toward the current whispers.

"I bet Catherine and Bert would be plenty proud of that girl if they were still alive."

"I imagine so, Frank. Especially Catherine. She would've been tickled pink to see her all dolled up the way she came in here. Nothing would have pleased her more, except maybe if she'd married a rich man. Catherine would have liked that. That's one thing I don't understand. Why she never married. She must be pushing thirty-five by now." Aunt Sophie. No surprises, even now.

"She has her reasons, I suppose," said Aunt Margaret. "Maybe the scars. Maybe the fits. Who knows. Though I can't say I've ever understood the girl either. Secretive. Buried somewhere inside herself, just like Catherine."

"At one point, there was some suggestion they might use radiation therapy to remove the mark, radioactive pellets, probably. But Catherine vetoed that and so did the doctor," Trudy said. Naturally, Ingrid thought. Trudy was the family nurse. "Apparently it was too low on the back," Trudy continued, "too close to the reproductive organs. She could have been sterilized, they said. Catherine didn't want that, of course. I mean, the reason they did it in the first place was because Catherine figured the hair might stand in the way of her getting married some day. And having kids, you see. Provided she did get married, which, as you say, Sophie, doesn't seem to be the case."

"If you ask me, there's only one thing we have to remember here. The girl was pretty close to the old woman. It's bound to hit her hard." At least one of them understood, Ingrid thought. No surprises. Again it was Uncle Frank who understood. Once, when Ingrid was nine or ten, she had had a seizure at a dance, a family reunion no less. And Aunt Sophie had put her on the floor of the cloakroom and everybody had crowded around above her and looked at her as if she had been an animal in a zoo. Then they had left, all of them but Uncle Frank. And when she sat up, he had put his arm around her. "Everybody gets them, Ingi, or something like them," he said, "sometime. Thing is, yours is got a name, that's all. You don't need to feel ashamed about a little name. As soon as you're feeling better, you and me'll have ourselves a dance."

But today, Margaret agreed with Frank, in a round-about way. "That's a fact," she said. "Ingrid spent most of her time with her grandma. Especially when she was little. And even when she was in school. Mom moved right up to Prince Albert to be close to Catherine and the kids. Though I never could see why. She'd been better off with the rest of us if you ask me."

"She's back now ain't she?" said Frank.

"You know what I mean, Frank. This is where she belonged. After all, the homestead's close by, and Papa's grave."

"I never understood that either, Margaret," said Sophie. "And another thing I never understood was the way Mom used to treat the girl. Always held her up like she was something special. That was part of the problem. Mom never seemed to care that she was marked, wouldn't even listen when you told her about the fits. Never believed she had them. Mom thought she was perfect."

"That's not so hard to understand," said Frank. "The old woman always believed what she wanted to and no more. I heard her tell us one time there was no such thing as surfing. We were watching it on TV and Gran pipes up and says, 'It's a trick. They got them strung up on wires. I lived by the sea for thirty-five years and I know it can't be done. If it could, then there would've been someone out there doing it.' And that was all there was to that."

Ingrid could hear laughter, assorted. She herself almost laughed, couldn't keep from smiling, no matter how bad she felt about it.

"And you should've seen her when they walked on the moon," continued Frank. "Pure fiction. No truth in it at all she said!" More laughter through the gaps in the weather stripping around the door. More. But polite this time, restrained. They would bury the old woman within hours.

Ingrid huddled against the door like a small hunted animal, alone and still and waiting for the owl. Musty coats hung on hooks along the porch walls. They smelled of sweat. Her stomach heaved. Parkas and scarves and sweaters all carried the enemy scent. There were extension cords and battery cables hanging from nails beside the door. Electrical apparatus. She never trusted it. There was always the possibility of malfunction. She had written a paper on it at university. She knew more about electrical malfunction than most people.

She looked away from the cords, toward the floor. Workboots stood empty on the porch floor. Head down, she surveyed the row of boots. The dizziness increased. She raised her head and when she did, she thought she saw the arms of a parka reach out, then lift their hollow sleeves toward her face.

Battery cables with metal clasps and silver teeth extended themselves toward her, hovered in the air above her head. Cords with pronged heads like snakes undulated, swung dangerously close to her eyes. This had to be an optical illusion, she thought, or hallucination. She needed to rest, to lie down. Then she would be all right. But she was afraid to lie down in case one of her aunts might come out and think she had collapsed. "The falling sickness," she remarked to herself sarcastically. Still, the porch walls menaced, began to close in on her.

And the screams began. Inside her head. "Grandma was right. She was right. There's nothing wrong with me. I'm the same as you. I am. I am. I am. I am. I am." So loud that she began to be afraid they might be heard on the other side of the door. That she would hear the others laugh again.

Because they were right too. Her grandmother did not believe men had walked on the moon, no matter who tried to tell her. One day in the nursing home in Prince Albert where Ingrid had visited her right up until the end, until they'd brought the body back here, Ingrid had tried to explain how it had been done, in a way she thought the old woman could understand. But she hadn't believed her. She had scolded Ingrid for filling her own head with sawdust, just so much foolishness, she had said. And what was to become of her if she believed everything she heard.

The night her grandmother died, Ingrid heard the voice of the old woman in her head. *Yes, Ingrid, there are angels.* At first, Ingrid thought it was a joke she was playing on herself, unconsciously. "Yes, Virginia, there is a Santa Claus," she had muttered, then laughed out loud. But by and by the mental apparition of the old woman grew stronger. She was twiddling and twirling her thumbs in her lap, a vestigial habit from her bout with St. Vitus Dance and the farm when her hair fell out and her hands would hold nothing; and china and time, everything, slipped through her fingers like water through a colander, smash and crack and crying all the time, even in the forenoon, the wash out on the line, the baby in the basket in the back bedroom. Sighing. Sighing. Einar in the field, breaking land, trying as hard as he could.

Yes, Ingrid, there are anyels. And right after Ingrid was notified of the death, had she not imagined her grandmother flying in her mind, wearing her street length lavender with the white lace collar, a nest of pink roses and babies'-breath pinned to her breast, reminding Ingrid of all the family weddings. Her grandmother's hair was silver and marcelled. The image was barefoot but for the pearl hose on the round feet and the injured winter toes. And the fact was there were these passing days men and women travelling through space wearing helmets enveloped in a thin film of gold, tubular wings of fire on their backs. No disputing that, she laughed quietly. How could anyone deny that?

The wind whipped the outside walls of the porch, tried to whistle its way through the keyhole of the storm door. Maybe the old woman had been as mad as a hatter. And maybe the others were right about Ingrid too. Why not? The old woman had pitied her, protected her out of pity. Snow flayed the window. A spray of silver sparks, like the ones that had spewed out of the frayed cord of her old kettle the night it short-circuited in the kitchen of her apartment. Enough of them could break through.

This time memory lifted her grandmother's arm, exposed it like the top of a snow fence whipped visible out of a drift by the very wind it meant to overcome, the same wind that had worked like a fiend to bury the fence in the first place. The arm, exposed, was immense. Fat and round and full of flesh. And when she slept at her grandmother's house the arm was always offered. Her pillow on the weekend nights was warm. She could hear its pulse, could feel the life against her face. The soft and steady solitude of flesh.

She lay in the crook at the elbow and she could feel her hair grow warm against her grandmother's skin, could feel the dampness, smell the rising of the wild rose arm, perfumed earlier in the hot bath she shared with the old woman in the deep white porcelain tub, the water rising around them, scented with the Avon oil. "To a Wild Rose." Always the same too sweet, too heavy fragrance. Almost always thick enough to make her gag. Her grandmother never saw the scars, or never said she did. Ingrid stayed with her every weekend, and on Mondays she was always better for it. She cowered less among the others. Believed almost that she was one of them.

She felt slightly better. The dizziness had passed although the nausea had not. But she was well enough to realize that she had to leave now. Otherwise there would be no time. The funeral was at three and it was almost noon. She opened the storm door as quietly as she could, hoping they wouldn't hear her leave, wouldn't suspect that she had heard.

She lifted her gloved hand to her head and straightened the sable cap. The cap formed a black frame for the frame of her light brown hair, properly coiffed, a Sassoon cut, a geometric cap, good for her face, still elfin in spite of her age. The upturned nose, the large brown eyes, the unmascaraed lashes.

Even the walk to the car was difficult against the wind. But she quickly remembered the best way through. You bowed your head and leaned into it. That was the only way. She smiled at the memory of Uncle Frank intoning the prairie cliché, usually around Christmas or New Year's. There was almost always at least one ungodly blow when everybody was on the road, heading home.

She unplugged the extension cord from the block heater. Frank had remembered to give her the cord the night before. She got into the rented car and turned the unfamiliar key in the ignition. Nothing. The connection must have been faulty, or she hadn't plugged it in properly, or something. No wonder she didn't trust the damn things. They were always malfunctioning. Finally the motor turned over. She left the car running, got out and with one gloved hand, swept the snow from the windshield and the back window. She had to be able to see a little, at least, when she drove through the city.

Although she hadn't been back here for years, Uncle

Frank's directions were precise. She had no trouble finding the place. Templeton's Funeral Home, stuccoed white and stippled with the snow.

The long, low rectangular building crouched near the sidewalk which had drifted in again, though it had obviously been recently cleared. Someone had tried to hide the self-conscious squat of the building with dwarfed cedar, juniper and storybook spruce. The funeral home didn't look real to Ingrid. It was like an imitation building, something a little girl would construct out of cardboard and paint white. Paint on stained glass windows. Paint on doors, dark brown. Only the child must have grown tired of the pastime, leaving it unfinished, or had forgotten to cut slits in the cardboard so that the doors and windows could be opened; or perhaps she had never wanted to go in, ever.

Mechanically, Ingrid reached for the handle on the door. She tried to pull it open toward her, against the wind. She became aware of a tremendous resistance. She couldn't get into the building. She froze to the step, afraid for a moment that the building was not real after all, that the whole thing was some kind of diabolical practical joke engineered by the rest of the family. Then she realized that this, too, was a trick of the wind. She remembered. There was always this fighting to open doors, always the tension back and forth.

She liked the funeral director. He wore an alpaca sweater over a madras shirt. No Dickensian shirt and tails. She was more comfortable than she thought she'd be. But this worked against her. The relaxation, the amicable appointment with this death. Initially, she had admired the young funeral director for his enlightened approach, for being able to create this relaxing atmosphere in such an unlikely place. After all, death was part of life. It shouldn't be so very different, so very difficult.

"And your name?" He spoke to her naturally.

"Ingrid Bale. I'm here to see Mrs. Lund."

"Yes, Ms. Bale. Mrs. Lund. Your grandmother?" Ingrid nodded. "I hope your trip wasn't too difficult," he continued.

"The weather's terrible. The roads must be terrifically dangerous."

"I flew."

"Well, that would be even more dangerous, I would think. I hope the rest of the family arrived safely."

"Yes, they did, thank you." By then, he was reaching for the handle on the chapel door. He opened it. The door which closed behind her made no sound. Ingrid stood for a moment. She felt abandoned, betrayed. There was no continuity. The comfort and ease and affability of the funeral director had left with him.

The coffin was open. But then, what had she expected. She felt uncomfortably warm, unbuttoned her sable coat. When she had the last perfectly upholstered button out of its silk cord button hole, she grew cold again and wrapped the fur around her, clutched the hair of the coat as if it were her own, as if she wanted it to cover thickly all her years, as if she wished it grew out of her skin, through pores, with roots and oil and softness all her own.

She walked down the short aisle, then stopped, instinctively, before she could see over the velvet rim of the coffin. She sat down on a blue chair in the fifth row from the front of the room and set her Gucci bag carefully beside her on the floor.

The chapel was quiet, not oppressive, but quiet. Natural. No heavy oak pews or phosphorescent crucifixes. Tasteful. Natural. Like someone's living room. Someone you'd know. Only there were chairs, wooden ones with blue upholstery. They were arranged in rows across the room. And at the front, the flowers, wreaths of pink and white roses on wicker stands, like the easels of an eccentric painter. The coffin was pink too, flesh-coloured velvet mottled with the petals of a thousand roses imprinted like fossils on the surface of the fabric. It was mounted on a stainless steel trolley, discreet and unobtrusive.

She waited. But whatever it was she waited for did not come. Finally she wrapped the coat around her and rose easily from the chair. She walked forward, toward the velvet lid.

She could see the body now. It was nestled in white satin folds. It was wearing a flowered gown, a family brooch pinned on its chest, like a medal, one birthstone for each offspring. Sophie's idea, no doubt. But they hadn't lied. The woman here was dead, and the woman had been her grandmother.

Ingrid leaned over the side of the coffin. She thought she heard herself call, quietly at first, "Grandma? Grandma?" This could have been inside her head. She couldn't tell.

Now she reached down toward the slate-grey hair and, as if she were in a trance, she observed herself caressing the hair with her glove. Someone had brushed the hair back, straight back, in a way her grandmother never had. She always had curls, Ingrid remembered, gentle grey-blue curls, like four-o'clock shadows on snow. There were bruises on the forehead of the corpse. Three of them, large and dark, as if someone had sketched them on with charcoal, an afterthought.

Ingrid was fascinated by the bruises and by the dark brown spots on the skin stretched and dried over the bones on the backs of the hands. Someone had stuck three artificial roses in the hands. The roses were made of light pink silk and Ingrid knew immediately why they had been put there. The hands were unco-operative. They declared the death with unruly rigor, stuck out their fingers awkwardly, displayed their stiff arrangement of blue nails. There were gold rings on the fingers and the rings were her grandmother's. Ingrid remembered them, not from her last visits with the old woman, but from her childhood. On mobile fingers lifting countless coffee cups toward the moving mouth. The rings were hers but not the hands. Someone had tried to hide them with the roses.

The arms had been delicately sheathed in flowered silk, but they still strained obstinately at the stitches of the seams. Just as before. The arms, immense and round and full of flesh.

Ingrid braced her hands against the coffin's edge, felt the velvet crush beneath her fingers. She raised her skirt and sable coat, then lifted one leg. She levered herself, lifted her body up and over the edge of the coffin until she lay face down on the corpse.

It did not yield, and though she felt the stiffness of the frame, at the same time she was aware that the shell was insubstantial, like the carcass of a dried grasshopper. She put her cheek against the corpse's face but drew back instantly because of the cold. The skin was cold, dry. She pressed her ear against the flowered dress, heard nothing, began to be aware of an unfamiliar odour, a little like formaldahyde or rubbing alcohol, but it was neither of these which she could have recognized. The smell wasn't strong, but she gagged. Then, quickly, like a small animal, she burrowed her head deep into the crook of the stiff arm. She closed her eyes, and it was as if a switch had been thrown in some secret box inside her head. All of the energy seemed to leave her body as if the simple climbing in had used up everything, all the reserves, and left nothing.

She was almost asleep when the whispering began. She could hear the others whispering again, just as she had heard them on the porch, just as they had whispered after her down all the stairstep years of her childhood.

"Catherine always dressed her up like a doll. In my opinion it wasn't good for the girl. Made her think she was something special." Aunt Dot, her mother's older sister.

"You're absolutely right, Dot. She thinks hers don't stink." Ingrid remembered the shrill, crude pitch of the voice. It belonged to her cousin Carla.

"She's always thought she was better than the rest of us," said Carla's mother. "You can tell by the way she walks, head thrown back, nose in the air. And the way she talks. Good god, Margaret, we could all go to the dictionary and look up some of them hundred dollar words for ourselves, if we wanted to put on the dog. She don't need to think she's putting anything over on us. It's not as if we don't know she takes the fits, though Catherine liked to cover up for her. Catherine always said the girl was tired, just needed a little rest, then she'd be all right. But we knew.

"You can tell by their eyes every time. You can spot them a mile away. I just hope she don't have one when I'm around.

108

I've seen them before, gagging and choking and twitching. Foaming at the mouth. Old Sam Sullivan's boy used to take them. Got so bad they had to wheel him around in a baby carriage, and he twelve or more. And after that, they had to use the wheelbarrow, he got so big. He had one of them big heads too, what is it they call it?"

"Water on the brain," said Trudy, "hydrocephalic."

"Yes, that's it. I always felt so sorry for Ginny and Sam, wheeling it around all over town like that. Couldn't leave it behind for fear of the choking. Though it never knew the difference, never knew where it was anyways. Everybody said it was a blessing when it finally died."

"But I never saw Ingrid foaming," said Margaret. "Did you, Dot?"

"No, but Catherine was always so careful not to let anybody see. Always said Ingrid had a different kind of fit, too. The ones that aren't so bad. But that was just her way of covering up. You know the way Catherine was. Of course Ingrid couldn't be the same as anybody else, not even in that. But to me, fits is fits. Dress it up any way you like."

"Thing is, Ingrid was marked too," said Carla's mother. "They all are, one way or another. With the Sullivan boy it was the head, and with Ingrid, well, the hairy mark. Born with it. But she was lucky there too. That was hid, was on her back, I think, though I never saw it."

"Oh I did," said Dot, "when she was a baby. I saw it when Catherine was changing her, secretive as usual, sneaking the baby into the bedroom, not changing her out in the parlor with the rest of us like we would have done. Always trying to hide the mark. But I saw it.

"You should have seen Catherine start when I walked in on her. And grit her teeth. She had two diaper pins sticking out of her mouth, the way we used to do, and I could hear the pins scraping over the tops of her teeth just like one of Frank's files over scrap metal. I just stood and waited because I knew sooner or later Catherine would have to lift that little bottom up to slip the clean diaper under and when she did, I saw it. A patch of long brown hair. Just like the hair on the baby's head. Just like a monkey, I thought at the time, or a gopher.

"Marked, though you could never tell it when she was all dolled up, the way Catherine used to keep her. She was the prettiest little thing you ever saw too. But I always knew. Right from that day forward."

"Sort of reminds you of the story Grandma Lund used to tell us about the huldermaiden in the old country, don't it. You know, the one about the girl with the tail. Seems to me the only way she could get rid of that tail was to get married, if my memory serves. And they used to say the tail dropped off right there on the altar in front of the whole congregation. I don't suppose there's anything to it, do you?"

"Don't be ridiculous, Norma," snapped Trudy.

Ingrid couldn't believe her ears. So they dragged all of that garbage over on the boat with them too. For people who were supposed to have travelled so light, Ingrid thought, they didn't seem to have left much behind. The old ways alive and well in the new world, side by side with the krumkaker and the lefsa, the gjetost and the pickled herring.

The next voice was more difficult to identify, fainter somehow. Sadie, maybe. No, not Sadie. "Trud's right, of course." It was Aunt Olive. "But you know, Bert once told me Catherine stepped on a beaver's back over at the meadow dam. Catherine was about eight months along with Ingrid at the time and they were on a picnic. Bert was there and he saw it. Mind you, you couldn't always go by Bert. Anyway, he said that was the cause of it all, the hairy back, the fits and all. It's a wonder she ever made *anything* of herself, when you stop to think about it."

"Well, that's not the way I heard it at all. I heard she *dreamt* she stepped on the tail of a beaver the night before the girl was born. Had to be something though; that's a fact." This voice was unrecognizable. Ingrid hadn't thought about some of these people in years, had never wanted to, would never have seen them again as long as she lived if she had had any choice in the matter. But she had no choice. She had to come to the funeral. She had promised the old woman.

"She still got that hair on her back? I mean, don't she shave it off or something?"

"I don't think so. I heard Catherine and Bert got her an operation. She was about five, I guess. Charlie and Kaye were up in Prince Albert then, visiting, and they noticed little Ingrid wasn't around and nobody said nothing, so finally Kaye gets Catherine in the kitchen and she asks her. 'Where's Ingrid?' And Catherine says she's at the hospital and she's had to have a minor operation. Then later Kaye asks one of the boys how long little Ingrid's been in hospital and he says he thinks about five weeks now. (That was the boy who went overseas, Ethel, to Cyprus). Anyways, I don't suppose it was too minor, do you Margaret?"

"No, I don't suppose so. I heard that story too. My Audrey used to take swimming lessons with Ingrid at the lake. Says she saw her back once in the changing room. Told me the scars are terrible—show's what you get for trying to get rid of the marks, don't it. I mean, they must be put there for a reason, I figure. Otherwise the good Lord wouldn't have bothered."

"I was always so relieved it wasn't one of mine, you know, and I—" The voice dipped, disappeared, as if the anonymous throat had sucked it slowly back into the anonymous body.

"But you have to remember Catherine and Bert thought they were doing the right thing," said Sophie. "Not only that, but the doctor who did it wasn't really in good shape, either. Catherine told me the doctor wasn't all there by any means. She didn't know it at the time, of course, but the man was an alcoholic; she found this out later. His wife had left him and gone back to England. Shortly after the operation, he did himself in. They found him in his office, cold as a stone."

Dr. Hill. Twirling his finger through her hair. "Hello." Her face was turned toward the hospital wall. Dr. Hill. At first she had thought he was her mother standing by the bed. When she saw it was him instead, she began to cry and she turned back toward the wall. And that was really all she remembered about him now. The sudden fading smile of Dr.

111

Hill. Then she remembered his mustache. She had never seen a mustache before. So he was dead, too. She hadn't known.

"Well, anyway, the whole thing makes a lot more sense to me now," Trudy said. "I mean, they say by the time you're five, the game is over. The way you act and who you are, they say it's all locked in by then."

"They teach you that at the hospital, Trudy?" asked Frank.

"Well, something like that. Some people even believe it's all set the day you're born, before that even." Silence. "Then again, I think they're probably all related, you know—the mark, the seizures, the poor circulation in the one limb and so on. All three or some variation of them frequently occur in cases such as Ingrid's and if that's so," she was on a run, "there could be a hereditary factor involved." Another lunge of silence. Lethal. Active. "Well," she continued finally, her voice hesitant, as if she'd been stunned by a blow, "of course, we don't really know." Silence. "Do we."

Ingrid stirred. Her sable cap fell off and covered the face of the corpse with rich dark fur. With detached horror, she observed herself strike the corpse's breast. She pounded the brooch with her gloved fist, willed the cloud of silver to reappear. Choking and pounding and heaving, she heard herself beg it to reappear.

The hand on her shoulder belonged to Uncle Frank. "Ingi," he said softly and without reproach. "Ingi, we have to go back."

She said nothing, kept her head bowed. He put his arm around her waist and helped her climb down. She retrieved her sable cap and put it on. She straightened and felt her legs stiffen under her. She buttoned her coat, walked over to the blue upholstered chair and picked up her purse, Gucci, $285. She opened it and took out a Kleenex. She put the Kleenex to her face, distractedly wiped away the mucous and the water.

They drove back to the house in Uncle Frank's car. She would pick up the rented one later. For a long time, they said nothing to each other. They were almost at the house when Ingrid spoke. They were just pulling into the driveway.

"Why did you come?" she asked him. Though it was only one-thirty, lights appeared to be burning in every room, but even from the driveway you could hardly see them through the wall of snow. "Someone must have phoned," she said.

Frank took the keys out of the ignition. "No," he said, "Dick Templeton was just calling the house when I walked in. I come on my own." Ingrid raised her eyes cautiously and looked at him. "For one thing, you don't know the city no more. There's been a lot of changes since the last time you were here."

"Some things don't seem to change at all, Uncle Frank," she said, her voice flat, cold. "I had no trouble finding Templeton's if that's what you mean."

"I know that Ingrid," he said. "I guess you heard." He rubbed his forehead hard with the fingertips of both hands as if he were trying to erase something written there. "The other thing is we got to talking after you left and they said you shouldn't have to go alone. Nobody should, they said."

She lowered her eyes again and began to fidget with the bone handle of the bag in her lap. "I don't know what to say to you," she said, "about me, about them."

"Then don't say nothing," he said. "There's no need. There's none of us understand it, Ingrid. Oh, I know we all have to chew it over every time a thing happens. Seems we somehow have to go through it all again, over and over. Once just doesn't seem to be enough for some reason. So we go on telling the same old stories, switching things around and figuring and figuring and carrying on. And sometimes we're right and sometimes, it's true, we're terrible, pitiful wrong. But in the end we don't really know any more about it than we did at the outset."

He opened the car door and got out. Ingrid watched him bend down to plug in the block heater. She opened her door and stood for a moment in the snow. She could see his breath rising over the hood of the car. She turned and walked slowly toward the porch steps, stopped at the base of the steps for a moment, took a deep breath.

Inside, she unzipped her boots and took them off. When she opened the door to the kitchen, everyone in the room looked up at her and she bowed her head. As she was taking off her cap and coat, she heard one of them ask in a hushed voice, "What the hell kind of animal is that anyway? Mink?"

"No," Carla whispered, "she says it's sable; she told Frank it's sable. He says it's worth ten thousand dollars if it's worth a dime."

Ingrid took her coat and hat into the living room. She laid the cap on the arm of the sofa, then spread the coat at one end over the cushions, fur side down. She smoothed her dress behind her with her hands. The dress was black virgin wool. That had been an extravagance too, but then how long would it be till she'd be able to go back to Paris, she had rationalized. There was so much work. She sat down on the coat, pulled her legs up under her, then settled them to one side. She crooked her arm and lowered her head until she was comfortable. Then she burrowed her head into the crook and closed her eyes.

She had begun to doze when someone passed between her and the bright light shining directly on her face from the lamp. She heard the lamp click off and felt the darkness, like a salve, between her eyelids and her eyes.

"A fit?" she heard one of them whisper from the kitchen.

"I guess so," Uncle Frank replied. She imagined that he nodded then, bowed his large grey head toward some wind.

"Don't wake her till it's time to go," he said.

The Metal Detector

Aunt Connie rented the metal detector from a mining equipment agency before she left Vancouver. She brought it all the way back to Trestle on the Greyhound bus. No one expected anything of the sort. Sylvia and I met the bus. Later Sillie would say we should never have laughed. But Aunt Connie was wearing brand new rubber boots. She was also wearing a hot pink cotton tee shirt which had FOXY LADY scrawled across the breasts in plasticized silver glitter. The breasts of a young girl, really, maybe sixteen or seventeen, though Connie was older than our mother by almost eight years.

Her face was a girl's face too, and her hair, though greying sparse, was fluffy, like down. Her grey eyes were full and round and proud, but the irises were splintered and everywhere I looked in them I thought I saw pieces of my Uncle Ace. Connie's trip back to Trestle marked the beginning of her first summer without him.

She appeared perfectly calm moving slowly past the bus windows, one hand settled patiently on the back of each aisle seat as she made her way toward the exit which was also the entrance of the bus. For a moment, Sillie and I expected her to disembark like Queen Elizabeth on television, gliding ceremoniously down the red carpet boarding ramp of an aircraft toward a state reception on the ground. But on the last step, Connie exploded into the air like fireworks, the starburst kind we had seen against the flat felt prairie dark after the grandstand at the fair.

"Well here I am!" she cried, and "How's your mom and dad!" But when the hugs and kisses were over and I looked into her eyes, all I could see was the negative of the starburst, the dark splinters of Ace scattered through the bright irises. And Connie was silent. Sillie and I stood beside her, waited by the mouth of the luggage compartment of the bus, our arms stuck to our sides, awkward, stiff, as if they'd never hugged anyone, much less Connie so hard only moments before.

Now, I think we had expected Connie's arrival to be altogether different from what it was, an imprint on our minds, perhaps, of what we had been led to believe it should have been. Like a computer read-out that comes out wrong and you have to start over. This, the moment when the screen is blank, again, before the beginning. We must have expected a sorrow of some kind because this was the first time we had seen her since Ace died. Mom and Dad had gone to the funeral by themselves. But other than the shattered irises, no sorrow in a sagging mouth or shadows under the eyes gave us any indication of the harrowing winter we imagined she must have weathered.

The bus driver came toward the back of the bus and opened the luggage compartment, exposing the squat suit-cases arranged in rows like many-coloured teeth. He removed a large red Samsonite suitcase and a matching train case from the mouth of the bus. They looked brand new. Red. The colour of celebrations and flags.

Sylvia and I each grabbed one bag and started toward the car in front of the hotel. But Connie stayed where she was and finally, when I knew she hadn't followed, I turned and saw her talking to the driver. Both of them were peering into the dark hole in the side of the bus. Then the driver crawled right into the hole. For a moment we thought he had disappeared entirely, he had gone so deep, or was it just the way the shadows worked that day; from where Sillie and I were standing, we couldn't really see.

But when he emerged, backwards, he withdrew a piece of machinery which from a distance looked a little like a vacuum cleaner or floor polisher, a long silver handle attached to a perfectly round contraption on one end. The bus driver set the machine on the ground, upright. It must have been heavy because Aunt Connie seemed to have trouble carrying it. Pretty soon she turned around and backed toward us, dragging the machine as if it were a belligerent calf and had no intention of making it easy for Connie to do whatever it was she had come back to Trestle to do.

Whatever she had come back to Trestle to do. Why she would come back at all was the mystery for Sylvia and me. She hated the town, the people, the prairie, and she made no bones about it, had never once looked back since moving to the coast years ago now, though she had always kept in touch with Mom and Dad and a few other members of the family.

Connie was my mother's sister on the farm. She still is my mother's sister, of course, but whenever I think of them together, really together, it is within the silver yellow photographic framework of the farm. Because that is all I have to go by — the family pictures in the cardboard box. The box of guilt, my mother used to call it because she always felt bad about never having assembled the family photographic record properly in albums; whereas I liked the box, the way the pictures were thrown in randomly so that every time the box came out was a surprise, like the fishpond at the church bazaar. The stories always came out in a different order according to which batch or booklet or photo you happened to pick up. In a way, I guess, there was nothing random about it, though, because whenever we got the box out it was for a definite reason. We were flipping and stacking and sorting for a reason.

Last night, in preparation for Connie's arrival, Mom had brought the box down, set it on the kitchen table and begun to sort through the heap of old photos for pictures of Connie and Ace taken when they lived in Trestle. Mom thought Connie might like to see them, talk over old times, though she said we'd have to pick the right pictures and the right time to show them to her on account of the fact that all the old times were not good times and Uncle Ace only died last year.

So we flipped and sorted and searched all evening and by eleven o'clock, we had a satisfying little stack of photographs of Connie, Ace and the kids, marked '48, '49, '52, including a large one of Ace standing in front of his blacksmith shop, a

117

small one taken on the farm of Connie in the school cutter, her toqued head sticking out the window carved by Grandpa Spese in the shape of a heart in the tiny door. Even a series in a booklet of Little Lyle by the slough on a windy day, trying to scare the water by saying "BOO!", the sizeable waves washing toward him. Kids think they can make almost any kind of bad or sad or scary thing go away by saying boo. Sometimes older people think that way too. Anyway, how could we know that Connie would not only not want to see the pictures, but that she would be hopping mad we brought them out at all.

When we got to the car, I put the key in the trunk and lifted the lid. I threw in the red suitcases and Sillie and I bent down to lift the machine. "No," Connie said, "I'll take care of it." And she did, bent, lifted and swung the silver machine into the trunk, pushing hard on the handle so it wouldn't stick out under the lid. I shut the trunk and we all piled into the car.

"So what is it?" Sillie asked as soon as I got behind the wheel and slammed my door. Sillie never could wait for anything. She had no patience whatsoever.

"What's what?" asked Connie as if her baggage were quite ordinary, incapable of arousing the least bit of curiosity.

"The thing you brought back from the coast — the machine," persisted Sillie. "What's it for?"

"I'm looking for something," Connie said, smiling, secretive, almost mischievous.

"For what?" I said.

"Time will tell," Connie replied, secretive again. Then she guided the conversation away from the silver machine with the long chrome handle, guided us through the tedious routine of how was the school year (of Sillie), what will you do after grad (me) and all the regular things aunts tend to ask nieces in these sorts of situations, arrivals, departures, parlour talk.

When we pulled up in front of the house, Mom and Dad were both out the door and waiting on the step. Dad came toward us to help with the luggage. "Hello there stranger," he said, pecking Connie's cheek. But Mom flung herself at

Aunt Connie in a prodigal sister hug, complete with all the prairie pats and squeezes which, to tell the truth, I'm not all that sure Connie appreciated, from the look on her face.

Sylvia and I went to the trunk of the car to unload Connie's luggage; Sillie was just pulling the machine out when Connie disengaged herself from our mother and raced toward the trunk. She finished extracting the machine herself and dragged it over to the porch step. "Well," she said, "here we are!" As if the machine were a person or something. Her travelling companion.

Anyway, at least she let Dad carry it up into the porch. "Not that it's any of my business, Connie, but what the hell is it?" he said when he got it through the screen door.

"It's a metal detector," she announced, proudly holding it up by the handle like a sap issued a new rifle. "I rented it from a mining company on the coast. Listen, Calder, it'll pick up anything, even silver." She rummaged through her purse, placed a dime under the machine, flicked a switch, and stood smiling while we listened to the apparatus shriek and heard the dime click to the round metal plate on the bottom of the detector.

"Oh," said Mom.

"Well that's something, anyway," muttered Sillie, sitting on the kitchen stool beside the fridge, "but what the hell's it for?"

"It's for finding metals and things — say you lost something, like that." Her eyes engaged a distance nowhere in the room, maybe nowhere even on the planet from the looks of her. "And I'm looking for something," she said.

"Such as?" said Dad. He had to say it twice and cleared his throat before the second time. "Such as?"

"Such as Mom's Viking warrior brooch. The silver one she brought over from Norway on the boat. She lost it in the pigpen on the homestead, Lila, remember? Must be at least fifty years ago now. And tomorrow morning I'm going out to the home place and I'm taking this contraption along. And I'll tell you another thing. I don't intend to give up until I find

119

that brooch. I didn't drag the damn thing all the way from the coast for nothing, you know."

Mom seemed to regard Connie with pity, seemed to have only just noticed the tee shirt with FOXY LADY silver glittered across the breasts. From the expression on her face, half startled, half sad, I could tell she thought Connie had lost her mind, thought Ace's death had somehow addled her brain and wasn't it a terrible loss, her own sister's perfectly good brain, addled.

"That's the old spirit, Connie," piped Dad, too chipper by half, I thought. "We'll take a few sandwiches out and make a day of it."

Later that night, when all of us were gathered around the kitchen table drinking coffee and eating freshly baked cinnamon buns sticky on the bottom with brown sugar goo and walnuts and spice, we planned to show Connie the pictures of her and Ace and the kids. But she would have no part of them. Actually we had expected the evening to be very quiet, subdued in fact. We had expected to sit respectfully at the table which had been decorated with a doily and my mother's milk glass vase containing the six orange silk tiger lilies Sillie and I had given her for Mother's Day when we were still in grade school. Mom had added numerous tufts of various prairie grasses including a liberal sprinkling of wheat. We expected Aunt Connie to reminisce and we listened for the sorrow we assumed had consumed her. But there was none.

Aunt Connie spent most of the evening teasing our mother whom she frequently referred to as an old prairie dog. She was animated and excited, from time to time jumping to her feet and smoothing the back of her slacks as if she were wearing a skirt. She entertained us royally, had Sillie and me in stitches most of the night. At one point she went to her room and returned with three sea shell sculptures which she had fished out of her suitcase, two small ones for Sillie and me and one large one for Mom. She had made them with oyster shells and sea horses, shiny beads, a palm tree each and two china seagulls perched on a plaster island base. Not to be outdone, our mother went to the china cabinet and brought forth her best ceramic elevator salt and pepper shakers to date, each decorated with a small orange tiger lily, guilded, the interminable word "Saskatchewan" written on both in a microscopic hand with gold paint. These she presented to Connie, satisfied, more or less, that she had evened the score.

After Ace died, Connie said, she had sold the house and bought a new condominium. It had a jacuzzi and a swimming pool. The grounds were beautifully maintained and the interior was posh, she said, deep chocolate brown rugs and fancy kitchen fixtures, harvest gold. A dishwasher, even. Sillie and I were impressed. Until two years ago we hauled all our water from the well below the yard. And even now, though we had running water in the house, it was cold and we had to heat it with the immersible. We had to ask what a jacuzzi was, even. Sillie did, that is. She's always the one who asks the questions. We were impressed all right, had almost forgotten about Uncle Ace altogether by the time we went to bed. It was as if he had never existed at all, or if so, only faintly, almost invisible through gauze or cheesecloth or in the picture left untouched on the table beside our aunt, the silvery old photograph of him standing in front of the black-smith shop in Trestle.

Before Connie went up to bed, she peeked into the porch. We teased her about having to say goodnight to a metal detector. I thought she might be thinking of taking it up to her room, maybe even tucking it into bed with her, the way she lingered.

The next morning she was up and at it, as she said, a high pink flush on her cheeks and a prospecting light in her eyes.

Sillie and I helped Mom make ham and cheese sandwiches. We packed cookies, hard-boiled eggs, dill pickles and crumb cake for the picnic at the home place. Mom filled two thermoses full of coffee and one of tea. Then she made a jug of lemonade. Dad and Connie were out in the driveway practising with the metal detector. After a while, Dad brought in three rusty bottle caps and a nail. This did nothing at all to

121

alleviate my mother's scepticism over the metal detector which she called a contraption, or the expedition itself which she called a treasure hunt. My mother always thought of herself as a sensible woman — both feet firmly planted on the flat earth, she said, was the best and safest way to live.

But to tell the truth, as much as we loved our mother, both Sillie and I leaned toward Aunt Connie and her foxy lady shirt. We had been leaning that way for some time, in fact, only we had nobody to hitch our leanings to. Aunt Connie was a windfall. Where we lived, women were expected to behave in a certain way — one certain way. You grew *up* and got married and settled *down*. It was the emphasis on the *up* to *down* that scared us. Only it wasn't all that easy any more. At school they were teaching us about women doctors and lawyers and judges, welders, executives, tailors and politicians. These now on top of the teachers and nurses we knew a woman could be. The trouble was we'd never seen any of these women around. It was almost as hard to believe in them as it was to believe in angels. And although Aunt Connie was none of these, she was something special, something we had never seen before, someone filled with the new light which seemed to glitter off her shirt.

She had very small breasts, unlike our mother's matriarchal mounds. I had more than I wanted already in this particular department, well aware that breasts weren't too fashionable these days. Sillie was lucky that way, tiny ones like Aunt Connie's. And today Sillie wore a tee shirt she had bought at the Battleford fair. "GRASS DOESN'T GROW ON A PLAYGROUND" scrawled in black across the breasts. Every so often while we were making lunch, Mom gave her a dagger eye, even one of which would have reduced me to a puddle on the kitchen floor. Sillie didn't seem to notice. Sometimes I wished I had her courage or her ignorance or both. I wore my faded blue kangaroo shirt and a blue floral scarf tied peasant fashion over my hair. I also wore a tee shirt I bought at the same time Sillie bought hers. Mine said "A WOMAN'S PLACE IS IN THE HOUSE OF COMMONS", but I kept it hidden under my sweat shirt. Mom wouldn't like mine any better than she liked Sillie's and I had not yet mustered up the courage for the unveiling although I was determined I would.

Finally we packed the metal detector and the lunch in the trunk. We all climbed into the car and set off toward the home place, past the spruce and poplar bush, the fields, the sloughs. Just before crossing the river, as we approached the barn-like pavilion which used to be a dance hall, Connie began to talk about Ace. Actually, she started a mile or two before the hall. There was a song on the radio, a song from the fifties, "Twenty-six miles across the sea — ", and I think that's really what set her off, just like a trigger had been pulled in her head. You have to wonder how the head works when something like a song can set you off like that. I heard somewhere that neurosurgeons in Montreal can stick a little wire in certain parts of your brain and you will automatically start to sing a whole song, say, or run through an entire conversation from years and years back. Things you had forgot or thought you had. That kind of thing happened to Grandma Spese too, toward the end. Sometimes she talked like a tape recorder — Mom thought she made most of it up — but I guess we all do as we go along. I mean, nobody has the same memories, really, or sees a thing exactly the same as anyone else. So it's all made up, in a way, as far as people are concerned. I suppose a certain part of what happens is real, if only you could know *which* part is right and real. But I don't really see how it's possible as long as people are gummed up in the works, because we all see a thing different.

"Well if it isn't," Connie said. "The old hall. Ace brought me up here to my first dance. I was sixteen."

"Fifteen," my mother said from the front seat.

"I'd swear on a stack of Bibles, Lila. I was sixteen. Because I remember Mom wouldn't let us date before we were sixteen."

"That's why I remember it was fifteen," Mom stuck to her guns. "Mom and Papa were pretty worried that night. Ace was so much older than you and he was known as a hell raiser to boot."

123

"We had a flat tire. Ace couldn't help that, Lila." Sillie and I smiled. "And there's lots worse things a person could be known as than a hell raiser. At least he wasn't dead from the ankles up."

"Whatever you say," Mom laughed. "It doesn't matter, Connie. We all went through it one way or another. Calder and I too. And now it's our turn to sit up and wait for the girls. Never worried much about the boys, but the girls — you gotta worry."

"Bullshit," Sillie muttered under her breath.

"Things don't change all that much over time, do they Connie?"

"Maybe not up here, Lila. That's why we had to get out. Once they got you pegged for something up here, that's it. You're shot. It wouldn't matter if you changed into a pink elephant or a bloody saint."

"Touché," muttered Sillie.

"Well, it's sure good to have you back home for a visit anyway, Connie," Calder said, his eyes on the rutted road ahead, hoping to avoid the potholes if only he could see them soon enough. "And I sure hope you find Grandma Spese's brooch."

"Thanks, Calder," Connie said. "I've been thinking a lot about it lately. I remember when she lost it. Mom and Papa had been out all night to a dance. They got home just before daybreak and Mom, who ordinarily would never have gone down to the barns in her good clothes, especially in the purple crepe, went straight down to slop the hogs that morning — she must have been in a huff, I think — and she was wearing the silver brooch when she went. And when she raised the pail of slop and bent over the pigpen, the clasp must have caught on a board and off came the brooch, flickered silver into the muck. She said she tried to catch it but no sooner had it landed than the old sow stepped on it and squished it into the muck. It disappeared. I can just imagine her. 'Oufta!' she likely would've said and stalked off toward the house holding

124

the pail stiff to her side as she went. She would've rather died than ruck through pig shit, even for a silver brooch from the old country. It was the finest piece she had. But according to her she left it right there and never once looked back. She never did go back and try to find it. So I figure it's still there."

"Maybe a pig ate it," I said.

"What?" She stopped for a moment, thought. "Well, what the Sam difference would it make? It would've just come out the other end of the old sow anyway. Like the clay beads Little Lyle ate when he was a baby, turned up in his diaper, didn't they? Every last one."

"I suppose," said Mom, reflective, maybe wondering as I was whether anything was ever lost at all except maybe inside everything else. The countryside flew by, the fields, the farms, the old granaries and abandoned places. Homesteads. It wasn't easy to make a living up here in the old days. Lots of people left. Lots of them went off to the war. Sillie and I had heard the stories of each place dozens of times.

"There," said Calder, "Connie, you must remember old Carl Shackle's place. Ace used to work for old Carl, back in the depression, when he first come up from the south."

"No," said Mom, "that's not the place at all. It's coming up on the left, just after this bluff. His place was on the left. I remember passing it hundreds of times."

"Well I'll bet you a dime on a dollar," said Calder, "that Shackle's place was on the right and back down by the slough."

"I hate to say it," said Connie, smiling coyly, but I think both your memories are failing. His place is down by the river. I used to go down there to see Ace when he helped build the new barn. He used to straddle the rafters and throw me peppermint candy wrapped in cellophane. In fact you went down there with me once, Lila. I remember how mad you were when Ace threw all the candies down to me and you had to wait, for a change, till I gave one to you. You were always the one they thought was so cute."

"Impossible," said Calder, determined. "I delivered a load of lumber up there one time and I know exactly where he was. I know this country like the back of my hand."

"In a pig's eye you do," Mom said.

Sillie and I looked at one another. We had to lean forward to do it because we were on either side of Connie in the back seat. Sillie grimaced. I raised my brows the way I have of doing. I have dark brows. My brow raising and Sillie's grimace were both a sign of *Here we go again*. We had been through this or something like it before with Mom and Dad, but now we had a third opinion — Connie's. And we were both inclined to believe her version. After all, she shone with the new light and she seemed more reliable to us because of it. Had she not come all the way out to the prairie on the bus by herself. Had she not had the presence of mind to rent a reliable, scientifically tested metal detector to assist in her search for the lost brooch, the treasure of our grandmother's past buried somewhere in the best aged natural fertilizer this side of Toronto. These were things people, especially women from Vancouver, seemed to know about life that simply didn't extend inland, and Sillie and I both intended to get some of it, by osmosis, if nothing else, for it seemed to literally ooze from Connie's pores. There was no doubt in our minds that she would find what she had come for. Mother was equally certain she would not.

As we came up over the hill, we could see Trestle, a small town like any other small prairie town, the railway pattern tattered by the time it got this far north. "Girls," Connie said, her voice rich and dramatic. She was smoking a tailor made cigarette which made her look even more *with it*, as we said in school. "Girls, this is where your Uncle Ace and I were married, in the Anglican church. Remember how it rained that day, Lila, and you spent the better part of the day before the ceremony kneeling behind the privy praying it would stop so you could go. You didn't have a proper coat and Mom wouldn't allow us to go to town unless we were properly dressed. And remember, it didn't stop. No, it did not."

126

"How could I forget," Mom replied, tartly. "It was enough to test the faith of a saint."

"And this," Connie continued, softly, "is where we had the kids. Your Uncle Ace was the blacksmith and town cop for years. That's where the shop was, right there." We already knew where it was. Dad pointed it out almost every time we came to town. "But you know," she spoke gently, seductively, "I hated the place, hated the people, hated the town. And the truth is I still do. If I had only known then what I know now, I'd have been gone years before we actually left. Hindsight is a damn sight better than foresight, though. If I was as young as you girls and had the opportunities available to me that you do now, it's hard to say what I would have made of myself. The world is your oyster nowadays. But I was just a kid when I got married. Don't for godsake make the same mistake. Still, it was the best move Ace and I ever made, getting out. Ace used to call it the ass hole of the universe," she said and laughed and peered at Trestle out the car window.

"Maybe you get out what you put in, Connie," Mom said, "and that isn't likely to change no matter where you go." It was her town. Sillie and I knew she was hurt. Her shoulders stiffened against the back of the seat, her greying hair set neatly in the finger waves of forty years ago.

"Now, Lila," Dad said.

"You think your way and I'll think mine," said Connie. "We had our reasons for leaving. I had my dreams. Before we left I had the wildest dreams. Once Evelyn and I were riding down the river road in a one-horse buggy and the next thing we knew there were all these bodies lying around on the river hills, all with their heads cut off, and I was whipping the horse, trying to make it go faster, and the maniac was closing in and closing in and then I woke up.

"Then one time I was walking along the riverbank with little Lyle who was twelve or so at that time. The bank gave way and I fell over and on my way down I grabbed hold of this willow clump, hollering at Lyle to pull me up and he just stood there grinning and I woke up."

127

Connie was on a run. As Calder breathed deeply, his shoulders rose up over the driver's seat. Then he sighed and they sunk back down.

"In the winter dream, I was walking along the riverbank with Sadie and I could see all the kids from town including my own skating along on the river. We just got to the edge of the bank when we saw a crack open up in a circle and all the skaters went down, all the kids went down in the cold water and drowned.

"The next night I dreamed we were all of us out from town walking along the riverbed and there was no water. All the water had disapppeared and there were gold nuggets and jewellery of all kinds flashing in the sun, lying along the riverbed and everyone was picking these up as many as they could when a wall of water started coming down from the north and just before it hit me I woke up."

I could tell by my mother's stiff neck, the veins from the neck to the chin taut, that she wished Connie had not woke up, or wished at least that she would just shut up.

"The last dream I had before I left Trestle was the dream of the white sails. I was walking along the riverbank with Sadie and there were sailboats on the river — a whole flotilla of white sails and there were whales. That's when I knew I was moving to the coast. And I vowed that when I moved to the west coast where no one knew me and who I was supposed to be, I would be myself. The funny thing is once we got out there, both Ace and I wound up working in Riverview, in an asylum, if you can believe it. Don't laugh, Sylvia. You wouldn't be laughing if it had been you.

"And a dream I had all the years I was trapped in Trestle came true too. I used to dream about a house on a hill with a winding road up to a garage. There were trees at the back of the house, an orchard of flowering trees beside a creek. There was a beautiful lawn all around the house and in my dreams we were always moving into that house. It had large empty closets and a glassed-in veranda at the back overlooking the orchard and the lawn. And there were so many rooms. When we went out to the coast we built that house together, Ace and me. We all have a right to our dreams Lila, our opinions and our dreams. And I'm just saying it was the best move we ever made, the only move we could have made. I'd rather be dead than move back."

"You always remember every dream as clear as that, Connie?" Calder asked. "I'd go nuts."

Sillie and I, though we never really painted the town so black as Connie, had roughly the same opinion about Trestle. As we drove through, I thought of Vancouver, of what it must be like. I tried to piece it together in my head from Connie's snapshots — hydrangeas and ferns, cedars and ships and the salt air of the sea. Shops and city streets and at night, lights everywhere on water. I could see Connie's point. Trestle had changed very little since Connie had left. The one paved street, the two cafes, changing hands occasionally, but two cafes, a grocery store, the bank, the hardware, the lumber-yard, the hotel-bar, stippled with brown pebbles, the elevators, one new, to be sure, but hardly anything you'd want to remember or care about really, unless you hauled grain.

The nine miles from Trestle to the home place were spent almost entirely in silence except for Mom who would periodically praise the countryside, which was embarrassing under the circumstances, as if she hadn't heard a word Connie had said when we knew very well she had not missed a single one. Still, it was beautiful, no one could deny it. Rolling and lifting gently, laced with small clumps of bush, coulees and bluffs and every so often a farm. Even Connie had to admit that conditions had improved since she was last up here. Better roads. Some farms with new houses, barns, machinery, and lots of stock. People seemed to be able to make a better go of it now, even Connie had to agree.

We turned onto the road to the home place. The road was overgrown with weeds and saplings so we had to leave the car and walk in, Dad carrying the lunch, Connie dragging her metal detector, and Mom with two large, empty plastic pails. The farmer who rented the place had planted rape almost up to the door. But the old man's beard still smothered the whole front porch, sagging now in the centre so you wouldn't dare walk in. Connie poked around the yard a bit, circled the house and looked in through one of the broken windows. Sillie and I were right behind her everywhere she went. When we stuck our heads in through the open window we saw the ceiling had fallen, the floor caved in. The crazed and tipsy linoleum was littered with broken glass and dank old newspapers, rags and magazines. The smell was something awful and as we withdrew, rather quickly, Sillie and I knew there was nothing of value left on the whole place, judging from the disgusted expression on Connie's face. Whatever her memories were right then, we wanted no part of them.

When Connie was finished inspecting the house, or what was left of it, Mom said, "They're gonna tear it down, he needs the land. So if there's anything you want to take back, now's the time. Calder and I might take the old grain sorter on the porch back to the house."

"What in God's name could I possibly want out of this old dump?" Connie glared at Mom, clearly, consciously challenging the widely held belief that any old piece of tin or metal on the prairie was to be regarded as a relic, a treasure.

"You know, Lila, when I went to Norway I saw the house Mom's great-grandmother was born in. It's still a beautiful, well-kept place, believe it or not, fresh coat of white paint, flowers, stone walkways. And it's in the country, Lila. There's still people living in it. And it was made of wood too. Those people knew how to take care of things. These old heaps of rubble on the prairie — people poking through the garbage as if they were about to come up with Captain Kidd's cache or something. It's sad really. It's pitiful."

"Maybe the weather's a little different here," said Calder.

"They got weather there, too, coming in from the sea. It's no excuse."

Sillie looked over at me and I let her know I thought Connie was being a bit hard on Mom. How could she possibly defend the whole prairie by herself, as if she were responsible for every rotting old wreck of a building between the west coast and the east. She couldn't and we knew it and we thought she was the one who was sad and pitiful, not the land. And I, for one, felt like a traitor; but I couldn't help it. Connie was telling the truth. What was left of the home place when all was said and done?

"You know, Connie," Mom said carefully, "the past there is no different from the past here, really. It's no better, if that's what you're driving at. But time. Time would be better off in a different place, it's true. It doesn't mean a thing to anybody here. A year, ten years, ten thousand years. Maybe here the buildings don't stand, but fall and rot. Quicker maybe, that's all. A man didn't have a lot of time to build or usually anything to build it with. So what Connie. So you find your bloody silver brooch, so what?"

"Let's get at it," Dad said. He had just returned from the car carrying a spade.

Mom snorted.

"All right," said Connie in her slow seductive voice, her prospector eyes alive again. She bent over to pick up the handle of the metal detector which was lying in the high grass. "The pigpen was just down here, if memory serves." She walked over, dragging her metal detector behind her, scouted around in the grass until she thought she'd found a ridge. "It's over here Calder, come on over here. This is where we'll start." Dad followed her over.

"Memory doesn't serve," Mom called out. "You're all wet this time, Connie. You're nowhere near where the pigpen was. You're right over the garage."

"Bullshit, Lila. We'll start here. I know where it was. If I had a nickel for every pail of slop I—" she trailed off, absorbed in setting up the metal detector.

"Well I remember it too, Connie," Lila pursued, still at a distance, refusing to take any part in the expedition, "and you're barking up the wrong tree." Sillie and I were raking through the grass with our hands trying to find the outer edges of the pigpen for Connie. Her foxy lady appliqué glittered brilliant in the high hot sun though there were clouds gathering overhead and the undersides of the poplar leaves blown up before the rain were silver too.

The metal detector was activated almost at once, a high whiney shriek that thrilled us with the prospect of seeing the silver brooch sooner than we had thought. Connie smiled and laughed and waved the machine back and forth over the find, so that it shrieked and stopped, shrieked and stopped, shrieked and stopped, coming to rest finally over the steady, shrill indication of buried metal. Dad took the spade and dug. We all hovered impatiently around the hole as he reached down and pulled out a giant bolt, a piece of machinery of some kind. Next he turned up a harrow disc, then two rectangular pieces of iron.

We looked over and saw Mom pick up her plastic pails and wave. "I'm going over to the coulee hill to see if there's still saskatoons down there," she called, her arm moving through the air, a silver line of light, like water along the underarm. "That used to be the best place to pick for miles around here."

We waved her away and went back to helping Connie. Pretty soon there were so many holes and mounds of earth around, it looked as if a colony of prairie dogs had set up a town in record time. The high metallic shriek repeatedly squirted through the lazy air of the old farm.

Calder pulled out a file. "Looks like Ace's work," he said. Connie's eyes filled with water. Next a ploughshare. Ace's work. We seemed to have come upon a whole cache of Uncle Ace's work. Sillie and I stood silent through all of this, the piercing squeal of the machine like a knife now every time in Connie, and still she moved it steadily over grass and over grass and still Dad dug and every time he pulled a horseshoe or a shard of metal from the earth, she cried. And every time she took her find and placed it carefully on the grass over by the house in a neat respectful row, memorial, as if she were unearthing bodies and laying them out parallel to each other, like we'd seen them do on television. Rusted bits of this and that, blades, an axe-head, all corroded and covered with dirt. No silver. None at all. And each time something different was unearthed, she'd say she'd take this back with her on the bus, back to the coast, this one for Gwen, that for Lyle, this for herself, all scraps, old scraps.

"Oh shit," Sillie said and she left the diggings and went over to the house and sat in the shade and waited. I stayed and watched.

After a long time, Calder said maybe we better pack it in. He dragged the metal detector back up to the house. Connie followed him. She carried the spade. He spread out a blanket beside the house and Sylvia and I unpacked the lunch. We sat down and ate, Connie and Sylvia and I quiet, Dad trying to do all the talking.

We were just getting ready to repack the lunch dishes when we saw Mom coming up over the ridge to the east. She was no different than she ever was, her wavy hair arranged as if it were marcelled, only almost white in the sunlight. I hadn't realized she'd gone completely grey. She carried two pails and when she got close enough she held them up, tilted them carefully so none of the berries would fall out. They were full of saskatoons and the silver sheen on their purple skin was remarkable to me and sad somehow in the sun. As sad and calm as Connie's arm resting thin on the chrome handle of her machine, almost invisible in the high grass.

The Garden of Eloise Loon

She wasn't one of them. She didn't belong here. She was not what they thought she was nor was she part of any other people. She nodded in the sun on the makeshift step, four large gallon ketchup cans supporting two grey planks, a spike driven through each of them into the tins for good measure. The stoop of the shack faced south and she nodded toward the sun as if to say yes. Whatever it wanted to do with her, it could. Melt down the body, even the moving mound in her round belly, render the fat, make soap, dry the withered hide of her and peg it to the ground, stretch it flat and smooth, scrape it free of all the filaments of flesh. Evaporate the water from the blood and scatter the rusted powder of her seed in the fields, wheresoever it should please. There was nothing left but the beginning of summer.

She hadn't seen Earl since two weeks last Friday. Sometimes he went up to work in the bush, but usually he said if he was going. This time he took his check, left without a word, and she hadn't seen him since. Nor had she any idea when she would see him again. She had no way of knowing. She had come to the point of not caring either. To fretting, she preferred moving her feet in small spiralling circles in the dirt in front of her, making smooth furrowed patterns in the grey dust, watching a film of dirt powder slowly, accumulate over her feet, her ankles, her shins. She had eaten nothing for two days.

The sun made her dizzy. She leaned her head back and watched the leaves on the poplar trees flutter in the wind. Poplars and spruce surrounded the shack. The leaves were round and green and looked like they were spinning, spinning green, almost lime, they were so new. Her belly was hard now, no longer high. The baby dropped three or four days ago, dropped closer to the hole through which it would make its way, like a worm. She cursed the lump. "Shit," she would say, circling the mound with her arms, laughing and crying at the same time. "Shit, shit, shit." And she rocked back and forth to the rhythm of the curse.

She closed her eyes. The lids flooded orange, then red, like thin hot blood. The red was all over her and warm as if it circled inside her brain and coated every cell with warmth the colour of a red rain. Now there were small black dots beginning to appear scattered over the clear warm red in her head. They expanded and grew, black and grey and elongated, like the worms. Finally they overlaid the red and she shivered and opened her eyes and blinked.

From the stoop she could see two other shacks through the bush. One straight ahead, one off to the right. Both were patched with cardboard and tarpaper. Eloise Loon was hanging out her clothes, grey and dripping, from a tin tub. She was silent and the flies buzzed round her head. There were chickens in her yard, all colours, chickens with ragged heads and one, almost pecked to death late one night, staggered with maggots near the outhouse.

The other house off to the right was grey as a grown over grave, silent in the heat. Usually there were many children. She didn't know how many; she had never figured that out except she knew there were a lot of them. All ages. Ragged little diapered ones and ones with fine new store-bought clothes and some with running noses, some with faces brown and live and shining round as the round round sun. But today, not one. Someone had driven up in a van a couple of days ago and now there were none.

She stretched her arms out. She wore a checkered blue smock from the Mission rummage, slid the sleeves up for more sun, her skin already a mass of freckles. Her hair was red and thin and she hadn't combed it since the day Earl left. There were freckles on the skin of her face, all over except for the eyelids and the mouth, which was now a round black hole, agape, a yawn.

She felt the first on her foot, looked down, batted off a long black worm with pale yellow ovals along the ridge of its back. But mostly black. The worms were mostly black. They were not really worms, she knew. They were tent caterpillars, by rights, but everybody called them worms.

Last year they layered the bush in a black mass, writhing over the walls of the shack, solid black and moving over the window panes, turning the inside black at the same time as the outside. She stayed outside, batted them off her ankles and her shins. Sometimes they fell from the roof in a clump and landed in her hair, began to move there over her scalp and she would fly from the stoop and scream and run around in circles till Eloise Loon would look up from her garden and laugh. But last year there was food in the house, at least.

And Earl was here. And sometimes he took her down to the lake where she swam. The worms covered the sand but they couldn't really swim. Only once had she seen a fleet, undulating, black, carried over the lake by the wind. Only once had she seen them land and writhe toward the high shore and the bush. They devoured everything in their path. Earl once said they were a lot like people that way. They ate everything in sight and had no natural enemies. But he said they carried their own parasite inside, sooner or later would do themselves in, and the cycle would end. The birds would have nothing to do with them. Even Eloise Loon's starving hens wouldn't eat them. Earl said a man from Chicago had brought a single pair over from Europe years ago. He figured he could make a fortune selling silk.

She remembered the night Earl rode out of the bush wearing a hood and shrouded in the white gauze of the worms, his horse lathered white, the calf a ghost of spun white. But as he drew near, she could see the worms, dropped from trees, black and writhing over the three, the man, the horse, the calf. When the worms were finished with the bush, there was nothing left on the trees but bones, the skeleton branches, like winter wounds, reached up toward the summer sun which bleached them clean and thin and white against the sky.

But this year, there wasn't even food for worms much less her. Much less the baby inside. There wasn't even Earl. There would be no eating off her this year, she thought, and coughed a small high-pitched laugh, spat toward the sun.

Last year the worms came into the shack too. There were gaps in the floors, knotholes in the walls, a ring of sky around the stovepipe hole. The worms used all of those last year. So let them come, she thought and shifted on the stoop. And let it come, the little one.

She wondered if maybe she shouldn't go across to the shack of Eloise Loon and ask for scraps. But the air was too warm, too thick, seemed solid between her and the shack of the brown old woman. And Eloise Loon would laugh. She always laughed, her fat heaving in round brown wrinkles, her eyes winking one, then the other, as if she had a tick, these flip-flop eyes. No, she wouldn't go over for a while yet. Maybe Earl would come back tonight.

She reached and batted two worms from her legs. One had climbed as high as her thigh, one only near the ankle bone on her right foot. She reached over and around the mound of her bellied child and picked a stick up out of the dirt and began to hurt the worms, first one and then the other, squashing out their jelly, green, a kind of green, not lime, but poplar, like the leaves they had devoured. Like the leaves, she thought and smiled upsidedown, her thin lips twisted in a small half circle, like a pale young branch bent by wet snow.

Earl in winter found her in the snow, half buried, wearing a ragged old coat. She had taken the bus from the city where there were banks and brokers, lights and water, pimps and grocers, singing in the bars. And other darker things, of course. But now, as the sun burned low, shattered black by the branches of the spruce, she thought especially of light, the many flickered city light. She could only half remember the rest. Then, the city a ring in her nose, a noose around her neck. She had thought that nothing could ever be worse, cursed the cracks in the sidewalks, broke her mother's back a million times. But she was wrong.

When she got off the bus at Trestle, she began to walk, stopping from time to time to talk to herself, to ask herself where she thought she was going with one cardboard suitcase and open-toed shoes, the snow blowing up her skirt, the cold obscenely creeping into the crotch of her panty hose. The noise, the whining wind, instead of dying, rose and covered her head with the sound of something white, all white and smothering and warm, a swarm of white, like cats in her head, a thousand white and mewling cats. Then howling, bitter ripping cats. Then no cats. Then no white. Then no sound. Only a lying down and a feeling of every round and silent moving thing surrounding her, taking her place, talking with her breath. Oh please. Oh shit, oh shit, and a feeling of rocking. Of rocking herself to sleep in a soft white drift.

Then Earl. In a truck. Earl had stopped and picked her up. Picked her up and put her in the truck and that led to heat and something to eat and bed.

He took her to the reserve. And for a while things worked out all right. She made him supper, peeled potatoes, roasted meat, everything ready every night when he came home from wherever it was that he had been.

She missed no one, none of the other girls who preened in the can at the Queen's every night. None of the Johns, not one. She picked berries all day long, strawberries and dewberries and red currants and black currants and lowbush cranberries and saskatoons, blue. Blue, her fingers blue, dyed blue and red and purple all through the summer into fall when great wedges of geese fell out of the sky and cried for the summer inside the hope, cried for the sun inside the north, the days the sun was dying south.

The winter was spent in the mouth of a long black stove. Shove, shove in the wood, split the wood, carry the wood. Then shove, shove, the sparks on the floor of the shack, the smoke, the long black pipe, a ring of winter silver sky around the stovepipe hole. Then no more wood. Then no more coal. The cold. Everywhere the cold.

For water she melted snow while Earl was in town running

around wherever he could find a woman white enough. Every day she hauled her tubs out of the house and into the yard. She filled them full with a spade, the snow sometimes dry like sand, sometimes crusted, sometimes so heavy her hands ached for hours inside the shack where she sat and watched the stove and waited for the snow to melt in the round tin tub. Sometimes she saw Eloise Loon in the yard with a tub and a spade, heaving and hoisting too, laughing and cursing the sun and the moon.

Sometimes she hid from Earl when he came home and the headlights of the truck shone in through the shack window. Sometimes she hid under the bed. But he found her and grabbed her by her thin red hair and banged her head and banged her head on the cold grey floor, till her nose bled and her ears rang with the roar of the stove and the white of the storm. He swore and dragged her all over the shack, backwards until he got tired and fell on the bed and started to snore.

The second summer came the worms, the walls of worms, the grey floor crawling black. She squashed them and gathered them all into a potato sack and threw them in the stove. She laughed. The summer passed and the poplar branches, stripped clean, began to leaf again, grow green. Earl went up to the bush. There were no berries because of the worms. She sat on the stoop and looked over at the shacks across the yard, watched Eloise Loon hang out her clothes, tend her tattered garden, weed and hoe and reap in the fall under the sun and the call of the great wedges falling through the sky around the curve, the round wound of the world.

The white of the following winter, a narrow hole, a silver needle with the dark of a hundred icy nights, back to back. The air flecked silver like glitter on glue. She peeled the potatoes and tended the stove, heaped wood in the box till the flue glowed dusty red as powdered blood. In the morning she walked in the bush, clumps of white powdered snow falling from the spruce, sometimes falling on her head, spreading a crown of crystal on her hair, spraying from there down the neck of her coat, down her spine, a thin line of white lumps under white skin, white as the skin of a cutworm in the garden of Eloise Loon.

And the wind blew. Earl returned for two weeks, nailed her to the bed two, three, one day seven times, the long hard line of his own fishing swallowed by her hole, the jigging ungentle, mortal, full of milk, full of resin, full of slime. There was a time in the middle when she could no longer tell the winter day from the winter night. And somewhere in the time of the winter worm, on the bed in the corner of the small dark room, the child began.

Now in the summer sun she sat rocking the round wound, circling the mound with her arms, laughing and crying at the same time, cursing both the sun and the moon. Finally the sun went down and she rose and opened the screen door, flack flack behind, stuttering the present into past, the past into the dark future, into the shack. As soon as she was inside she saw the worms begin to move across the floor.

She lay on the bed and regarded the pain from the distance of stars, the moon through the window welding arcs of shimmied light against the wall of the shack, her back a rigid arc, a wall of ache. The hole of the night narrow in her throat, the skin of her bloated belly shiny, white as the face of the moon and tight, too tight, the skin splintered with the silverfish of too much light inside, as if she would explode if ever there were another long hard night of arcing time.

In the morning she sat on the edge of the bed with the bloody child. The sun rose red. In the morning she took a rag out to the rain barrel and dipped it in and pulled it out dripping. She carried it back to the shack and wrung it out over the grey scum in the basin on the washstand. Then she began to clean the child which did not utter sound. But moved. Moved a little, flinching like an open wound. When she had him clean, she leaned over him and sang a song with no words, a song which found its own articulation deep in her throat, a curve of sound drawing honey from the bush and from the lake and from the wild and cunning throat of Eloise Loon. She wrapped the child and held him to her close.

140

Most of the morning she sat on the edge of the bed and suckled the child which clung to her breast like the rest of men do to the world. And she thought of the thing that she could do, deliver the child to Eloise Loon and beg for scraps. That was the thing that she could do. Just that. And then she wondered if the van might come and she could talk to the man who drove the van and deliver the baby to him. She smiled, her smile thin and dry, a kindling branch.

Finally she took the child acradle on her arm and she went out of the shack to sit on the stoop where it was warm. With the sun today had come the worms, in swarms, hanging from the eaves in clumps, their gauze in all the branches of the trees. The black of millions lying on the leaves, eating quietly. She saw them moving over the ground, around the stoop, a black mass thick and round on the rain barrel. Over the way, the garden of Eloise Loon, once green and full of bloom, now was black, undulated toward the stoop of her shack, looped over her clothesline, onto her roof.

And still there was no sign of Earl. Earl, if only he would come, could take her to the lake where she could swim in the wide water, a water full of silver and no worms. But by late afternoon, Earl still had not come and she sat on the stoop, suckling the child and drumming the fingers of her right hand on the grey plank and wondering what she could do.

Watching the worms move, she grew sleepy; the lids of her eyes were low. The clump of worms fallen from the eaves onto her hair began moving now, moving slow across her brow, curling round her ears, up into her nostrils, flowing down her neck, down the white line of lumps marking her spine through the thin white shirt. She looked up at the sun and closed her eyes. For a moment she saw the shadow of Eloise Loon against the lids which flooded orange, then red, like thin hot blood. The red was all over her and warm as if it circled inside her brain and coated every cell with warmth the colour of a red rain.

Now there were small black dots beginning to appear scattered over the clear warm red. They expanded in her

141

head and grew, black and grey, elongated. Finally she brushed them away from her eyes and raised the child in her arms, held him out toward the sun, stood up still holding him high, sighting along him as if he were the barrel of a gun, sighting the poplar and the spruce and the wide water. She left the stoop and began to run toward the garden of Eloise Loon. There she laid him down among the worms. As many as she could gather in her arms, she heaped high in a black and moving mound which began to spin a canopy, a shroud, delivered him to the dark, surrounded by her own laughter and the high arc of the only sky.

At Mrs. Warder's House

From the kitchen window above the sink I can keep an eye on Eric and his friends while I work. I see Stephen Willis is wearing a poppy today, pinned to the chest of his blue and white striped muscle shirt. Mrs. Willis should be shot. It's too cold today to be sending a four-year-old boy out to play in a shirt with no sleeves, and the poppy has an open pin which is a foolish thing to be sticking on a little boy.

Same thing every year. Passing poppies. They'll never learn. Stephen's poppy irritates me, reminds me they must be holding Remembrance Day services in schools all across the country. I was the one most years chosen to read the poem at the service—

> In Flanders' Fields the poppies blow
> Between the crosses row on row
> That mark our place...

There can't be many of us who don't know the words by now, after all the shuffling dusty afternoons, squirming on hard-backed stacking chairs, itching to get out and rip off the sad little red velvet cardboard corsage with the black felt dot for a centre, to rid ourselves of the pitiful poppy which along with the teachers, the compulsory minister and the Veterans' Affairs Department, conspired to make us all feel the sorrowful same—which we would not do.

The teachers said they chose me for my voice because it carried, and I knew the implication was that I should be honoured. But for me it was no honour. For one thing it separated me from my friends. I had to sit on the platform with the minister and the pianist. I could see my friends, their pony tails bobbing silly in the distance. And I was given to giggling back then, spent a fair amount of my platform time trying to control it.

The other reason I could feel no honour in having been chosen was because I knew I didn't deserve it. Because I knew what I was supposed to feel when I didn't. I had no excuse. I had felt it many times before, once at Mrs. Warder's house and the rest of the times with my grandmother. So if my schoolmates remember my solemn face, small and white, surrounded with a wreath of curls, my poppy red and lying for me on the lapel of my best white blouse, they recall a fraudulent respect, a sadness in my round white eyes which was not sorrow, but guilt.

Now, I work full-time for one of the largest accounting firms in Alberta. I am a Certified Accountant. I consider myself highly competent, but I'd be the first to admit having trouble coping with the double day, as they call it — eight at work and eight at home. I save most of my housework for weekends and, as usual, I seem to be spending half of it at the kitchen sink, which is not ordinarily this unpleasant. I can look out the window and listen to the radio while I work. Sometimes I even sing along, "If I were a carpenter, and you were a lady, would you marry me anyway, would you have my babies..."

It's not just the poppies. It's other things. Like the berry blood my small son brings in on his hands, squeezed crimson dye from fallen clusters underneath the mountain ash in our back yard. And the hedge of cotoneaster lying like a wreath around my neighbour's yard, the leaves all speckled red and gold from early frost. And for some reason, voices always seem to carry farther in the fall. Maybe that has something to do with it. I feel this way every year when the leaves are not quite gone, like thinning hair on men. Sometimes it's later; sometimes no leaves at all by the time I get around to it. But always and eventually, I do remember Mrs. Warder's house.

This morning I put down twelve more quarts of pickles. Beets this time. A part of my past I can't seem to let go of, although I know I have no time for this sort of thing anymore and the accountant in me says I don't really save any money with the cost of sugar and jars these days, and my time into the bargain. But it's a kind of compulsion with me, makes me feel right somehow, putting things down for winter, making provision. Ritual. My mother, her mother, her mother's mother — God knows how far back it goes. As far back as there is, I guess, for women. At least as far back as honouring the battle dead.

Beets are messy though. For some reason I always forget from one year to the next that they bleed all over everything, stain the white arborite on the counter top, dye the wooden spoons a colour not unlike menstrual blood. And now I'm faced with cleaning up the mess again, scouring the stains from pots and spoons and saying — Jesus Christ why am I doing this — some people never learn — half mutter, half chant, always a little surprised by the comfort that comes from the repetition, even of curses or bad news.

The news is over. The tone signal. The time. The twelve o'clock news. It is worse every time I listen. The broadcaster just said the situation in the Middle East is so serious the United States government is asking all American men and women of military age to register with their nearest draft board office. Now they're calling women. I try to put it out of my mind, try not to think about it. But the season works against me, the cold clear air coming in through the kitchen window. Now they're calling women. The possibility exists, no matter how I try to avoid it. I might be called up someday. Not soon, I know that, but someday maybe. "Called up" as my mother used to say, "your Uncle Olaf was called up." Her brother. "After he was called up, he never came home. We never saw him again." Irrational, of course. Then, it didn't necessarily follow that being called up meant you never came home. I know lots of men who served, men in my father's generation, my father himself.

The worst of it is there are women who want to go. I've even met a few. So we all edge toward the front line, wherever that may be in this day and age, rather more like a ball of yarn, I suspect, than a line, intersect and then around, intersect and then around and around and around.

145

Ordinarily I like to look out the window. But Stephen's silly poppy aggravates me. Even the sight of Eric himself, crouched under the mountain ash, makes me angry. Eric has straight blond hair. "A perfect Aryan," my husband once said, half joking (he is, after all, half German), "except the hair will never lie exactly flat — maybe he's safe." The window is open and I can hear their conversation under the tree begin, quietly at first.

"Do you know my guinea pig got killed?" asks Stephen.

"Who killed him?" says Eric.

"I don't know. He just got murdered. My mom found him by the fence. He got a wire stuck in his stomach and he just got dead."

"And blooded?" asks Eric, with too much enthusiasm for my liking. "And did his bones got squashed?"

"I don't know. No, I don't think so. I think he just got a wire stuck in his stomach and he just got dead."

"But how did he get dead?" Eric pursues.

Stephen is hollering now. "I don't know I said. I said he just got killed, that's all I said. He just got murdered." He picks up a stick. And Eric picks up a rock lying in the circle of dirt under the tree.

"Hey, hey, hey," I call out through the open window. "No more of that, you guys." Both of them look up at the window, surprised they are not alone, curiously surprised they are being watched. Stephen puts down his stick and Eric throws his rock over the back fence.

I look down at my hands, limp in the sink, the water a cloudy burgundy now from the beet juice. I'm a little startled by the colour, not so much by the colour itself as by the fact that I've been wallowing in it for almost twenty minutes without noticing the colour. Mindless. Up to my elbows in dishwater again. Which may be the main reason I started to think about Mrs. Warder. She always smelled of soap. Not Ivory Snow, not gentle fragrant soap. Sharp soap. Lye. Which I remember reading somewhere is used sometimes to cover uncoffined corpses, outside prisons, I think it was, asylums maybe, or in wars. Why, I don't know. The reason wasn't really given. But it's lye soap I remember at Mrs. Warder's house.

Mrs. Warder lived in Trestle. She's dead now, but she used to live on a sidestreet in a small house the shape of a chicken coop, grey clapboard with a roof that slanted from the front to the back. The house was fenced with chicken wire. I used to go there with my grandmother sometimes when I was on summer holidays.

Mrs. Warder's house was surrounded with poppies, squat orange California poppies sprinkled with babies'-breath, pretty really, if you like that sort of thing. And closer to the house were great red opium poppies opened up so wide I could see their throats, wide as if they were screaming something I couldn't hear. And over the house itself, a blanket of lobelia, small purple flowers on a bed of scalloped leaves, climbing in vines up the ladder of lumber till they almost touched the roof. I used to wonder what would happen when they crawled up over the top, what they would reach on Mrs. Warder's roof that would make the climb worthwhile.

These purple blossoms everywhere on green were vaguely shaped like valentines; not exact, like the ones I cut out of books in February, not symmetrical, each one just different enough for me to see that they were not the same, though all of them were purple. At school, we had been learning about the body in Health Class — the skeleton, the lungs, the brain, that sort of thing. The last lesson before summer holidays had been on the heart, and when I looked up at Mrs. Warder's vine-covered porch, I couldn't help thinking of all the blood those purple flowers must have known had they been hearts.

My grandmother and I walked over to Mrs. Warder's house. It wasn't far from Aunt Ida's where we stayed, only down the ravine, across the highway, then the main street and down two blocks. I don't believe they named the streets in Trestle back then, or if they did, I never knew. There were a lot of things I never noticed then. For instance, years later, I

147

learned from cousins that everyone in town said Mrs. Warder had bats in her belfry. They told me she threw pots and pans at any of the kids who came near the house. Whacky Warder, they used to call her. But I still find that hard to believe because she was always so good to me when I went there with my grandmother.

We both had to get all dressed up to go — I in my lilac taffeta and she in her rose print. And a hat. A pink straw pillbox with two small red rosebuds on a silk band. Her hair was already completely white. I held her hand when we walked over there even then, though I must have been ten or eleven years old by that time.

When we got there we went in through the gate and to the back door. We stood on the stoop and Grandma knocked. Mrs. Warder came to the door. She smiled, flapped open the screen door and hugged me hard which I didn't like. She smelled so strong of soap.

"Hedvig!" she said to my grandmother. "Come in, come on in." Mrs. Warder was fat and had a round face. She wore a dark brown hair net over grey pin curls and some of the bobby pins stuck out of the net, making her look a little like a porcupine, like an illustration out of Beatrix Potter. She wore an immaculate full white apron.

Her whole house smelled of lye soap and cabbage. She led us through the kitchen to the living room, small and full of doilies and china dogs and faded ice box flowers. The far wall was hung with pictures. A baby picture in a small oval silver frame. A Boy Scout picture, a pale adolescent hand raised in a two-finger salute, like the Scouts at school on Remembrance Day. A high school graduation picture, still a boy, I remember, a round fat face framed with one of those black hats with the diamond cardboard tops. And centred among these, a large, tinted, ornately framed photograph of a young man in uniform with wings on the shoulders. I distinctly remember the wings.

I sat on the couch across from the photograph wall and looked at them or rather at him. You could hardly do otherwise at Mrs. Warder's house because the couch and two chairs were arranged in such a way in the tiny room that you really had no choice. If you didn't look at the photographs, you pretty well had to look at your shoes. Now I recognize this to be the nature of shrines, this uncanny ability of making you bow your head without even knowing why.

Grandma and Mrs. Warder sat at a round oak pedestal table in the corner. Mrs. Warder picked up a pencil and continued work on a crossword puzzle left unfinished when she had come to the door. At the time this didn't seem peculiar to me, I suppose because my grandma appeared to accept it as a natural course for the visit to take, as if she had been through it before. Grandma sat and watched her for a while. They didn't speak. Nor did I. And time suspended itself, as it sometimes seems to do, out of neglect, I often think, or maybe in this case out of an awareness of its own silliness, of how little difference it really made, in this house in particular.

Pretty soon Mrs. Warder looked up at Grandma and said, "What's a seven letter word for forgetting, Hedvig?"

"Forgetting what, Frieda?" Grandma said.

"Forgetting everything," Mrs. Warder replied and smiled. "You know. Like what happened to the boys overseas. Olaf and Carl."

"Oh dat," said Grandma, remembering. "Amneesha."

"That's it," Mrs. Warder said. "Only it's not 'amneesha', Hedvig, it's 'am-ne-si-a'. Isn't that so, Irene?" She looked at me. "Am-ne-si-a," she repeated, "you're a clever little girl. I'll bet you can spell 'am-ne-si-a'."

"No," I said, "I can't. I don't know that word. We never took it yet."

"Well it's where a person loses all his memory, you know. Like Carl and Olaf, in the war. So's they can't remember who they are or where they come from. Even who their mothers are. So's they have to start all over again. In England, say, or somewhere overseas. You think they're back in England, Hedvig?"

"Vell, dat could be I guess," Grandma said quietly.

149

I couldn't believe my ears. I had spent every Remembrance Day since grade one with my grandmother. In Saskatoon. In the morning we went to the parade and the service at the cenotaph where all the soldiers were. We watched them lay the wreath. We wore our poppies. We walked back to her room in the Ross Block on Third Avenue by the old Eaton's and we sat together for the rest of the day. She crocheted and I read or played with her jewellery, all of it except for the silver cross in the black velvet box which was empty today because the cross was pinned to her grey wool coat. Sometimes when I got really bored, I would sit by the window watching the traffic moving below on Third Avenue. The cars were scarce because Remembrance Day was a statutory holiday then, everywhere for everyone.

Toward late afternoon, usually just as it was getting dark, early in November, she would get the pictures out. They were in an album she kept in a small cupboard by the radiator. She kept her books of Norway here as well, and I always got to look at them too which was good because they were full of beautiful pictures of fjords and blossoms and boats. We looked at these books first, a ritual we had of pretending to go over everything and just happening upon what I now call the real pictures, the pictures of Uncle Olaf on a horse in front of a granary when he was a boy, tow-headed, like Eric. And Uncle Gunar who died of diphtheria when he was four on my grandparents' first homestead near Viscount.

The picture of Gunar was strange, old and yellow — a picture of a miniature coffin with a window in the top. And through the window I could see the boy in a white embroidered bonnet and the top of a white embroidered nightie which I now realize must have been his christening gown.

She held the picture in her lap for a long time, not even looking at it. I guess after all that time she didn't have to, had it somewhere in her head more clear than what was left on cardboard. And then she moved to those of Olaf and did the same. Held them each in turn for what seemed like a long time to me then, although it must only have been minutes.

And finally she wept, head up, eyes open, making no sound. The only way I could tell in the half-dark was by the water on her face, illuminated red and green at regular intervals by the revolving neon sign of Day's Paint and Wallpaper attached to the brick wall beneath her window. Even then I knew she wept for both, indiscriminately. The one she'd lost through pestilence, the one through war. It didn't seem to make any difference to her how they'd died.

Those nights, she always let me stay up late, and when the cenotaph clock struck eleven, she turned on her television set and we sat and watched the CBC news. Every year the same. Some mother unearthed somewhere in the country who had lost two, three, maybe even four sons. They always had her lay a wreath in Ottawa at the cenotaph there and I got this idea that there were cenotaphs everywhere you went, like houses or like churches, everywhere the people were. And I was right, I think now, almost everywhere you go.

I nearly spoke at Mrs. Warder's house, in that matter-of-fact way children sometimes have of speaking. I almost said, "They're dead. My uncle Olaf and Gunar too — and Carl. My grandma told me so."

But Mrs. Warder said she thought they'd make out pretty well. "Carl was always so clever," she said. "He won every trophy Trestle High School had to offer. And it was worth the effort. That's what I always told him," she said, "every bit of the work is worth the effort. When he got low and wondered what he'd do and where he'd get the money to go to the city for university. And why he studied so hard anyway and wasn't out there with the rest kicking up his heels. 'It's worth every bit of the effort', I told him — and you should remember that too, Irene," she said turning her head and nodding at the couch where I sat, bored to tears, my hands limp and sweaty in my lap. "And I said it to myself too, Hedvig," she continued, "when I was up on the hill scrubbing out Mrs. Stirling's kitchen, down on my hands and knees. I always said I'd scrub every floor in Trestle a thousand times over if I thought it would help him along. And I know he's doing fine,

Hedvig. And your boy, Olaf," she reached across the table and touched my grandmother's arm. "I know he'll make his way. He was always so good with his hands, Hedvig, and you couldn't hope to meet a lad more thoughtful. They're probably married by now," she said and smiled. "You think they might have kids?"

"Ja, I imagine so," Grandma said without blinking, without so much as a hint to Mrs. Warder or to me that there was any doubt. They both had kids. I was dumbfounded.

Mrs. Warder served us tea which tasted as if it were brewed with bathsalts, and scooped Neapolitan ice cream out of a waxy brick, half-thawed and sudsy on the outer edges. It tasted old and awful. After tea I watched them play Canasta until it was time to go.

On the way home I held my grandmother's hand. By the time we reached the boardwalk crossing the ravine, I had made up my mind I would ask her. "Why does Mrs. Warder smell like soap?" I said, sneaking a look up at her soft white face.

"Ssst." Grandma said.

Then, "Why doesn't she keep her ice cream in the fridge like other people do?"

"She doesn't hef one."

"But why does she think — "

"Ssst." She looked down at me quickly, her face a flat iron square, and she squeezed my hand hard, a hurting hard I thought had broken fingers. But I never forgot and I never asked or thought of asking the question again. I guess I didn't really need to because I knew, right from that time forward — things can get so bad you can't forget them; sometimes they get so bad you can't remember. She must have thought I was too young to know and even if I did, too young to remember. But children do. They do remember. And for me it always comes back this time of year, each day a little shorter, each night a little darker than the last.

It's worse this year, for some reason. The news maybe. It certainly doesn't help to listen to the news. And Eric throwing stones, of all things. I've never seen him do it before. They say all kids try it but it took me by surprise, a boy who still needs to be rocked to sleep sometimes — throwing stones.

I lift the stopper out of the sink and watch the water, coagulated dark and soapy, circle down the drain. Eric has just come in from outside. He looks cold. His cheeks are red. I should have put a jacket on him.

"Stephen's guinea pig got tooken to God's Jesus!" he shouts, exultant.

"I doubt that very much, Eric." This comes out too sharp, I know. I dry my hands on a tea towel hanging on the oven door and bend down to kiss him. His flesh is cold and I draw back. I can smell the rotting leaves in his sweater. The fall. It's all around him. Seems somehow inside him. He holds a cluster of smashed berries in his hands. They're smeared on his shoes and I can see where he has tracked them in sticky patches all across my freshly scrubbed floor.

"Get into the bathroom and get that mess cleaned up," I yell, "and don't you ever bring any of those stupid things into this house again." I grab a spatula from the cutlery holder in the drying rack and almost throw it, watch it in my mind slow motion hurtle end over end awkward through the air, clatter against the far wall of the kitchen and drop to the floor. I can't believe I almost threw it, look down at the kitchen tool, my hand, inspect it as if it belonged to someone else, as if I were looking for an injury of some kind. And then I begin to pound the soft edge of the hand against the sharp edge of the counter, pounding and pounding till the hand slips and knocks over the box of soap sitting too close to the edge. The soap flakes spill over the counter edge like a waterfall of snow, forming a small mound on the linoleum and spraying around my feet.

Eric and I both watch the last flakes trickle over the edge. Then, still staring at the floor, I step out of my own footprints. When I look up my eyes meet his. Ordinarily he would have laughed. We both would have. The footprints are so clear, like cartoon steps, the kind you see pasted on sidewalks as a joke, leading nowhere. But he doesn't laugh. His eyes are frightened and confused, as if I were watching him with Mrs. Warder's eyes, as if he were afraid I'd pick up the coffee pot next, or the Dutch oven.

"It's only berries, Mom," he says finally, trying to defend himself against something he has no way of knowing, "it's just the berries from the yard."

Irene, I tell myself, he turned four last month. He's four years old, for Christ's sake, like Gunar in the little box. And I want to tell him it has nothing to do with berries, nothing to do with kitchen floors. Most of all I want to tell myself it has nothing to do with me or the smell of lye soap or pinning poppies on the clothes of my children. But I don't have to say anything. He runs up to me and grabs me around the leg and I take his head in my hands and press it hard against me. He doesn't cry. He is too scared. But I begin, the water moving slow and cold over the skin on my face.

"Get into the bathroom," I say again, quietly this time, "and wash yourself."

The Fathers of Her Friends
—for friends

A piece of green plastic stuck out over the edge. At first Miriam thought the plastic was light green, mint, the kind of plastic florists sometimes use to wrap cut flowers, and she felt an overwhelming relief. The casket was filled with flowers, not her father.

She was happy and saw herself eating cake and drinking wine from a long-stemmed crystal glass, talking easily with people whom she did not know. She set her glass on the lid of the casket and began to finger the plastic protruding from the lid. It was smooth and dark. Dark. Not for wrapping flowers. It was dark and dark and she slipped on the smooth edge of her fear and began falling. Falling through the open mouth of the bag, plastic, a dark green plastic, almost black. A dark green plastic bag which began to remind her of garbage. Glad. A Glad garbage bag was really what it was and now she was afraid. The casket filled with garbage, not flowers at all. Then she was all right again and poured more wine and drank from the crystal glass, twirling the stem between her fingers, filling her head with light.

Her father stood beside her on a platform made of wood. He was smiling and talking to a man. The platform seemed to be a loading platform outside a warehouse of some kind where trucks backed into numbered stalls and merchandise was loaded in and hauled away. She moved toward her father in her dream and woke.

Externally she was calm but her organs felt as if they'd disappeared, had been replaced with air the consistency of jelly which shook with every step she took. The worst of it was the way the double image overlaid in dream. Once she was awake, she couldn't seem to separate them. They seemed to have fused the instant of her waking, at exactly that moment

155

when sleep breaks off and dream is severed from the head like a hand from an arm. Fused, like a shadow and a man at the high point of the sun. The garbage and the flowers fused. That was the peculiar part of the feeling — the severing and fusing felt the same. Miriam worried about it, wandered around distracted, the dream top-heavy in her head all the following day.

After work, when they had settled themselves in the Heidelberg Lounge in the Gasthaus, Collette asked her how things were going — in general — Miriam knew she meant "in general", but she blurted out the dream, whole, garbage bag, loading platform and all, to the astonishment of both Deborah and Collette.

"That reminds me of my dad," said Bev, predictably. Miriam bowed her head. How could she have forgotten about Bev's dad. "Don't worry about it, Miriam," Bev said, "it's not your fault. Nothing to do with you really. Everything seems to remind me of him these days."

Deborah and Collette shifted a little in their chairs and straightened noticably, one after the other cupping their hands around the bottles of Heineken set on the round oak table in front of them, cupping the bottles as if they were trying to hide the labels, their luxury, when they knew very well right across the street and down two blocks Bev's father was dying in hospital, maybe tonight, maybe tomorrow, but certainly soon. And they knew because of this, as in all their recent excursions to the Gasthaus, Bev would be able to stay with them for only a little while before visiting hours began and she had to go up to see her father.

Collette had diagnosed the brain tumour without ever having seen Bev's dad. She was able to do this sort of thing with terrifying accuracy, had been able to do this sort of thing since she was a very small girl, since her mother died, she said. Even she had no idea where the ability came from and she knew very well there was no empirical proof of her peculiar skill, that it was especially suspect in the field of medicine. But the three women with whom she worked and with whom she now sat around the wooden table in the lounge, speaking in one low, carefully controlled, homogeneous voice, knew Collette's ability was fact. She had been accurate too many times. Over and over, her voice like a dull bell described the course of imminent disaster, especially death, long before the actual event took place. The saving grace was that Collette could also "perform", as she called it, in good things, like winning prizes. Like the time Miriam had come first in the Light Horse Show and had found herself accepting the magnificent silver trophy in the centre ring at the Stampede Corral with a dead centre calm which came off as good grace, humility and good sportsmanship to the audience, but which she herself knew to be the same dead centre calm she had felt after her conversation with Collette before she left work the Friday night before the show. "It's yours," she said, "it's in the bag." And so it was.

Miriam found herself staring at Collette now, across the table. Her colleague's face was white. Miriam was beginning to be able to pick up the signals, like the warnings one of her clients had described preceding seizures. But this wasn't the only reason Miriam found herself staring at Collette, the watching for signal. Collette was a beautiful woman, not a frivolous or even a dramatic beauty in the usual sense. In fact, she considered herself plain. But Miriam loved her face, the cheekbones high and shadowed blush naturally on the under rim of the ridges. She wore no make-up. Her eyes were large and wide and grey. Her hair, very dark, from the French, she had told them once. "And maybe too," she said hopefully, "from the 'prairie princess'." Collette had told Miriam and the others that her great-grandmother was the daughter of a Cree chief. "Imagine a princess in Saskatchewan, of all places. A blue blood," she had said and they laughed. "Imagine me a bloody blue blood. You'd never guess it by my salary."

Staring at Collette now as she spoke to Bev, quietly, her head tilted toward their mutual friend, Miriam couldn't help wondering how that head could work the way it did. Which led to a sudden speculation as to whether Collette might know exactly when Bev's dad would die. And together with the pale face, the thought crossed Miriam's mind that maybe it was tonight. What if it were tonight. And again she was awash in a kind of panic. Another overlay of last night's dream. Garbage and flowers this time superimposed over the image of Bev's father cranked up half-tilt in a hospital bed, reaching for the button on the intercom above his head, calling for the nurse. Only the man in the bed wore the face of her own father.

She shivered and picked up her glass, became aware that Collette was now staring at her, had been for who knows how long, her grey eyes blank, her face inert, pale as porcelain. Miriam felt as if she were looking into a crystal ball from the inside out, as if Collette should be wearing a bright red gypsy scarf with tiny black and yellow daisies all over it. Instead her head was circled with a dark ring of hair, cut blunt like a high fashion model from Rome, say, or Paris. Very chic actually. Like something out of *Vogue*. Ridiculous, Miriam thought, ridiculous the way her mind seemed to be hopping into all sorts of unlikely, surprising places. She had the jitters was all it was, doubtless because of Bev's dad. And talking about her own dream in front of Bev hadn't helped the situation any either.

"I know it sounds crazy," said Bev, trying to comfort or forgive, Miriam couldn't decide which, "but it wouldn't much have mattered what you said. Really, right now everything seems to remind me of Dad. The silliest things sometimes, not that your dream is silly — and the connection is pretty damn obvious in this case — you probably wouldn't even have had it if it hadn't been for me. It's just that I'm getting so tired of the whole thing. It sounds awful, I know, but I wish it were over. I really do." She said this thoughtfully, but flat, not sad or anything, just as if a whole lot had happened since she had begun to speak. In reality, Deborah had been the only one even to lift her bottle and pour in the interval, and even this she had done cautiously, Miriam thought, setting the bottle down and then the glass, with unnatural care, as if the glass were very weak, had some sort of flaw or maybe just was delicate and could be broken easily, with something as soft as breath against the rim. Like fine old crystal. Which of course it wasn't in the Heidelberg Lounge.

Deborah was uncharacteristically quiet tonight. She had hardly said a word since they left work together, in pairs along the snow covered sidewalks, along Fourth Street, four abreast crossing the interesection at the lights, over to the Gasthaus. Their favourite watering hole, Collette called it. Their only watering hole, as far as Miriam could remember.

Deborah was a lady. At least she was Miriam's idea of a lady — fine features, fine clothes, furs, china, jewels, the whole shebang — but all of these things taken together were nothing compared to her head, as brilliant and hard as emerald. Miriam regarded the head, swathed in hair the colour they called strawberry blonde in the beauty parlours.

Ordinarily Deborah would have been full of words. Which were her greatest gift — companion to her mind. She was one of the most articulate people Miriam had ever met. And the words had found themselves the medium of a rare voice. Miriam often found herself spellbound by the texture of the voice alone, an instrument of enormous advantage in what were euphemistically called "the helping professions", professions in which all four women were engaged together every day at the clinic near the hospital, the hospital where Bev's dad was right now — as far as they knew he was still there — all of him and who knew how much of Bev.

So although it was Bev's voice which moved across the table through an almost solid air of fantasy and beer, the lounge decor a large fluorescent mural of old Heidelberg set in stone on the far wall, Collette and Miriam looked toward Deborah. Deborah who was expected to speak, expected to direct the conversation tonight especially, probably toward the comfort of Bev who needed to speak of fathers. Deborah said nothing, remained still. But her silence was filled with energy, an active absence. Maybe she was just plain beat,

Miriam rationalized, she's just exhausted after a heavy group session or something. God knows the whole week had been rugged enough to strike anyone dumb.

Collette was the one who finally spoke. Collette was always more uncomfortable with nothing than she was with something, no matter how bad that something was. Miriam suspected Collette didn't even believe in the idea of nothing, let alone its actual existence, felt there was always something, no matter what you called it or what absence it indicated — it was still a name for something. She was fond of telling the story of poor old Marconi, as she called him. "The poor old bugger was locked up for years," she'd said, "just because he thought he could send sound waves through air without wire — what can you expect from fools on a flat earth?" And they had laughed at that too.

But there had been no laughter the day Collette diagnosed Bev's dad's tumour without ever having met the man. He had been away on a business trip and had gone off the highway into the ditch near Lethbridge, Bev said. All four of them had the same information; the doctors, of course, had even more. Now wouldn't you think, Miriam thought, that Collette would have had to sort through the logical alternatives too, like the rest of them — he fell asleep at the wheel, had been drinking, a simple seizure, diabetes — there were a thousand things it might have been. And yet Collette seemed to have been lit with it, knew right then the precise nature of Bev's dad's predicament. And the worst of it was she said it — out loud. Miriam would never forget it; it was one of the rare occasions when she doubted Collette's judgement, considered her in fact irresponsible, unfeeling, reckless in her speech. Although even Miriam could see it was almost as if Collette *had* to say what she did, as if it had to be out of her as soon as it was in — a certain pressure in her head and mouth. Almost exactly the same feeling Miriam herself had when they had first come into the bar, before she blurted out the dream. A few weeks later, the diagnosis was confirmed. Malignant. Terminal.

"How is your dad, Bev," Collette said now, matter of factly, the same way she had said, "It's a tumour Bev. It's a brain tumour." No hysteria, no dramatics — as if she'd said "There's a button off your blouse, Bev."

"Just about the same I guess," Bev replied, "except thinner — and he already — " They all knew anyway. They'd been through it before. By last Monday, he was down to less than eighty-five pounds. " — and he was always such a big man," she finished finally. Within the last week she had slipped into a kind of litany. Many of their conversations had ended with the same words, uttered mechanically, like an afterthought, "such a big man", as if by the very repetition of it she could come to believe at least in his physical transformation if not the psychological ones such as his determination to buy new skis during the mid-winter sales even though he knew, had been told.

A big man. A big man. And Miriam's father was with her again, in her head. *A big man.* He was standing on the loading platform in the memory of her dream. Tall. Taller than he really was. Even now she sometimes thought of her father as a big man, though he was not, by comparison with other men she had come to know along the way. Not tall at all. If anything, he was on the small side of a medium build, applied to men. She shook him off, lifted her glass and took a long swallow of Heineken. She couldn't be the only woman who always saw her father tall — taller than he ever was, even when she had moved away from home, even when she was no longer a child.

Neither Collette nor Deborah responded to Bev. Perhaps they had talked to her before about the physical change in her father, sometime at work, between interviews and groups. That was probably the case, Miriam thought. She herself said nothing, remained silent, lifted her glass again and took only a small sip, relieved the light in the Heidelberg Lounge was dim and blue.

Her father's face suddenly back. His body shrinking. The shrinking speeded up, racing unmercifully, like a film on fast

161

forward or air escaping from a balloon. She shuddered, quickly dropped her eyes toward the floor, as if looking for her lighter or something fallen from her purse, afraid Bev may have known somehow and would be hurt by the overlay, the displacement. More likely Collette would know, she thought, not Bev, and she lit a cigarette, still embarrassed, especially by the sudden visible shudder.

"You chilled, Miriam?" Bev said. "Why don't you take my sweater. I'm all right."

Miriam said, "Thanks Bev, I am cold," took the sweater offered over the table and draped it round her shoulders. A blue and white Norwegian sweater. Bev dressed in a way that made Miriam think of her as Scandinavian although she wasn't — fine wools and things — and she liked to ski a lot and was fair with blue eyes, had somehow a nordic look, but fine-boned.

"You look tired, Miriam," said Bev. "Didn't you get much sleep last night? Are you all right?" And who is comforting whom here, Miriam rebuked herself, feeling worse than ever. Wasn't the purpose of coming over, tonight in particular, to be with Bev before she went up to the hospital to see her dad. "Maybe the dream, Miriam," Bev said, "I forgot about the dream."

"I suppose," Miriam answered casually. "I guess I didn't actually get much sleep after that, now that I think about it. But it was only a dream, Bev," Miriam said and laughed and lifted her glass. There it was. Exactly what she didn't want to say. "I didn't mean —"

"I know," said Bev, "it's all right."

"How about your dad?" Miriam said, backtracking. "Is he able to sleep?" Collette nodded. Deborah did nothing, only looked at Miriam, a knowledge and sadness on her face Miriam had seen that morning when she had first told Deborah about her dream. Deborah seemed to know exactly what it meant but wouldn't say. She had a fair amount of experience with dream analysis which Miriam did not, and Miriam expected something more from her. But Deborah wouldn't say, only nodded slightly when Miriam had finished speaking. And now Miriam began to feel the sadness on the face had not only been for her but for Deborah herself. And not for Bev at all. And everything seemed upside-down somehow and not right.

"Are they able to control the pain any better now, Bev?" Miriam persisted, wading through the wall of inertia, withholding, her eyes level now with Bev's, avoiding Deborah's. The conversation was going around and around the table like a roulette wheel, it seemed to Miriam, and whenever it stopped all four of them crowded close, their elbows on the table as if looking for numbers in the bottoms of glasses — a win, a loss — and the one who seemed to be the winner was the loser and had to carry the words into the next spin. And that winner who was the loser leaned back in her chair, leaving her beer on the table while the others drank in the dim blue light. And there was hardly anything said in all that time, the words so heavy in the mouth, the air beginning to thin and grow tight so the words would hardly even hang in it at all let alone travel over the table. They seemed to deflect or ricochet or boomerang back to whoever had uttered them.

The other tables in the lounge were empty now but for one couple in a corner, their faces dark under the far end of old Heidelberg. Sepia. Lit dead centre from above. Marie was on tonight. She wore a leather apron over a blue German folk dress. She cleared the empty bottles from the table and Collette ordered another round. Marie was back within minutes. She seemed to sense what was going on when she returned and she set the bottles down carefully. She said nothing.

Bev waited until she was through. "I don't think he gets much sleep any more," she said, "not real sleep. The pain is actually a lot worse." She lit a cigarette. "Which is only to be expected, I guess," she added. "So they're giving him a lot of morphine now." She paused, as if there were a decision to be made as to whether or not she should say any more. She looked at Miriam and went on. "He's started hallucinating.

My mother calls them visions. But they're strictly from the drugs. This is the hardest part of it for me so far, to see him like this. He was always so rational. But now, as I told Miriam yesterday, when I went up to see him in the afternoon, he told me they'd put him in one of those Kleen-pac garbage bins — the nurses had, I guess he meant. And he thinks they've got all these bins lined up on a railway track behind the hospital where there's a kind of loading ramp by the back doors. And they just put all the dying people into these bins and take them down to the tracks and ship them off.''

Miriam lowered her eyes to her lap again, could hold Bev's no longer, the connection to her own dream painfully obvious, embarrassing to everyone. How could she not have remembered?

"I mean, what can you say," Bev continued, "it's not as if he were one of my clients. He's my father for Christ's sake.'' Miriam raised her head, looked at the eyes, no longer dry. Finally. "It all makes sense," Bev said. "I even went to his window when I didn't know what else to do, what else to try. I was going to say 'Look, Dad, I checked it all out and it's fine, everything down there is fine.' But there really *was* a garbage bin under the window, three stories down. And I'm sure he had seen it earlier, when he could move around a lot better. And I know the tracks are pretty close and he must hear the trains. I can see it all makes sense, I know it does, but it doesn't help. For one thing, he doesn't know. How can he know. And I can't tell him, I can't even — ''

Collette, dry-eyed, bright-eyed, wide-eyed, pushed her chair away from the table, jumped to her feet, a terrified child, her voice amplified. "That's it. That's it. I'm leaving. I've had enough," And she was gone.

Miriam wasn't the only one who had been taken by surprise. Deborah and Bev looked just as stupified as she felt. "What's wrong with her?" Bev said. "I mean, I've never seen her do anything like that before. I hope I didn't — what happened to her, for God's sake?''

Which was exactly what Miriam wondered and Deborah

too, obviously, because she had already pushed her chair away from the table. "I don't know but I intend to find out," she said; and over her shoulder, "Order me another Heineken, will you, if you can catch Marie. One for Collette too." She disappeared against the backdrop of Old Heidelberg, her red hair swinging shoulder length, smooth and soft. As if she had been a doll wound down and someone had wound her up. The Deborah they knew was back, confident, professional, decisive. Not that she hadn't been concerned before, only she seemed to Miriam to be distracted by some calculation, some argument inside herself. And as Miriam stared at the dark doorway through which Collette had disappeared and Deborah only seconds later, conversations drifted back toward her out of the new dark. Deborah was the only one among them whose father was already dead. And mother too, for that matter. And Collette, with Collette it was her mother.

"I shouldn't even be talking about it; it's all I ever seem to talk about these —" Bev began, but Miriam cut her off.

"No Bev, you need to talk about it and they want you to. It's just that they've been through it already and we — well, I haven't — yet," Miriam faltered.

"It's all right, Miriam," Bev said, placing her hand on Miriam's arm. Miriam suddenly felt as if she were going to cry. You'd have thought she was the one who had lost her father or was about to, the way she was acting.

Deborah came back without Collette. "Did she go home?" asked Miriam.

"Nonono," said Deborah, waving her hand, the burgundy nail polish catching and holding the faint light. "She'll be out in a few minutes. She just wants to be by herself for a while. She'll be all right." She withdrew a cigarette from a soft brown calf case and glanced around for her matches which must have fallen to the floor when she got up to follow Collette into the washroom. "Gretel", Miriam remembered, an odd thought now, but the bathroom here was called "Gretel", calligraphy burned on a small wooden plaque. Little girls. Lost. Bev leaned over and lit Deborah's cigarette.

Deborah settled back in her chair, took three deliberate draws.

And the silence was with her again. Her insidious silence circling the table, closing in and closing in. At last Deborah turned to Bev, focussed sharply as if she were the bull's eye on a dart board. "Listen," she said, "I know what you're going through. When my father died, I had to take a flight from Calgary all the way back to Halifax. I will never forget that flight as long as I live because he had already been dead for hours before I set foot on the plane. And every mile of that trip I argued with him in my head. All the way back. I'm warning you, I have never been so Christly furious or hurt in all my life and I don't ever expect to be again." She delivered this calmly. No details, Miriam observed. No details from the woman who made a practise of sharing her own experience with clients if she thought it would help in any way.

What kind of man must he have been, Miriam wondered. Whoever he was, he hovered over the table like a hawk, a cloud, unholy, dark. A chill. No details. "We had a lot of unfinished business," Deborah said. Which was an interesting way of putting it, Miriam thought. They would never know what it was. Just the sound of no sound. Miriam was still cold, drew Bev's sweater more tightly around her back, and the dream of her father surrounded her again. Now she was hunkered up against the table, her arms crossed as if she were protecting her belly, the soft underside, hiding, head bowed, the casual brown curls divided in an uneven part at the crown.

"You still have time," Deborah said after a few minutes.

"For what?" snapped Bev, an edge to her voice now. "For what? Besides, we couldn't have been closer. Our whole — we got along very well, Deborah. I'm not going to say it again."

"*Are*, Bev. You mean you are very close. He's still here. Tell him. And leave room for the rest."

"There is nothing else. For the last time, there is nothing else." Bev's voice, almost loud enough for Marie to hear her in the bar kitchen, suddenly dropped. "Besides, he can't talk.

He can't even listen. Not even to the good times, not even to that."

"You can," Collette's voice, calm and emphatic. "Who knows how much gets through, Bev, or even how for that matter." Collette was back, a woman again, tall and sleek in high black boots, self-assured. "Sorry, Bev," she said right away. "I'm sorry but I just couldn't take any more of it. For God's sake say goodbye." She turned abruptly to Miriam.

"And your dream, Miriam," she said, composed, almost aloof. "Ask me about dreams." She paused. "My mother died in the Trestle Union Hospital when my brother Maurice was born. I was four and I was there. The nurses brought me into her room to give me her ring. To say goodbye. You know, the nurse bends down to the little girl and says 'How would you like to come and say goodbye to your mom now. You come along with me.' There were basins of blood — bloody rags they must have been — but to me they looked like basins brim full of blood. My mother's blood. She hemorrhaged. She was thirty-eight. I only have four more years."

"Collette!" Deborah blurted.

"I'm serious. I only have four more years. So I live like that. I always have — as if I only had thirty-eight to start out with — if there's more, it's a bonus. I've used up thirty-four. Time sure flies when you're having fun, eh?" she laughed.

"Anyway, I got scared. After I got the ring I got scared. And I ran out. And I never even — " Her face, so carefully controlled until now, only a few seconds ago lit with her own black laugh, crumpled suddenly. But even before she began to cry, she was reaching down into her bag for Kleenex. Bev passed her a clean one. "For God's sake say goodbye, Bev," she sounded cross, "that's all you have to do," water moving freely from her eyes, over the high cheekbones, toward the corners of her mouth.

"You were four, Collette," Miriam said, dumbfounded, unfolding herself and leaning over the table top toward her. "You were only four years old."

"All I had to do was say goodbye. Goodbye, for Christ's

167

sake. One word, Miriam." She wiped her face and blew her nose properly, hard, and her eyes were wide again. Opened up too wide, Miriam thought, like a child just out of nightmare. The others waited, silent, circling their wound.

"So that's the way it was," Collette continued, shifting down. "After Mom died the nuns talked Dad into sending us to the convent. Said a man couldn't raise three girls properly alone. Mom was a good Catholic, they said, and would've wanted the girls raised in the faith. So off we went to the convent and the baby went to Saskatoon, to my aunt's place.

"I nearly died in the convent I got so thin. And just about the only thing I remember from there is polishing the silver, of all things. Polishing, polishing. What the bloody hell for? What the bloody hell for? And this one nun kept telling us our dad was going to hell because he didn't go to mass. As if we could make him go. We couldn't make him go. And little cards with pictures of Mary on them they gave us for polishing silver, for Christ's sake.

"Finally the doctor told my dad I'd die if he didn't take me home. So he did. And all us girls finally got home and he told the nuns he didn't bloody well give a damn if he was going to hell or where he was going, they were his kids and he'd do the best he could. And if that was the kind of God there was, the nuns could have him all to themselves and hell maybe wasn't so bad after all, compared to the convent." They all laughed, even Bev who was Roman Catholic.

"As soon as I got home," Collette went on, "I started having the dream. Every Thursday night for the next four years I dreamed the same dream. Giving blood. I was giving blood. It was for Dad and I knew it was for Dad so it was all right. To keep him going, I guess. He told the older girls that if they'd had more blood at the hospital, Mom never would have died. Since he was all we had left, I figured it was the least I could do, I suppose, somewhere in the back of my head. Every Thursday night till I thought he could get by, I guess. Who knows what a kid thinks. I can still see the dream sometimes at night before I go to sleep, just before I close my eyes. I had it worked out that we were taking turns, the other girls and me, every other night, and Thursday was my night.

"Dad made out all right too, we all grew up. When he had to work late at the garage he took us with him and while he worked underneath the cars we played with the staplers and paper clips in his office till we got tired and then we fell asleep on a pile of greasy overalls in the corner beside him. When he was finished work he wrapped us up in his ball jacket and carried us back up the hill to the house, one by one. Spic on weekdays and boiled chicken on Sunday. That was all he knew how to cook." She paused. "So I know about dreams."

Miriam nodded. Who could argue.

"He called us 'gifts from God'," Collette said quietly. "He still says kids are gifts from God, if you can imagine, in this day and age, after what happened to Mom."

Bev had on her coat and a blue woollen cap, was on her way out the door, by herself. And Miriam paid the bill, left a tip for Marie; Collette and Deborah ran ahead to catch up to Bev. And Miriam followed them out the door, out onto Fourth Avenue, toward the hospital, her scarf trailing along behind her on the ground, the face of her father ahead, no matter how fast she ran.

Barbed Wire and Balloons

"What the hell did you do to yourself this time?" Jordan was not a reticent man. But neither was August.

"I'm telling you Jordy, it feels as if I got three bands of barbed wire cinched round my middle and some jackass is just a drawing them tighter and tighter every time I take a breath."

Stella was upstairs in the back bedroom. She was only half awake but even so she recognized the voice right away. It belonged to August Pickard Moon, her mother's older brother. There wasn't another man between here and Battleford with that raunchy rhythm to his words, that molasses resonance. He was a great storyteller if nothing else and Stella decided to get up and go downstairs.

Her favourite story so far was the one he told about the bull. When he was just a young buck, he said, he got himself a bull calf, a black one with a slobbering snout. He said his calf gained a pound a day. And every day, he'd lift the little begger up over his head. Every single day. And because it gained only a pound a day and because he always figured he could lift one more pound with no trouble at all, he planned to lift the animal when it was fully grown. "And by jumping Jesus, that's exactly what I did," he said, "and the bastard fully growed weighed in at damn near a ton. I lifted him, without a word of a lie, I lifted him right up over my head, right there at the Meadow Lake Stampede, right in front of the crowd. Clap! You never heard the beat of it. Clapped till they bust out in blisters!" Stella loved it. She could see him clearly in her head, grunting and hoisting his big black bull, till finally she saw him pivot slowly for the crowd, so everyone could see.

"That's a lot of bull all right," her father had said. Later, after August left that night, he said to her mother, "August never was a farmer, Iris, you know that as well as me. He don't know a damn thing about livestock. Your folks never had no cattle, only the grain, and he was no help with that either. Galavanting around to sports days was about all he was ever good for. That and drinking, of course. But he sure knows how to shovel shit. I'll give you that. Born in him."

Her father's case was solid. Stella knew that much, even then. But she loved the story and the way he told it and she had learned to keep certain things safe in the back of her mind where her father couldn't get at them. Things like Uncle August's bull. She grabbed her balding blue chenille kimono from the closet hook and shoved her feet into a pair of rabbit slippers, tufted and worn through to the hide where her feet rubbed together when she walked. Wrestling with the kimono all the way down the stairs, she flung herself headlong toward her uncle's voice.

Her father and mother were in the kitchen and both of them were in the process of examining August, who was for the moment silent. He revolved stiffly, all two hundred and seventy-five pounds of him weighted on the heels of his cowboy boots, setting up a linoleum creak which flattened the ears of the dog. Her mother already had the coffee pot ready to go on the stove. She was clutching a half-empty bag of Nabob coffee to her chest, like a stethoscope, looking at August as if she intended at the first appropriate moment to use it on him, to find out for herself once and for all what made the man tick. Her face was pale and serious under the bare light bulb hanging off-centre from the kitchen ceiling, and from the look of her, Stella figured the situation must be pretty bad, whatever it was.

Uncle August, in one of his slow circles, stopped like the winning or losing number on a roulette wheel and faced her mother. Without speaking he stuck out one of his long heavy arms toward Iris and nodded. Stella was by then standing beside her and, without looking at the girl, her mother stuffed the coffee bag into her hands, which were already open, ready to receive something, like those of an altar girl.

171

Iris took the end of her brother's jacket sleeve and slid it off the arm with that particular gentleness usually reserved for undressing babies. August was wearing his lime green ball jacket, though he did not play ball. It had a red and yellow crest on the back that said "Hub City Sockets" in bumpy appliquéd letters with a matching bumpy black wrench underneath, though as far as Stella knew, he had no particular affiliation with the Hub City Service Centre any more than he played ball. But August got around, she knew, and she supposed the jacket was just another one of the spoils of his fly-by-night way of life. Along with the peaked John Deere cap he wore, to the side, pulsing yellow with a small green deer, antlered and leaping on the crown at the front of the cap.

The first sleeve fell away and her mother began to peel off the other. Her father, who until then had been standing behind August, rubbing his whiskers and hitching up his pyjama bottoms, reached out and caught the jacket just before it hit the floor. He hung it over the back of a chair.

"Jesus H. Christ, August. What the hell kind of contraption you got on your back?" Jordan spoke to the back of August's head. August had just rolled up the last of his tee shirt and was preoccupied with the final unveiling of his most recent burden.

Stella could see what her father meant. It was a contraption all right, a back brace. It was ribbed and looked a little like Grandma Moon's old flesh-coloured corset, but it was white and padded thick with foam, like the neck brace her mother had to wear after her whiplash a couple of years ago. Except this brace circled the massive circumference of Uncle August's chest and back. His belly button, which should have been buried like a winking eye in the folds of his belly, remained unfettered, a saucy protruding bump, exactly like the ones she had seen on the bellies of babies. Stella saw her mother's eyes scrape open another notch when she saw the brace and the button.

"Now let me see," August began slowly as if he weren't

quite sure himself what had happened to him. "I guess I'd have to say it had something to do with the cows, and God Almighty," he sighed, "I guess if I was pushed, I'd have to say it had something to do with the Indians, too." Stella picked out a chair directly opposite to the one with the lime green jacket hung over the back. She wanted a good seat so she wouldn't miss anything.

"Well, hell, it's a long story," he began again, "and of course it's late and if you folks are pressed for time —" This part was rhetorical. There was no question about whether or not they would listen to the story.

"You gonna tell the damn thing standing or sitting?" Jordan asked.

"Sitting, Jordy. I been standing for a week. Help me get this goddamn contraption off." The request put them all at ease for they knew then that the brace was more like a theatrical prop than anything else, that whatever had been the matter with August, it must be almost over. He wouldn't have to wear the contraption forever. They relaxed. Stella pulled another chair over close, put up her feet, and wrapped the flaps of the old blue chenille around her legs.

She looked as motheaten as her slippers. She hadn't even taken the time to run the brush through her hair, which was like her mother's, only redder. It looked a little like someone had set fire to a bramble bush. But she wasn't really worried about her hair. She knew Uncle August didn't care how she looked because she wasn't *on*. He was *on*. He played fiddle with the Rowdy Roses, played for all the dances for miles around, all the way from Battleford to Lloyd. He had a stage sense not everybody has. And a sense of timing. Stella was audience, and audience could look any way it liked so long as it was there.

While her father helped August unhitch himself from the brace, rolling his tee shirt back down over the enormous liberated belly, her mother measured six teaspoons of coffee directly into the boiling water in the pot, set four cups on the table along with a jar of spoons, sugar bowl, creamer, and an ashtray. Uncle August smoked. "It'll be ready in a flash," she said and sat down.

"Maybe August don't want that kind of lightning, Iris," Jordan said. "Maybe he needs a shot. Whadaya say, Aug?"

"Now you're talking, Jordy. I got a lot of pain in my condition. I tell you, if it were any closer to Easter, I'd think I was carrying the goddamn cross."

Jordan poured two glasses full of Three Feathers and set them on the table. August made his way to the chair with the jacket on the back and lowered himself slowly to the seat. He took off his cap, drawing the back of his right hand across his brow as he did so. Iris took the cap and put it on the arm of the sofa, which served as a barrier between the living room and kitchen of their farmhouse.

While she poured coffee for Louella and herself, August fidgeted in his chair, straightened, stuck his right hand behind his back, reached under his tee shirt and rubbed so hard Stella thought he'd flay the skin right off. He took a long, sucking sip off the top of his drink, taking in more air than rye. Jordan lifted his glass and drank half the amber liquid straight off.

"Get on with it, Aug," he said, rubbing the line of whiskey on his lips downward into his whiskers, like a salve which smelled a lot like Zambuck or Zinc to Stella the only time she'd tried it.

August lifted his unoccupied hand to his broad forehead, splayed his fingers and ran them over the shiny skin on the top of his skull as if there were hair, handfuls of it. "Damnit," he said, "I'm just trying to recall here what time it was it happened. I know it was a Thursday — no, by God, it was a Friday — payday for the other guys on the run. I don't worry about that no more, Jordy, since I bought the truck. Now I'm my own boss. Anyway, I know the sun was about halfway down the other side of afternoon, three, maybe pushing four. I'd made seven trips already, up on the grid near Meadow Lake, up past the reservation there, forty-five, maybe fifty miles from here. Hauling gravel. And every time I come back empty, well I had a scrap of time to think."

August had bought himself a gravel truck in the spring. "God knows where he got the money," Jordan had said. "He never has two cents to rub together." But Stella thought August had always been very enterprising — in his way. He'd been in and out of more occupations than they could count, wheeling and dealing his way through farm machinery, the manufacture of rapeseed oil, grave digging and landscaping, the oil rigs, insurance, janitorial services, taxi driving, and bread delivery — these were only a few she could remember from the stories. Now he had bought himself a gravel truck and all the relatives hoped he could make a go of it this time. That was how her father had put it. Make a go of it.

Stella didn't judge August by whether or not he could make a go of it and she didn't think it was right that most of her relatives did, with the possible exception of her own mother. Stella was in grade ten and the threat of having to make it on her own hook was at least a year or two away. But once in a while, usually late at night, the prospect of finally being responsible for all her own decisions worried her. Then all the vague and nameless future decisions buzzed her like the random, mindless threat of bees. And she saw herself, like Uncle August, turning every which way in life, trying to figure out the best or safest or most lucrative or most worthwhile way a person could live. And her worst fear was the never ever *knowing* what the right one was. The *right decision* rose like the ghost of Marley, every year more and more rarified, more remote, more guilt-laden, and especially more threatening. She had her dreams, but they gave her small comfort. For one thing, they had to do with painting pictures, an idea she got after she had been to the Imhoff Art Gallery near St. Walburg. This was not exactly what her mother and father thought of as a levelheaded sort of plan. And dreams of any kind were under suspicion around this house since Uncle August was, above all, a dreamer.

"So I'm coming back empty the seventh time," August said, "and I'm listening to the radio and I'm looking around, seeing which crops are ready for threshing, here and there looking at the cows — that sort of thing. And I begin to think. And you won't believe what I'm thinking about, Iris."

Stella started involuntarily when her mother jerked and opened her eyes. Iris began to fuss with the lace around the collar of her brightly quilted red robe — this animation instantaneous, as if August had just pushed the "on" button of a machine. Stella noticed that her mother's hair was no more respectable than hers tonight. She had managed to find her new glasses with the amber plastic frames, squared off on their owlish edges, but they gave her no protection from August.

"I'm thinking about *cows*, Iris, the cows I been passing fourteen goddamn times already. Finally, it registers — them poor bitches is dying, I says to myself. The hides, I'm telling you Jordy, them hides was hanging like gunny sacks. You could've hung your hat anywheres you wanted to on the poor buggers. Their bones just stuck out like goddamn coathooks and their hair was all matted and the tufts were just a flying in the wind like puffs off an old dandelion."

"Now hold onto your horses a minute, August," Jordan said. As Stella suspected, her father had definitely not been sleeping. "Where in hell are you talking about? You don't mean to tell me every bloody farmer between here and Meada Lake is starving his cows, because it ain't so."

"I was getting to that, Jordy." August raised his thick black eyebrows as if to let her father know he was nobody's fool. He tipped his head back and closed his eyes. The sausage fingers of his left hand cradled the remaining amber in his glass. Louella always wondered how a man with such thick fingers could play the fiddle the way he could. His right hand was still behind his back and kept right on rubbing, as if pain were his lot — external or self-induced, it made no difference; he had to bear it. This constant rubbing had a great effect. She had to hand it to him.

"To get to your point, Jordy," he began.

"I'd be grateful," Jordan said, rolling his eyes away from the dark half-moons which had risen beneath them.

176

"The fact is," August continued, "them cows was on reservation pasture. And the goddamn government give them Indians the cows so's they could start a herd. You and me, Jordy, the goddamn government don't give us a plug nickel, and we're scratching, ain't we, hard as we can, just to make a go of it. Not a nickel, let alone a herd of cows. In fact, they're sucking us dry most of the time."

"I don't give a damn whose cows they were, August. They have to belong to somebody. And I'm not sitting up all night talking politics, neither." Stella was afraid her father had decided to go to bed. And August would leave, knowing he had pushed him too far this time.

But Uncle August groaned and Stella was amazed at the speed with which her mother jumped up and grabbed him a cushion from the sofa and tucked it behind his back. He said she shouldn't have — she was a saint, he said, and she was too good to him, and he was no good for nothing anyway, and he should be moving along so they could all get to bed.

"August Pickard Moon," said Iris, as if she were scolding a small child, "what's a sister for?" Although, to look at them, Stella couldn't tell they were related at all. A difference of night and day, people always said. "You tell us your story, August," her mother said softly, "we're all ears."

Jordan stood up, raised his arms over his head, bent them crooked and clasped his hands behind his head. Stella thought she heard his knuckles crack. He left the table and she thought he was finally fed up and was on his way upstairs, but he headed for the back door, flapping his slippers on the linoleum as he went. He stood at the screen door for a long time, looking up. Then he turned and flapped back to his chair and sat down. "Full moon tonight, Aug," he said.

"I seen that, Jordy," said August, smiling, "and I see your point." His voice was feathery, like the pillow Stella knew her father would rather have had. "It don't matter whose cows they were. The fact is they was starving. That pasture was just about as bald as Jordy here." Her father's hair was totally grey and was beginning to thin, but Stella could see you'd

177

have to be half blind not to notice he was by no means as bald as August. "They even ate the goddamn twigs. I mean there wasn't a leaf on a bush nor a blade of grass nor nothing. That's how poor it was. And the bastards were too goddamn lazy to move them cows to decent grazing.

"The cows were all standing in a row along the west fence with their heads bowed, stuck through the second and third rungs of barbed wire. Twenty-five, maybe thirty head, black and white. All with their tongues hanging out, drooling over a field of alfalfa on the other side. And it was one of the finest alfalfa fields I ever seen, even if I do say so, regardless who planted it, white men, Indians, or Jesus Christ himself."

"'Nough, August," Jordan said, nodding toward Stella.

"Maybe so, maybe so, Jordy, but the fact is them cows were starving. They'd chewed a swath about two feet wide all along that fence, picked her clean as a chicken bone. I bet you couldn't have found a ounce of vegetation on that swath if I'd a paid you a hundred dollars."

"For a hundred dollars, I'd a taken it out of my own hide," Jordan said.

"I bet you would, Jordy. I bet you would. Thing is the poor bitches couldn't reach no further. And I mean, what the hell'd they ever do to deserve that, I'm thinking to myself. Starving to goddamn death right beside the best field of alfalfa on the face of the earth. I mean, they're innocent, the poor buggers; they may not be as smart as you and me but they're sure as hell innocent." August adjusted the pillow behind him, pulling it up higher so that one of the tassels tickled his right arm, just below the armpit. He reached around with his left arm, awkwardly, in a way Stella thought would've hurt his back, but he didn't flinch or groan. Just flicked the tassel up and tucked it under the pillow.

"Well," he said, "the point is I got to thinking about all this on my dry run. I get back to the pit and they load her up and I see that all the other trucks is through for the day. I'm the only one making the last run back. I crank her up and away I go and pretty soon I come to the pasture, which was on

178

reservation land, Jordy, whether you like it or whether you don't."

"This story don't seem to have a damn thing to do with Indians, August, if I ain't mistaken. Could've been anybody. Fact is you don't really know for certain whose cows they were. Everybody around here rents pasture from the reserve, for Christ's sake."

"Maybe so, Jordy. But it seems to me that it do have something to do with Indians. Problem is I ain't quite sure what yet. But why else do you think I brung 'em in?"

"I believe I need another drink, Aug. Throw me the bottle. I'm damned if I can make head nor tail of your goddamn cows, August. How about you, Iris?"

Stella could see her father was fairly near to being lit by this time, which was unusual for him, but her mother had never been one of those women whose greatest need in life is to ride herd on other people. She smiled like a young girl, her freckles like the spots on the photographic negative of a fawn's back Stella had seen in the science lab at school.

"Give him time, Jordy. Maybe he's got something to say," she said.

"Thanks, Iris," said August, humble now and nodding his head toward her. "But I believe I need a little lubercation too before I go on." He poured a drink. Then he pulled a slightly flattened pack of Player's cigarettes out of the back pocket of his pants and lit up. His fingers had grease in the creases at the joints, and his right index finger was yellowed from the top joint to the nail. The nail was completely yellow except for a thin ring of dark green grease around the cuticle.

"Them things are gonna kill you one of these days, August. Why don't you give em up before they put you under?"

"Now Jordy, why'd you have to go and say a thing like that? You should know by now the truth ain't always what a person wants to hear — or needs to. Though I ain't saying it's so in every case. Sometimes the truth is what you have to have, like it or not. I'm only saying it ain't always that way."

They had all but forgotten about his back, especially

August, who had discarded his cushion altogether and now sat straight up in his chair, by turns moulding and poking and pinching the air with his hands as if it were made of bread dough. "Like I say, I'm close to the pasture —"

"I thought you said you was there already," said Jordan.

"And from a distance," August continued without pause, "I could see the pitiful creatures lined up like they was in a bread line for what I guess must a been their fair share of heaven, such as it would be for a cow. And I says to myself, 'No, goddammit! If he don't treat his creatures no better than that, the good old Lord don't deserve em. The old bastard's gonna have to wait.'

"So I shuts her down right then and there but she doesn't roll to a stop till about fifty feet past the fence. I open up the glove compartment, take out my pliers and away I go. I walk a ways back and as I'm going along I'm looking around. And there's not a soul anywheres, no machinery, no buildings, nothing. I don't see or hear no cars. Just the wind and the sun and the high sweet smell of tall alfalfa. And the great big blue sky. Not even a cloud.

"Pretty soon I come to the fence, so I straddle the ditch and spread the wires and I'm through. Took me a bit more time than I figured on account of not having snips, just my pliers. Fact, I caught my finger on one of them metal barbs — like thorns, Iris, only they don't give. Opened the sucker up about a half-inch deep. This here's the scar, Iris." He stuck his afflicted finger about six inches from her glasses so that momentarily Stella saw her eyes cross over to the bottom inside corners of her lenses. "And bleed," he said, "that sucker bled till I thought there'd be no stopping it. I damn near passed out."

Stella leaned forward to get a better look at the evidence, white scar tissue already starting to form a layer over the tiny red fissure in the sausage skin. Even she had a lot of trouble believing that so much blood had come from so small a wound. Her father just bowed his head and shook it back and forth slowly, like an aging buffalo.

"But I opened up that mothering fence in four places, about thirty or forty feet apart," August continued, more agitated now, his fiddle voice almost a half-octave higher. "And when I'm just about finished the last hole, I look back and —" He could hardly go on, he was laughing so hard, slapping his spread thighs and wiping the water from his eyes with the wide back of one hand. " — them goddamn cows was all through the *first* hole. And I been working like a bugger for nothing!" He made a whistle sound like the sound he made with his bow at the climax of "The Orange Blossom Special", high-pitched and thick and compressed. Then he doubled over and held himself in his own arms as if the pain had somehow wriggled from his back around to his belly.

Then he grew serious, as if a dark cloud had moved over the sun in his storybook sky. "That ain't the worst of it," he said, "that's the best. When I get back to the truck, I look up at her box and I see my load has shifted on the way out from the pit. I'd figured as much. I'd hit a bunch of pot holes about five miles back. Anyways, there was little turds of gravel rolling off already just like they do on the new mounds at the graveyard outside town." Then to Jordan he said, "This job ain't much different from when I was grave digging, Jordy. Same kinda thing. Just laying down dirt and stones as far as the eye can see. Anyway, so I climb up to the cab and get my spade out from underneath the seat. Up I go because I have to skim the high part of the load over to the other side of the box or I'll lose most of it before I get up to the goddamn site if I haven't already.

"I no sooner get up there and I'm straddling the hump I have to clear and I look up at the sky and down at my little herd which is having a field day, filling their faces to their hearts' content. I can hear them from all the way up there. And you know, Iris," he said, looking deep into her bifocals as if he were trying to locate her under water, "I never felt better in my life. Just like August Pickard, the fellow Dad named me for, the guy in the balloon that climbed the highest of us all. I know what it must've been like. How he must've felt. Felt that way myself, Iris, on top of my truck."

181

Stella remembered the story of how Grandpa Moon had come to name her uncle. In those days her grandfather spent his waiting time reading the *Western Producer* or the *Farmer's Almanac* — anything handy to take his mind off the back bedroom labour until the midwife brought out something more certain than herself. That particular occasion, the third of its kind in as many years, August said, Grandpa was just clipping the silver metal arms of his spectacles together when the midwife came out with a boy — the first Moon son.

According to August, Grandpa Moon rose from his chair like a king and solemnly declared that if that was the case, then the boy's name would be Auguste Picard, only he pronounced it August Pickard, having had a hard enough time learning to read English, August said, and no one had taught him to read the French. August Pickard, in honour of the man in the last article he had read — the man who had got him through the worst of the waiting. The man who that year, 1932, set the record for having flown the highest of any human being on the face of the earth — in a hot air balloon. And who would later set the record for having sunk the deepest, in a deep-sea diving bell, a bathyscaph, August said. But Stella's father always maintained that August came ill-equipped. No balloon and no bell. And he didn't think much of Auguste Picard in the first place.

"*That* poor son-of-a-bitch," Jordan muttered now, "thinking he went so high. No more than a flea on a dog's back. About the same size hop in the general scheme of things."

But August didn't seem to hear him, and regardless of what her father said, Stella couldn't remember when she had ever seen her uncle's large brown eyes so bright. "No shit, Jordy, I felt so good I stretched out my arms," he said "like this, high as I could, to see if I could get ahold of the big blue bugger and give him a helluva hug. Then, just as sure as I'm sitting here," he continued, bolting upright in his chair, "I slipped. And down I went, just like that." He raised his right hand high in the kitchen air toward the ceiling light bulb, straightened the thick index finger and dive-bombed it onto the yellow arborite.

Stella heard the finger bones crack. "Just like a bloody bird, froze and falling through the winter sky," he said.

"Landed flat on my back. Right on a goddamn bed of gravel. Not your fine stuff neither — boulders, I'm here to tell you. Jordy, you're always the one bitching about your boulder roadbeds — well this was one of them for sure." Stella imagined August on the boulder bed, his muscular arms stuck out perpendicular from his sides, his legs spread, his tee shirt lifted a little, exposing his innocent belly button to the elements. "They say He sees the little sparrows fall, but to tell you the truth," said August, "I got the impression that if He saw me going down at all, He didn't give a damn."

"The going down was bad enough," he said. Stella's mother nodded and shook her head alternately, but always sympathetically. "But when I tried to get up," he continued, "I thought maybe I broke my back. The pain was way worse than when I got my foot caught under the stoneboat, Iris."

Stella could tell her mother remembered by the way she winced. Though Iris was forty-three, Stella knew she had better recall of the minute memories of her childhood than she had of last week. Her father sat like a stone, patiently, as if he were waiting for something, his eyes turned upward, inspecting the ceiling. Trying to figure out a way to straighten out that light fixture, Stella bet. He could never stand to leave a thing off centre.

August continued anyway, undaunted, figuring part of an audience was better than none, Stella supposed. "The pain was so bad at first," he said, "that I figured I'd be better off not fighting it. So I just lay back and looked up at the sky. But all I can see is that great big blue bastard and finally I can't take it no more. So I look Him straight in the eye and I say, 'Jesus Christ, you would've done the same goddamn thing if you'd a been here, now wouldn't you, you son-of-a-bitch?' But I don't get no answer of course. Dead silence.

"By and by I think it could get a helluva lot worse if I don't get off the middle of the road. After what I said, I figured He'd probably send one of them big semis straight up from the city

183

to do the job. And I'd be flatter than the bloody province of Saskatchewan. So I worked at it and pretty soon I could get up. But I still got to wear *that* goddamn contraption," he sighed and pointed at the brace hanging harmless as a limp dishrag on the knob of the cupboard door. "Doctor says maybe I gotta wear it the rest of my life, off and on. Isn't that a bugger? But by the lord Harry, it was worth it!" He stretched, settled back, and smiled.

Stella wished she could clap, but now her father spoke. "August Pickard Moon. You are a goddamn fool." His speech was dangerous, precise, separating every word from every other word with a thin slice of silence.

"Now wait a minute, Jordan," her mother interrupted gently. But Jordan clenched his fist and thumped it on the table, not only making the spoons rattle, but causing them to hop around, clinking metallically, directionless on the yellow arborite.

"You stupid bastard," he said, "you killed them cows just as sure as puss is a cat, just as sure as if you put a shotgun to their heads and blew their brains out. Damn it, August, you should have known better. If you'd a gone back the next morning, all you'd a seen is thirty fuzzy black and white balloons, dead and rotting from the inside out. You might a seen them in the air, in fact, like your Mr. Pickard, they'd be so goddamn bloated. Jordan straightened up, stiff and self-righteous in his chair, his back erect. "There's only one way they could a been saved, Aug," he said quietly. "And that's if somebody'd a gone out there with the sharpest knife he could find and drove it straight through the hides to the high point of the bloat. Saved 'em from their own hot air. But I don't suppose nobody done that."

From the sad, immobile, disbelieving face, Stella could tell that August had not known better, that the fact her father had just brought to his attention had never even crossed his mind. All the cups and glasses on the table were empty now, even the bottle. There was a terrible, dry silence. Stella began to watch her rabbit slippers with the kind of intensity which suggested they might come to life, wriggle off her feet and run back upstairs to hide under the bed where she wished she had been right then. For a while she couldn't bring herself to look back at Uncle August's face. But after a respectable silence, she did. And when she did, she saw that the MacIntosh flush on his fat apple cheeks had disappeared. She looked back at the Three Feathers bottle, half hoping it was full again.

Finally her father spoke, "'S'at it?"

"'S'it," said August, suddenly heavy with his own weight. Stella thought he looked like any man would, just come down out of a storm in a hot air balloon, finding himself on earth again, forced to walk around on two legs like everybody else, at least until the weather cleared, always an indefinite period of time around here. He rose slowly, stood, and lifted his tee shirt.

Iris already held the back brace positioned in air, spread and waiting for August's massive girth. He stuck out his arms and she laced him up quickly. The quicker the better, Stella thought. He rolled his tee shirt down over the brace and Iris helped him into his lime green ball jacket. She plucked his cap from the sofa and handed it to him. He turned the yellow cap slowly with his sausage fingers till the peak was in its proper place and the miniature deer leapt above his forehead where it belonged. He pulled the peak down so that it shadowed his eyes. Stella had never seen her uncle's eyes so dark, that dark black-brown of limb holes on the skin of hard wintered poplar. Her mother was a good foot and a half shorter and a good hundred and fifty pounds lighter than August, but she reached up and tried to circle his trunk with her arms anyway.

"It don't matter, August," she said. "You did what you thought was right. That's the important thing."

"Well, Iris, I don't know about that," he said sadly. "I got no way of knowing if I'm damned or blessed or nothing at all. But I'll tell you one last thing. When I got up from that gravel bed, I felt just as if I was giving birth to a goddamn roll of barbed wire."

185

"Sort of like your story, Aug." Jordan's voice was softer. He had made his decision. "Take care of yourself," he said.

And Iris had made her decision. "Come again soon, August," she said. "Thanks for dropping in and letting us know how you've been getting along."

"Yee-uh, and thanks for the shot, Jordy," August said. He turned and made a stiff, cumbersome exit through the door which Jordan held open, formally, like a funeral attendant. "Bye, Stell'," he almost whispered over his shoulder before he left.

Stella was the only one who had not yet made up her mind. There seemed to be a lot of pitfalls in the business of making decisions. She couldn't even seem to figure out for herself whose cows they were, much less whether Uncle August had been right or wrong about what he had done. She went to bed, but couldn't sleep for thinking about the whole thing. She got up and went to the window which was long and high, two double panes of glass, one on top of the other. Her father already had the storm windows up, even on the second storey. She levered the bottom window up and propped it open with a stick she kept on the window sill. The bottom of the outside frame had a rectangular wooden flap which she now lifted back, revealing three small round holes of cold clear air.

She stood there for a few minutes just breathing and watching the full moon, thinking maybe she might see it move one way or the other, up or down, if she just kept a careful eye on it. But it didn't. The sky was clear and the moon stood exactly centred in the upper pane, balancing a brilliant bull of stars.

The Children's Bin

The first bird sings at half past three. By quarter to four the
shadows leave the hollows of the hills. Another night without
sleep. Another day of work without rest. I wish I could leave
or forget someone died in this room. Not even one room or
one person, for that matter, but many of them. They died in
rooms with numbers on the doors, new numbers layered over
the old ones, in this building once consumptive but restored
and freshly painted. I still have to stay here one more week.

I have a habit of walking in my dreams, like my mother.
But since I've been living here, I don't sleep well and so I do
my dreaming wide awake, in the early mornings walk the
hills of the hypnotic valley like a long dream, narrow in the
breaking east. Usually the valley understands the dark, seems
reluctant to let it leave, pockets shards in the cleavages of
hills, covets and collects the remnants of the night. This
morning the valley is troubled by the reappearing light, like
an old woman who hoards swatches of black cloth in memory
of a brilliant patchwork quilt she laboured over as a girl.
Sunburst.

My mother had a recurring dream. Every night she climbed
a high hill and every night she couldn't make it down, could
never find her way. She said she was a prairie girl. She said
she sometimes dreams it still.

I always make it down again, repeat the pattern every day
so I am certain I can make my way among the cacti and the
grass humped in small mounds on either side of the path.
Passage is all I ask. For all of us.

Yesterday I met a woman on the boardwalk in front of my
pavilion, near the bandstand. She was a small, grey-haired
woman with mottled cheeks and cataracts. She had come
back to see the place, she said. She was happy to see it the way
it is now. I asked if it had changed. Hardly at all, she said,
hardly at all. Except for the dining hall.

She was a patient here, she said, as a child. And did I know there used to be a morgue in the basement of that building over there, right under the dining hall, of all places. I said I did; the drawers are made of some fine wood, oak, maybe.

My friend and I used to sit at the window, she said, and watch them bring the bodies out the back way. There were lots of them. For awhile we kept count on her flowered notepaper. Just for something to do until we were well enough to go to the school on the hill. Just for amusement, I guess you'd say. We had a pretty dark sense of humour in those days. I guess we needed it too. One time they served us ribs for the evening meal. I had had seven removed and she three. So I said she should give me enough to make up my seven and that left her with only the three. I remember we laughed. I wonder whatever became of May, she said. It seems so funny here without the bells. They used to ring them every time a patient passed away. So we all knew. We used to count the bells too, May and I. And tally them with those who went out the back way. To make sure they kept things straight. Still, it's good to hear the children play. I'm glad I came.

You're all right now? I said

Who me? she said, surprised, and turned toward the lake which I'm sure she couldn't see because of the cataracts. Oh yes, she murmured, I'm okay.

I have my own dreams. They're not dreams, exactly, like my mother's, but only seem that way in memory, pursuing me. Before I came here, I decided to write about them but so far nothing comes except the sleepless nights. There is something vaguely amusing about this process. They pursue me and I stalk them relentlessly. Images, elusive while I sit, strong and clear and full of stinging light when I walk among the hills, the grounds, around the lake.

A small girl, four, in a corner bed in the nursery of a city hospital. The name on the bracelet is Velma David. She has had one kidney removed. She is set apart from the other children. Presumably the rest of the children's ward is full. There are few visitors. She cannot remember the last time she saw her mother. Parental visitation is discouraged because it disturbs the children. She spends her days alone. There is a window. There is light shining in through the window. The child is lying on her stomach. There is an inverted metal cradle over her back, a semi-circle of charred ribs. There should be a sheet over the cradle but there is not; it has fallen in a rumpled heap against the wall. She is naked. There are scars on her back. She is very still. She is listening.

There are rows of babies in glass cubicles in the nursery. They are crying, all of them seem to be crying at once. She is very still and listening to their cries. Her eyes are wide and wide and dry and suddenly she sees the babies from a height, rows of babies strapped to boards. Needles in their arms, tubing hooked to bottles in the air. White tape across their stomachs and their eyes. Bruises everywhere. And all the air is full of crying. She cries but can not hear herself above the others.

Later, when she is older, she will think she sees a crucifix, the infant on it taped, needles in its arms, tubing hooked to bottles in the air.

Later still, when she is much older, she will meet a man with long hair and a beard. She will meet him on a psychiatric ward. He will tell her he knows his last name, Christ. But he will sorrowfully say he has lost his middle name — it might be Karensky, he says. He has a sore back, he says, his back is very bad, and does she have a match. She will light his cigarette.

Her back looks sore as well, he says. She remembers babies strapped to long thin boards in the children's ward. She remembers water pouring from the wound on her back, cracked; she remembers floating. He is right, of course. He is right about her back. She will look for resurrection everywhere. She will work with very little light, wander the earth like the ghost of Goethe at his death who cried, "More light! More light!"

But I am unable to write about these things. It is as if there were a concrete wall between the memory and me. Maybe the late philosophers were right: there are no connections. I might have made them up. The possibility exists. Only the walking helps. This used to be a place where people came to heal or die. Perhaps it still is.

On my way down the hill I resolve that I will try to work again today. I stop half-way to look at the buildings nestled in the dawn, a small town. The power plant with its enormous red brick stack, the greenhouses, trade shop, residences, administration buildings, pavilions, all of them arranged just as they were in 1917 when people were first brought here for the treatment of tuberculosis. It's easy to see why they chose this site. The lake, the trees, the air. Coming back I take the road past the incinerator, the land fill and the old dump where you sometimes see the sides of old tin cups, bed pans rusted out, paint tins and half-rotted shoes. Past the snake pit and the gnarled black convoluted trees of the ravine. Past the greenhouses, the residences, the trade shop, and in through the tunnel dividing the main building from the West Wing where the children from the music school are billeted for the summer. This morning, as I have every morning since I arrived, I will turn right, move toward the West Wing and climb the stairs to watch the children sleep.

Drum.

David heard the drum first. Then he heard the horn. The flute. The drum again, this time the thundering drum. The drum and clarinet, a trilling which tickled his neck. He wriggled and tilted his head as if some big hand were tickling him just beneath the rim of his hair, as if he could squish the big man's hand between his chin and head and stop the tickle. But in a way he didn't want to stop the tickle or the hand because it reminded him of his dad. Because it was fun to be tickled along his spine, under his chin.

The trumpet again. David mimicked it, moving his mouth but making no sound. He looked over his shoulder as if he were thinking of doing something wrong. The nurse was gone so she wouldn't make him stop. She was the one who told him there was no sound. David answered the trumpet out loud. Giggled. Boom. Boom. Then together, all of the sounds together but he couldn't answer them all at once so he only sat, his jaw slack, his face pale, his large blue eyes round as the blue marbles his mother gave him the last time she had come to see him.

He had rolled them around in the children's bin, then rolled them out through the water spouts, two small holes at the base of the concrete walls of the bin to allow the water to run off the balcony. The holes were like eyes, and if he lay down on the balcony floor on his stomach, he could see outside the bin, the walls of which were taller than he was. Even on tiptoe, he couldn't see over the wall. Only if he jumped but he was too tired to jump anymore. Besides, the nurses didn't like it when you jumped. Or made trumpet sounds.

Down on his belly, squirming, he watched in silence as the blue marbles rolled out the spouts, down the little hill and disappeared in the bright green grass. Every marble, one by one. Gone. Swallowed by the long expanse of sloping lawn he hardly remembered from the day he had come to this place, a long time ago. Only remembered in daydreams the board-walk which wound all around the place from one building to another, past the bandstand, making it look like a little town. But not like Trestle; it was more like a far away town, a painted town in a picture book. He liked the boardwalk because the boards thumped hollow with every step you took. He had jumped then, too, but his mom had said he was too tired to jump so he had stopped. There had been big spouting sprinklers on the lawn which made a whishing sound. He could hear them now from the balcony, could smell the short wet grass.

Sometimes he remembered the lake at the end of the long lawn, remembered how he had begged to swim in the lake. *Oh Mom, please,* and *just this once.* But no, she said, stooping to look at his face, cupping his cheek hard with her hand as if she had never touched it before. Which made him afraid. She cried and even Dad cried and all he had asked was to go to the lake. All he wanted to do was go swimming that day they came to this place. Because it was a very hot day, really hot. Even Mom and Dad said so in the car all the way down from Trestle.

But when they cried he was very sorry he had asked at all. Though he couldn't figure out what he had done wrong except maybe look out the car window at the lake and wish he could go down to the water in his red and white trunks. Maybe that was it. He had left his bathing suit at home, forgot.

They had packed his clothes in the middle-size suitcase. It was from the set. It was the one his mother always used when she went to Saskatoon to see Aunty Cloe. It was dark blue and it had white stripes around it and a hard, shiny top. The inside was light blue and slippery to feel. It had puckered silky pockets on each side and a kind of wrinkled, silky piece of cloth that hooked the hanging clothes into the top half of the case. But he didn't have any clothes he had to hang up. He only had his sweater and some shirts and two new pairs of trousers, one blue and one black. Also new undershirts and shorts and socks. And when they got to Regina, Mom and Dad had bought him a pair of pyjamas with horses on them and moccasin slippers with a kind of fur inside and fringes around the outside and strings that tied on the tops to keep the slippers on your feet. But they weren't packed in the suitcase. They were still in the store bag and Dad carried them up from the parking lot when they got here.

When his mother had finished packing his suitcase, she asked if there was anything else he wanted to take and he said his shovel and his wheelbarrow that Grandpa gave. But she said no, he wouldn't be able to use them just yet, not for the time being. She always said that, for the time being. What did it mean? But she promised she would bring them along later when he had had his rest. What about books, she said. Yes, he thought that would be good. So she put in the books he brought to her from the shelf above his bed. He brought three books. *Favorite Fairy Tales*, *The Ugly Duckling*, and the book he liked the best. It was called *The Pied Piper of Hamelin*. It had a picture of a castle on the front and about a billion rats running around the castle. At the top of the picture were the faces of a bunch of little kids from a long time ago, and at the bottom was a picture of a silver pipe with about a trillion little black marks coming out the end of it. The little black marks were the notes, his mother had explained, and they were a way you could make people see music. He had told her he would have used a drum to scare away the rats if it had been up to him, not just a little pipe. A drum like the one Uncle Floyd used in the Legion parade. Yes, she said, she thought a drum would do nicely too.

But when he wanted to go swimming that day, he knew he should have told her to pack his swimming trunks instead. He never read his books anyway in this place. It wasn't the same. He had left his bathing suit at home, forgot. Sometimes that sort of thing made his mother upset. But not Dad; usually not Dad. In the car he got mad at both of them and he started to cry. When he was quiet again, he tried to figure it out. But he couldn't do it, figure it out.

Finally he thought it was because he was only a little boy. Sometimes his mother said he was only a little boy when he did something wrong and that made it all right somehow. But sometimes she said he was a very big boy. Like now. She said he was a very big boy, she knew he was, and Mom and Dad had to leave him for a while, and she just knew he would be a real big boy for the nurses and try very hard to be good, now wouldn't he.

Yes he would. He said he sure would. And he expected her to smile. But it only made her cry a lot harder and he couldn't figure that out either, though most of the time he really did believe he was a pretty good big boy and could figure most things out.

They took him to a place where there were ladies in white

dresses and white shoes and white hats and all white stockings. And then they gave him to these ladies and they said good-bye; Dad not even stooping for a hug, patted him on the head and held his own head way up high so he couldn't see his face. Then they walked away, leaving him behind. And he ran after them, but one of the ladies ran after him and caught him very easy because he was too tired.

At home, he remembered his mother telling him he was a very tired boy and he had to have a long rest and he had to go away to rest. And he said no. He would just go lie down on his own bed and when he got up in the morning he would be all better. But she shook her head.

She picked him up and held him on her lap. Sometimes now he thought he was too big a boy for that. But he liked her lap, so sometimes he thought he was only a little boy, after all, and it would be all right. She spoke very soft. He had to say, "Mom, you'll have to speak up! I can't hear a word you're saying," the way she did to him sometimes when he was talking too soft. Then she said very loud that they were going on a trip, they were taking him to a hospital where people went to get better after they'd had a little rest. And he told her no, he thought he'd just go up and lie down on his own bed.

He heard a sound like little bells. A xylophone. He had one in his own toy box. You had to hit a row of coloured pieces of tin with two sticks that had wooden knobs on the end. The sticks came in the same package as the xylophone. He got it from Aunty Cloe last Christmas. Then a *blaaat* in his head, big horns, like elephants. Dad had told him what sound elephants made and had made the sound himself so David could hear. He had laughed. Sometimes Dad did it with cow sounds too, and moose.

"David Gwyn, you better come lie down," said one of the ladies who took care of him in this place. And he knew he'd done something wrong. Nurse, he called them now. Nurse put you to bed over and over and over again. That's mostly what she did, put you to bed what seemed to David like all day and all night. And she gave you medicine and fed you,

194

but on trays, not like your mother did. Nurse was not your mother.

His mother came to visit him but after she left, it was as if she had never been there. Sometimes he dreamed he'd never see her again. Sometimes he dreamed that she was dead and couldn't move and couldn't talk and couldn't come to see him ever again. He woke up soaked in sweat as if he'd wet the bed and he cried and called out, "Nurse," toward the still, dark hallway.

"Come on now, David, I'm not going to ask you again. Come in and lie down on your bed." He did. This was the nurse he had told about hell and god who lived up in heaven. He told her god and hell were friends but sometimes they fought. She hadn't argued with him about that. She followed him into the room where his bed stood white as anything he'd ever seen, the blankets, sheets, even the bed itself a white steel arch with bars, white as teeth. He climbed up on the bed and lay down.

"I think it's time we had a little talk," she said, closing the door behind her. "Now tell me, David," she said, "what do you see when you look through the holes on the balcony? Why are you doing that?"

"I'm trying to see the lake."

"Well honey, you can't see it from here anyway. And we've told you before it's not good for you to be lying on the cold floor, right?"

"Right." The orchestra had followed him in. A drum roll in his head, then a clarinet.

"It will make you sick, right?"

"Right." Another drum roll, speeding up until he had shut her voice out altogether and lay on the bed, his damp head settled on the white pillow, his eyes fixed on the ceiling, white.

"David. David Gwyn," she touched his arm and he rolled around to look at her. "Try not to do it again, will you do that for me. You try and be a big boy and don't do that again. Listen," she said, "what is it you hear in your head?" Toots and flutes and violins. "David? David?" Louder, "David

195

Gwyn." He looked at her. "Why don't you play with the other kids any more? Are you feeling bad again, you feeling pretty sick?"

"I'm not sick, I told you before. I only need a rest."

"All right, all right, little man, don't get your dander up. So why won't you play with the other kids?" The drum and flute together now, a cymbal too, a horn, another violin.

His jaw slack, he looked thinner to her. Tomorrow he would be weighed and the doctor would see him. She made a notation on the chart. He imitates violins and drums and all manner of musical instruments. On the balcony, he refuses to play with others his own age. He grows too thin.

His mother and father came. They saw him in the Recreation Room that day. A door opened onto the concrete balcony where the children played. Those who could no longer play had been wheeled out in their beds for the air, which was the cure. The door was a dutch door and the top was open for the air.

David would not speak but only sat in the chair, dangling his feet over the edge, swinging his legs, swinging his legs back and forth, gazing toward the light of the half-opened door. His mother tried to hold him but he sat rigid on her lap except for his swinging feet, swinging faster than before, as if he'd done something terribly wrong. He turned his head so he could see the balcony door and the light.

His mother wore a mask, a white mask which covered her mouth and muffled her voice, making it sound very far away. She asked him many questions. So did his father, also wearing a mask, kneeling on the floor in front of them, one arm around his wife, one big hand resting on David's thigh. At first he tried to make him laugh. He whinnied like a horse. Then he tried to make him speak. Then only catch his eye.

Before, when they had come, David would sometimes cry and carry on and beg them to take him home with them. This time he did not ask. This time the nurse drew them aside and told them the doctor had made a referral to another doctor, a different kind, someone who would try and find out what was going on inside David's head. She said he no longer uttered a single word and refused to play with the other children. He imitated instruments, she said.

The next time they came, they found him confined to bed. The nurse had wheeled him out onto the balcony where he could see the sky through a canopy of leaves and needles, spruce, maple, apple, elm. On one side he could see the tops of hills, a fragment of the rim of the valley. His mother brought him grapes and Chiclets but he would not eat. When evening came, they wheeled him back into the dim room. He was very thin in the shallow light. His mother's lips were dry. She kissed him on the forehead which was hot. His hair was almost wet, the small white ears like shells. She straightened and went to open the top of the dutch door, leaned out and looked across the grounds toward the row of long pavilions half hidden in the shadows of the hills. There were pipers from Regina on the lawn. He had been a very good boy, the nurses said, the whole time.

Shortly the children will wake and make their way first to breakfast, then to their lessons. They will be carrying bassoons and French horns, flutes and clarinets, violins and music stands. They will be walking with their friends on the board-walk and racing around on the grass. I'll watch them from the sun porch off my room. When I'm tired of trying to work, I'll leave my desk, move out to the porch and press my face against the screen so I can see. For a while I'll stand and listen to them tapping out patterns of sound with their feet on the slats of the wooden walk.

Now I move into the lower West Wing through the stair-well door, making sure it doesn't slam and wake any of the children before it is time. On my right, a sign is tacked to a door. Eva Bauer, Oboe. On my left, a sign above the door marked Recreation Room. The room is large and full of percussion instruments, kettle drums, xylophones, smaller drums of all kinds. There is a plaque on the wall. "Children's Recreation Room Donated Through The Kindness Of The

Swift Current Ladies Auxilliary". This used to be the children's ward.

There is a row of dutch doors which open onto a concrete balcony. Sometimes the children practise here, out in the fresh air. All of the windows on this floor are lower, the doors smaller, the old washrooms designed for children. An autoclave has yet to be removed.

By nine o'clock, the air will be full of music, the buildings alive with flutes and violins. Admittedly some squawks and shrieks. A horn, a clarinet, a drum, all together. When I first came here to write, a friend of mine who is also a poet drove out from the city to see me. "Why on earth can't they all play the same tune?" he asked irritably.

"They do," I replied, "but not necessarily at the same time."

"You'll be stone deaf by the time you get out of the place, Velma."

"I don't think it's all that serious, John," I laughed. "Anyway, wasn't it Beethoven who said on his deathbed, 'I will hear in heaven'. And he was as deaf as they come."

The children rotate through the school at two-week intervals. I have attended their final concerts all summer long. They are held in the open air in front of Pavilion 31. Last Sunday the sun was so bright it hung like a flower in the mouth of the tuba, the outer rim reflecting a ring of spruce, maple, apple, elm.

This is the day the parents come to take their children home. The lawn in front of the administration building is littered with their luggage, pack sacks, music cases, totes. Some of the parents take pictures, move in and kneel near the orchestra to get a closer shot of the particular child. The orchestra is arranged in rows according to instrument, not the size of the musician. Consequently, some of the children do not appear in the official photographs. The pages of their music flap in the wind, held to the music stands with clothespins. I am amused by this innovation.

Last Sunday they played Bach, "Come Sweet Death", which struck me as an odd but appropriate selection in this particular setting. "This is a short piece with sustained notes," the conductor said, "and not here played under ideal circumstances; but we will try and fill the void with sound," he had added, conducting the air.

Tonight there will be a faculty recital, "Andante and Rondo" by Doppler, "Calm and Anger" by Richewandowski, "Intrada" by Otto Ketting, and Sonata (Movements 2 & 3) by Saint Saens. Next week there'll be pipers on the lawn.

In the evening, after my transcription is done, I'll walk the hills again, stopping from time to time to turn and watch the lake swallow the sun. I'll stay at the summit for a long time because from here I can see far down the valley on both sides, can see the lakes on either side of this one. From here I can see three of the four lakes in the Qu'Appelle chain, Pasqua and Mission; Echo is below. I can't see Katepwa from here. It is miles to the east; it's too far. At the summit the valley climbs onto a wide plain, flat as the hand of a man, where grasses blow and the sky holds both the sun and the moon at the same time.

On my way down, I'll stop halfway and sit until the lights come on in the buildings below, tentative as stars. From this distance the students are invisible as those who died. It is as if the buildings breathe, keep their own time. With the last of the light I'll walk back down to the valley. Exhausted, as usual, and unhappy with the little I have been able to do, I'll climb the stairs, enter my refurbished room, lie down and close my eyes. After a while, I'll get up and try to write what only seems.

The first bird sings at half-past three.

The Bid

Cassie left the work unfinished on her desk. She could not remember making a conscious decision to leave. She couldn't remember selecting a destination, had no previous plan of which she was aware. Nevertheless, she was on her way home. Not to her apartment on 25th Street, but home. North.

The campus was unearthly quiet in full term. This is the only difference so far, she thought. A stillness in the air. Not unlike the ordinary stillness in the fall but not the same somehow. She pulled out onto College Drive at the Memorial Gates, registered a numb, synthetic calm.

She had taken nothing with her. She had been researching certain linguistic transformations, changes in usage. St. Mary of Bethlehem Hospital in London to Bedlam, for example. Stages of transition. Initial compression related to convenience — Bethlehem. To Beth'lem. Then a colloquial modification, a conversion primarily due to dialect. Bedlam. Not a bad example of inversion, either, she had reflected before she left her office, before the news had come.

Over the bridge. No bottleneck. The others must not have had time to collect themselves, or perhaps they were merely staying where they were. The river metallic in its bed, the banks a riot of fall, the leaves like twirling yellow coins, the swoop of gulls.

On her left, the Bessborough Hotel, the prairie castle; even the fairytales she remembered hearing as a child had to go some to surpass the pink and white turrets of the Bessborough rising out of the early April river mist, pink and grey, she on the Broadway Bridge on the number four bus, her mouth a small round yawn. Over the arches of the bridge carefully concrete drawn on the map of a comfortable farm roughly a million square miles around. Her childhood wrapped in a hazy high blue dome. She had never known hunger, had never seen a gun.

On Hallowe'en she carried a collection box for UNICEF and, after an evening under the streetlights, a controlled dark interrupted at regular intervals with a beacon on the corner of every block, she had turned in her copper coins, fancied she had cured the children blind and halt and hungry, covered with sores and scars, come from other lands, their hands outstretched as she had seen them on a poster one clear morning in her school. Which was new. And brightly lit with many windows which in winter gave out on the snow. The school had a goldfish pool near the entrance to the girls' cloakroom and a wishing well where you could stop and look at the beautiful fish when you came in from the cold. Often she would stop there before moving on to her home room. She stood and watched the goldfish swimming around and thought about wishes, about "The Fisherman and the Goldfish" and other fairytales she had heard or read from far off lands.

Pushkin. A. Pushkin was the man who wrote that one, her teacher said. Remarkable how a little detail like that will stay with you, she thought now, smiling, for nineteen years later, half a world away, she had seen it again. "The Fisherman and the Goldfish." A. Pushkin. In the largest bookstore in Leningrad. On an educational tour.

She had been there with a group of teachers from the prairie. In the days when Russia had opened up again, relaxed a little. Salvage and restoration everywhere. Even in Moscow. The magnificent golden turrets of the churches within the Kremlin Wall, right off Red Square. Their preservation had taken her by surprise. The icons of Rubeloff, the eyes of Christ burning among the columns of lapis lazuli and malachite, hovering over archways above the wooden doors, under the domes of fresh gold leaf which shone like a cluster of suns beneath the high blue frost, just as before. The previous year she had taken the West Coast tour, Disneyland, Monterey, Big Sur, San Francisco. And three years before that, the Oriental tour. Impossible now to believe she had actually been there, stood in each place. Remarked to herself the marvellous circumference of the earth, the expanding dimensions of the corporeal universe.

How had she come to be thinking like this again when she swore she wouldn't dwell on what she could not change. She would concentrate only on the immediate goal, imagined herself walk in through her mother's door and stand before the fragile cabinet, spend whatever time was left peering through pearly glass inspecting the porcelain set of Snow White and the Seven Dwarves, the two-headed Stavanger troll and all the other bric-a-brac. The elves. One new, in a red hat, holding a lady bug. Cassie had brought it back from the Black Forest. The leprachaun from County Down. The Honolulu girl whose grass skirt swept the china cupboard glass, appeared to lightly dust the oak floor of her shelf. And beside the dancing girl, two old farmers made of straw stuffed into miniature denim overalls; one stood, one sat on a small, three-legged stool made of wood. Now she knew. Turning right at the bottom of the bridge, she knew exactly why all of this had come unbidden back. The Bessborough. The Bess-borough backward through the fairy tales, fast forward to St. Basil's and Red Square.

By the time she had passed the old Sion on Idlewyld Drive, she knew she would be too warm driving in her coat. This morning she had worn the cocoa suede with the mink trim. She pulled over to the curb and took it off, folded it over her arm and placed it carefully on the back seat which was black, warm from the sun. She wiped her brow, brushed her brown bangs away from her eyes. She returned to the front of the car, got in and pulled away again, passed the turn-off to the Master Bakery (ordinarily she would have stopped there and picked up bagels for her mother). The thought of the bakery reminded her she should be hungry by now. She had had no lunch. But she wasn't hungry. Under the circumstances, how could she be.

She caught up with the traffic at last, bumper to bumper out on the highway, and so hot in the car, stuffy, but if she opened the vents, she would get all the exhaust. She rolled her window halfway down. There was still frost on some of the fields although the sun had melted most of it off. Almost all the crops in swath, the harvest late this fall. These fields may as well be the whole world, she thought. And then she was struck by an odd and inappropriate thought. She was pleased that she could now see well, especially now. The blue bell sky bright, the right colour, the clear consistency of childhood skies.

Late last spring she had had something go wrong with her eyes. A kind of inversion of vision. Everything dark appeared to her as light, and all the places common to the light presented darker than a swallowed star. She had been utterly terrified throughout that time. Almost three weeks. The Coutts-Hallmark image of a butterfly on her calendar had metamorphosed into a sinister creature not unlike a leech. Or a medieval winged beast. Everything awry. A print of "The Potato Harvesters" hanging in the foyer of the library became a pack of ghosts reaping god knows what deadly fruit; the winged caps of the stooping women were all she could see, their dark bodies lost for a time like priests in the dark and umber fields which before her very eyes turned blizzard white. Over which hung the now black wings of reaping things. A configuration of the mind as much as sight, finally. There had even been a time toward the end when she wished she couldn't see at all.

But now especially, she was grateful for her sight, relieved she was able to see well. She knew all the towns on this line. She'd been over the road so many times before. Their order a personal litany — Dalmaney, Langham, Borden, Radisson, Fielding, Maymont, Ruddell — At Langham she read the sign. "Repent: Acts 3 —" something or other, the print too fine to read at this speed. "Of what?" she asked out loud, "Precisely what?" she almost yelled at the blue Ford in front of her, furious. On the sign there was a rudimentary picture of a clock like a cardboard clock on a kindergarten wall used to teach children to tell the time the old way, where there was a past, a present and a future, all together, time one round, comprehensible whole. These days there were children who couldn't even read such a clock, Cassie realized. Everything was digital now; there was only now. Five to twelve, the old clock read, stopped, but Cassie was gone, halfway between Langham and the next town.

The words were coming numb, undone. The poet was right. The fancy could not cheat so well. San Francisco and St. Basil's. How long, she wondered, how long did she have. How long would it take? The words were coming numb, undone. And the flying off into fantasy would not work this time. The content gone.

Why she would give a damn about the yellow river hills now was a mystery to her. But she did. She still did. She wanted to see clearly, now more than ever. A steady eye. She resolved she would no longer lie, even to herself. And yet she had to confess that part of her wanted to lie. Wanted to imagine a loophole, the eye of the needle, slip through and leave all the others behind.

Which was how it had been for a while now with words, she thought, the living lie. Because it was human and merciful to hide, to long for an imaginary place where the story was done, where you could protect everyone and everything within the spine of a book, confine the evil, give wings to the words of the good. Where magic was with the world again and time was one. Where fantastic creatures walked among us. Elves and trolls and dragons and the lot. And prophets talked. But what would they say now, Cassie wondered. What was there left to say. *I told you so* echoing all down through the tunnel of conscious time. *I told you so. I told you so.* Hell bent for Rangnarok. Their time finally come. What little satisfaction there must be in that, whatever version. For there were, as Cassie knew, many versions and many subscribers to each.

She had not been alone. At first. Those left on the faculty floor had been numb as well. Many did not feel the need for any empirical confirmation, intuitive powers being what they are. For a department whose very existence depended on words, there were precious few uttered and fewer yet were actually heard, she was sure, because of the shock. Articulation dumb and for a certain time there seemed to her to be a high sweet hum in the air, of wings, and in that space of sound, everything around her went on as usual. Someone asked if there was any mail, for instance. Victor placed a paper on Loreen's desk to be taken to the steno pool for typing. It was to be ready for Monday, he said, when he would be delivering "The Word," as he called it, to a group of businessmen on convention. Over his shoulder, Cassie read the title page on the desk. "Linguistics and Commerce." Ironic now, but at the time it had seemed perfectly relevant.

Loreen took the paper and walked toward the door. Cassie assumed she planned to take the paper over to the steno pool, but she did not. She dropped it on the floor. Then she took her coat from the rack and left, never looked back or said good-bye. By that time doors were opening all along the hall, 324, 328, 326; one after another the scholars emerged, up to and including the department head. "I am going home," Victor said. And Cassie left her work undone, lying on her desk.

Langham, Borden, Radisson; Fielding, Maymont, Ruddell. A rosary of towns. And like rosary beads, the towns were similar, one to another. The names of towns. Unlikely litany, her chant. But probably as effective as any other just now. The alphabet would surely do as well, she thought.

They had been given to understand they wouldn't have much time. But if there was one thing Cassie had always known it was that Trestle, Saskatchewan was not likely to be the target of a first strike. This used to be a joke around home. So Cassie figured she might have a couple of hours; if she were lucky, maybe a whole day; if things moved in the manner described in the projections given with various alterations over the years, depending on the oil fields and the proximity of the base. For they had been at this business of projections for a very long time now. Cassie was familiar with the pattern. She had made herself familiar with the pattern, in spite of herself.

Nevertheless, her foot was to the floor. But she did not appear to be gaining on the blue Ford ahead of her. Around the curl of the lip of the hill and down toward the old Borden

205

Bridge, three arches of concrete drawn over the river calm and winding quietly, small brown eddies swirling in the warm, familiar sun. Red willows and the dry grasses on the bank. The berry bushes not yet picked full clean by birds, the canners taken all they mean to do by now. Do down, do down. This was the season of preserves. The sealers whirled. The sealer rings, the rubber rings, everything began to spin. The words were coming numb, undone, just as her sight had come undone before.

Denholm, Brada, North Battleford. Normally Cassie would have stopped here for gas. From the outskirts, North Battleford, too, looked the same as it always had, maybe a winter Sunday afternoon sort of silence. She passed the familiar sign which still amused her. CEMETERY in bold letters on a diamond-shaped sign. A thick black arrow pointing straight up. Why not. In a world where one million three hundred thousand dollars a minute had been spent on building bombs while in the same minute thirty or more children died of starvation or disease, anything was possible. Anything, she thought. Why not. What an obscenity to pretend we even tried. It was true. The fancy could not finally cheat so well. Her prophetic sign seemed pathetic to her now. The cemetery in the sky.

She turned right at Territorial Drive which circled the heart of the city and headed North. As she left the city limits, she remembered having heard a doctor speak one evening in the composite high school here. He was from Saskatoon and she had been on her way through one weekend, on her way to Trestle. He had told them that even if they could fight a limited nuclear war, as civil defence departments would have liked them to think, Saskatchewan would essentially be devastated by radiation from attacks on missile bases in North Dakota and Montana. Not that they'd ever heard of Saskatchewan. Not that it mattered now. Cassie had met many people in other parts of her own country who had never heard of North Battleford. Then again, there were many places in the country she had been unfamiliar with as well.

This had been, after all, the second largest country in the world.

But the good doctor had his point. There really were an astonishing number of people who had thought they were safe up here. Even intelligent people who had paid little more than lip service to the whole matter while there may have been time to do something about it.

"Nausea, vomitting, and diarrhea would occur within a few hours of exposure," he had said. "These symptoms would disappear during the honeymoon period. Then hair would start to fall out and bruises would appear from spontaneous bleeding." No. She had told herself a thousand times before. No. There was no point to this anymore. She would make this an inviolable vow. She would stop thinking about it altogether. She would stop. "An individual will start to die within two to three weeks. Usually not quickly, but slowly by bleeding and from the infections that start to take hold." No. "The very young, the unborn —" No. "and the very old will be especially susceptible." As usual, Cassie thought, and then *NO*. The sweats had taken hold. This time she wished the words would come undone. Scramble. Delete. Erase. Whatever would remove them from her head.

She had promised herself before that she would not think about this or speak about what she had come to know over the years, even to herself. This was a machination of the mind, the memory, the words. As if she were under interrogation in a small dark room beneath a funnel of bright light, listening to her disembodied voice played back to her at an intolerable speed, measured, slow. If only there were a way of erasing the fact that she had known, they had known. For they had known. For some reason this was the part that bothered her the most. If only they had not known; possibly that would have been forgiveable. But to know and still proceed. A trick of her black track mind again. No.

The light was beginning to fade. There was no mistake. She would rather go blind than to say, but it faded into grey hills like ash near Jackfish Lake, just over the first rise but before the descent into Cochin. Just over the rise and then the falling away into all the smaller, countless hills; cattle on a thousand hills, and the image of the promised land gone still and blind behind her eyes.

She began to wish it were completely dark. Anything to extinguish the gold, the ghastly light. The whole country lacquered in it by the time she hit the Cochin Hill, habitually diminished speed as she moved down into the town, toward the shrine.

She was tempted to stop at the shrine. She braked and pulled into the driveway of the church, the gravel rumbling under the wheels of the car. She was intruding, making too much noise. A shroud of silence surrounded the shrine. She parked and got out of the car, started toward the clump of figures huddled around a small white plaster shell beside the lake. The Lady, like an expectorate pearl, remained kneeling, inert, before the plaster cast of the Deity within, all lacquered in an underwater light, grey and yellow. Right now She seemed to Cassie more like La Belle Dame Sans Merci than the Holy Mother of Bethlehem. And when Cassie drew closer, close enough to see the faces of the huddled frightened few, she knew she could not stay with them.

There were old women wearing work moccasins and rubbers, young men with long dark braids wearing high school hockey jackets with crests sewn on the back, the shoulders, the sides. There were men in peaked caps and wide-brimmed straw hats. Young men clutching small girls, their braids secured with red and yellow and turquoise loops of small glass beads.

Cassie had once seen the world champion hoop dancer on the Reservation near Trestle. At the Pow Wow. He had danced the creation. In the final movement of the dance, the imaginary whole fell apart and all the hoops, so cleverly constructed in the shape of a sphere around the body of the dancing man, had dropped to the dancer's feet and the little wire world had disappeared in the tall grass. The people at the shrine were from another Reservation nearby, Cassie thought. It must seem like the second coming of the end of the world to them. They have already seen something similar before. From within. Of this she was sure. But she could not stay. She was intruding, once again. And she knew she could not pray, not now, even with them. She turned away and watched the sun trace the last of the passing day with a grim impersonation of the light.

When she was back on the highway, she resolved she would not think at all, nor would she observe. At least not until she got to the next town. Not until the fall of the actual night. By then it would at least be dark. The twilight was intolerable, the in-between time.

But it didn't work. No sooner had she made the resolution than she began to think: we have all been through this awful day so many times before, in our heads; the dress rehearsals in the press, the poets and the novelists, the old myths: the rather tardy invocations of the high priests of the new myth. Laboratories, shrines. What difference had it really made, in retrospect.

At one point, they saw fit to inform the general population of the onset of the long winter after the event which no one was supposed to mention specifically. The Southern Hemisphere would not be exempt, they said, because of the dimming of the sun, the cold, the coming catastrophic cold. Well then, Cassie had thought at the time, in this part of the world (and in Russia too, she supposed) there is nothing we know better than the cold. And little which commands as much respect. Fire and ice. By a man named Frost, if you please. How do the poets know. At any rate, she thought, ice was not imaginary here, not fragmented myth, although it was sometimes full of light. The day of the triple dog sun, for example. Providing the sun hit the ice crystals in just such a fashion as to fill them full of light. This was true. But with the dimming of the sun, Cassie supposed the ice would be blacker than the clichéd ace of spades. So much for hemispheres. And for her resolutions.

Actually, toward the end, Cassie's family had finally made a resolution of its own because their gatherings had become so grim. Surrounded as they had been with good food, home-made wine, abundant and beautiful children, each other (this must have been the promised land or the closest thing to it, Cassie thought now when she looked back, although she would not have postulated such an arrogant premise at the time), their after-dinner conversations repeatedly engaged, in one form or another, the unspeakable event.

It got so they almost dreaded seeing one another, because of their conversations at such gatherings. They had to set limits. No one was to say anything about *the event* ever again, no matter how many wood lilies bloomed or patches of lady slippers found (and wouldn't it be a shame). The images had, over the years of apprehension, worn thin, become trite, but not the pain. Ironically, that remained intact the whole time. No matter how many fish caught, no matter how many bushels to the acre, no matter how many pounds of blueberries put down for the winter. The event was to remain literally unspeakable.

Not that they actually did anything to prevent it. That was the worst of it. What could they do? They knew people who sent letters to the government and marched against the deployment of various weapons along the way and things like that. But for some reason, they had done nothing at all. Hardly anybody had, when Cassie stopped to think about it now. Hardly anybody all over the world. But for a few brave souls. There was sometimes a price to pay, after all. Green-ham Common, Cold Bay and the like. These were women, mostly mothers.

But before the family ban, Cassie remembered, they'd had convoluted, lengthy discussions. Most of the time Cassie talked to her brother, Soren, who was a man of science. He held no hope for the species but he was of comfort, ironically, to those who had lost the faith, or any faith. Which by that time was most of them. He especially seemed vulnerable to the talk about the end of the world. Cassie thought it might have been because he was so very close to his children. He had one boy and one girl. But Soren could be persuaded to talk about field physics on occasion as well, and he was far more familiar with the concept of infinity, for example, than were many of the others. During those days, he, of all people, had been their greatest source of something which resembled metaphysical hope; though he protested, he protested in vain. For it had been he who had reunited them with the plausibility of eternity and the presence of wonder and all that would remain when they were gone. Soren. Soren had all the wood for his house milled in this town, Cassie thought, as she approached the sprinkle of light on the horizon.

She passed the mill on her right, just before the grain elevators. A sign along the highway said "North to Meadow Lake"; she planned to take the turn after the water tower, the narrow road north, home. But the light from the dim sun setting through the red haze frightened her again although all the way from Cochin she had done well, thought mainly of her mother's cabinet and of the pale, intricate pattern on the Hardanger runner and of the elves. At last count, her mother had forty-three elves. Cassie had contributed many of them herself. Souvenirs of her travels. But the last few miles, the burnt haze of late light through the thickening brush had begun to look like red teeth, the stand of trees a sulfur mouth. So she pulled off the highway into the town and parked in front of the auction mart on the corner of the main street. It was directly opposite the Co-op Store and down from the Post Office. There were many cars and half-ton trucks parked on the main street and on the highway down past the cafe and the motel, all the way down to the burned-out gas station at the far end of town.

The auction was in progress. The side door of the mart was open and a shallow light leaned toward the street. She rolled her window all the way down. She could hear the auctioneer from the car; his voice was like gravel but his words were clear. She opened the car door, got out and rolled the window up.

For a while she stood leaning against the open door, her arms folded across her breast, resting. She discovered she was

211

stiff and the muscles at the back of her neck were rigid. She massaged them slowly with her left hand. What time was it? Anybody's guess, she thought. Her watch had stopped. The auction mart was long and grey, clapboard, a false front facing the grocery store, but this side was long and unadorned. It could have been a barn. She slammed the car door and started walking toward the lighted entrance to the auction mart.

She slipped in through the light and made her way to one of the benches at the back. She sat down near a young woman. The auctioneer's right-hand man wore a red peaked cap and had a long soft face. He held up a sack of onions and a number, 34. The auction was only beginning. The auctioneer was doing food. Cassie had stopped here several times before on her way home and she was familiar with the routine. The food came up on the block first. Bagged carrots and beets and crates of apples and oranges were stacked beside cases of juice and Kleenex and paper towels along three walls of a raised platform lit by two lightbulbs swinging shadows slowly forth and back, back and forth. A woman sat at a plywood table on the platform keeping track with lists of consigned goods lying before her, lined up in the correct order.

The auctioneer was a jovial man, tall and heavy set but not fat. He had a full red beard and a moustache and an enormous bush of wiry red hair which puffed out from under a black cowboy hat. He wore a black silk western shirt with pearl buttons, a red rose embroidered on either shoulder. When he turned and bent toward the onions, Cassie saw he had three roses on his back.

"I want to tell you folks something," he said. "There are three important things a good auctioneer has got to remember, and this is fact. Number one: get good before you get fast. Number two: stay clear so people can understand you. And number three: there is nothing, I repeat, folks, *nothing* in the world which cannot be sold by auction. Which really means there's nothing can't be bought. World champion auctioneer told me that." And then he began to chant, "Whatamibid

whatamibid. Onions. Ten pound sacks. Five to the man in the straw hat. Ten to the Blue Boy Cafe. Five to the lady in pink at the back. Five to the back. Ten more sacks. We've got to move ten more sacks. Whatamibid whatamibid —"

Dazed, Cassie looked around the room. The sound of the man's voice ricocheted everywhere. Her ears rung. A chant for ninety-eight bales of hay, a case of ketchup, a crate of eggs, seventy-five bushels of seed grain, forty gallons of antifreeze and two black calves which bawled outside the double doors to the left of the platform. There were long tables set end to end the length of both walls. A buffet of clocks and burnished copper oil derricks, knick-knacks of all description, monkey-pod salad bowls, velvet paintings, garden tools and spice racks. Butter churns. Depression glass.

The auctioneer hoisted a crate of grapes. He tilted the crate and held it out to the crowd. The grapes were large and dark purple. They were in a California crate. "Whatamibid whatamibid," he bellowed into the microphone. His left black boot caught the cord and he slid a little, staggered back and laughed out loud. "No bid? No bid. They're all yours. Compliments of the house." He laughed again and reached into the crate, grabbed a bunch of grapes and threw them hard. A small brown boy in the front row caught them and ran toward his mother who was standing near the coffee urn at the back with the rest of her people, a dark knot from where Cassie sat.

Everywhere arms in the crowd, waving, reaching out, and the grapes flew from the auctioneer's hands till the crate was empty and the right-hand man passed him a box full of boots and shoes.

"You, Lou" said the auctioneer, pointing to a man in green overalls standing by the wall halfway down the room. "You need these shoes. I know you do. I know that for a fact because I sold you a box of shoes last spring and there wasn't a thing in that box a man could wear, no soles or tongues or laces in a single pair. How about it, Lou? Whatamibid whatamibid. You're too late, Lou," he finally said, sadly. "I got a bid over here. Whatabuy. Lou, my friend," he said, gesturing to him, "another golden opportunity has just passed you by, flew out these double doors over here on my right. Time waits for no one, my friend. Not time. Not my old man time. Don't matter where you live. In Livelong or in gay Paree — (Lou here is from Livelong, folks) — it's all the same to me. In the end." He turned and bent, heaved his black buttocks into the air and undulated twice. Then he was gone. The crowd roared.

Cassie couldn't believe her eyes. The bulbs on the platform swung from side to side. The door through which she had entered slammed shut with the wind and the lights died. But the voice began to rise. "Whatamibid whatamibid —"

An enormous postcard appeared before them, floodlit the full height and almost the whole length of the platform. First the mailing side, the back. "Leningrad, Pisskariovskoye Memorial Cemetery, Statue of Motherland, 1960, Sculptors: V. Isayeva, R. Taurit; Architects: E. Levninson, A. Valyev." Then it flipped over in a flash of light and on the front was a photograph of a statue, a woman carved of stone holding what looked like a net in her outstretched arms. She was elevated on a marble base. A knot of random men and women stood at the base, the backs of their heads to the camera so you couldn't make out a face. But Cassie recognized the stone woman and in her mind she surveyed the half million mounded in mass graves surrounding the monument. Civilians from the siege of Leningrad. Singing floated from the back of the auction mart. A female voice. High and slow and operatic. A dirge. And now Cassie remembered the music too, the chill April afternoon. And the guide who refused to answer whether or not it was true: that the female-male ratio in Russia after the Second World War had been seven to one. (Although you would never have known it from the Presidium, Cassie thought. There were no women in the Presidium. Not one.) They must have thought few people knew. Give us back our sons, implored the stone.

"Whatamibid whatamibid. From the USSR. Complete with birthing rope, the Ring of Glory and of hope," the auctioneer chanted. "This is a motherhood issue, folks. You bet your sweet life. Whatamibid, whatamibid. SOLD!"

The young woman beside Cassie had raised her hand. She turned toward Cassie now and frowned. Her hair was clean and long and blonde. Her face was wet, lit with reflected light. She fondled a tattered quilt in her lap. Apparently she had brought it with her to the auction mart. It hadn't come up on the block. It was made up of patches from the great coats, uniforms from World War One, grey and blue and brown. Canadian coats come home. Four numbers were stitched on a corner square, 1931. It had taken someone all those years to put it together, thought Cassie. Or maybe there wasn't a need until then. Depression. Anything to keep the family going, keep the family warm.

The room grew cold. Then filled with sparks and smoke. "Are you ready folks," the auctioneer began, "from China. Whatamibid for the Harbin Ice Lantern Show. Direct. The genuine article. We got to move this *now*, folks. Everything's got to go." The voice of the crowd exploded in one startled OH. Cassie's and the young woman's among them. Ohh. An arc of ice and coloured light appeared on the platform. A rainbow. And above it an arc of multicoloured fireworks against a dark sky, red and green and purple and yellow and blue. "This ain't chinoiserie, ladies and gents. This is the real thing. Whatamibid whatamibid whatamibid — SOLD! To the owner of the Blue Boy Cafe. I guess that's only right folks, whatdaya say?" The people roared.

Cassie herself placed no bid throughout the auction, although I was aware the whole time that the author wished she would. I don't know which I would say was more difficult, all said and done. Working for Chicken Littles like Cass' creator or for one of their counterparts who have been running around whispering, "The sky is not falling in; the sky is not falling in. I believe you, brother." Neither of them makes the least bit of sense from my point of view. Not that my perspective interferes. The assignments appear to be indiscriminate and right now I am here with Cass and this loony auctioneer.

215

The fact is I, too, harbour soft spots for the Honeyman Dunes on the Oregon Coast and for Tofino and the new Roy Thompson Hall, Vigeland and Mount Hoodna; the Grand Canyon and Madison Square Gardens and, for old times' sake, the wild and steamy two-room suite in that deliciously seedy hotel in the Bahamas. Nonetheless, there are certain things on which I will not bid, regardless of creative pressure, regardless of the apocalyptic vision of yet one more writer. And, although the plaintive quilt may function as a fine image in some ways, I suspect it will emerge that most women have had it up to here with the quiet, fatalistic weeping over the systematic mutilation of human beings, their literal handiwork thus far.

So, for the first time, I refused to deliver the lines assigned — what were supposed to be my last words in this case. For one thing, nothing is so plentiful these days as apocalyptic visions. They are a dime a dozen. The cliché of our time. Nothing easier to imagine (on a superficial level, at any rate) than the logical progression, the obvious end, the earned increment of ten thousand years.

My decision remained firm. Even so, I was sorely tempted twice. In the assignment of this role. In the voice of the character, Cass. It was all I could do to refrain from bidding when the Hermitage came up on the block. I have had many Russian assignments in the past, some in the Winter Palace itself and, over the centuries, I have watched the collection amass from Catherine onward. Lately I have taken a particular fancy to the large canvasses of Matisse, especially "The Dancing Women" series, these because I have recently been in demand for roles which focussed on the liberation of the female spirit. I have also recently been stoned to death because I was wearing perfume in the former land of the former Peacock Throne. Before World War Two, the Russians crated the most valuable works in the Hermitage collection and hid them in the Ural Mountains.

The last temptation came when the whole room started to spin and Cassie found herself peering out over the rim of a large Blue Willow teacup in Disneyland. Tinkerbell was just beginning her ascent over the castle in Fantasyland trailing stardust from her toes which not only took Cassie back to the Bessborough in the fall and the banks of the river of her home town and ahead to the Palace of Congresses in the Russian spring, high in the cold air, the sparkled gown of the Prima Ballerina of the Bolshoi Ballet dancing "Don Quixote" before a sell-out crowd, but also forward again to her mother's home near Trestle and to her china cabinet filled with fairies and with matadors, Snow White and the Seven Dwarves.

It also took me back to the Pacific Rim off the West Coast of Canada and another story I am to be involved with later on. I am to be a man who walks along the sand at night trailing bits of light behind him. A phenomenon called bioluminescence in which light is produced by the aggravation of an organism called phytoplankton found both in the sea and in the sand. The working title is "The Totem of a Modern Man."

Yet I was never as tempted to bid as when the man said "Whatamibid, whatamibid, whatamibid for Disneyland?" Cassie often travelled in other lands and she always brought back something for the kids.

The Lineman

Three minutes to twelve by my time. Pocket watch. Damn thing won't stop. Just like the clock these scientists are supposed to have somewhere in Europe. This clock is supposed to tell how close we are to blowing ourselves to smithereens or something. So what? I mean, what the hell can the little guy do about it anyways, the man in the street, the man in the sticks, like you and me? They figure it's all set to go at high noon, too, only it's about five to twelve on their clock whereas it's already three to twelve on mine.

They gave me this clock when I left the CNR and I have to admit she runs like a damn. Best workings in a clock I ever saw. Swiss, I believe. And the train's coming in right on time. Probably the loveliest sight you ever saw in all your life, even the diesel. Just like a bullet, a sure shot, slipping along the track, clickety-clack, clickety clack. There's just nothing like a bulling engine as far as I'm concerned, steam, diesel, it doesn't matter which to me. I guess I'm a bit peculiar that way. As long as it's on track it's got my vote.

So what's a better way of getting us all back together again than blowing us to bits, eh, right to kingdom come and back again. Misdeal. No deal. Reshuffle the cards for Christ's sake. The way things stand now, it doesn't look as if there's much of a choice anyway, no matter how you cut it. We've just about finished the job — and I have a right to my opinions whether the railway saw fit to retire me or not. I listen to the news.

I always did like working for the railway. Lineman all my life. I never wanted to be an engineer, didn't appeal to me at all. He can't see himself coming the way I can. Too close, if you know what I mean. For me, the best thing is standing by the tracks where I can see things coming, just where I am right now, in this exact same spot. I love the tracks. I just mind the tracks. That's my job. After a while of working for the railway, I got a pattern in my head that covers the whole country. It looks a little like a game of snakes and ladders, as I see it. And it all hangs together that way, you know.

At least that's the way it hung together for a long long time. Still got them patterns in my head, never left me, not one. I bet if you took a picture of my head you'd see them all up there. All the tracks ever laid. Up south, down north (which is where I wound up finally and don't intend to leave now or any other time, not for anybody, not even for my brother Owen from Vancouver who thinks I'm a nut). Anyways, I bet if you took a picture of my head, you could see all the stations, all the crossings, switches, trestles, practically every bloody tie in the province of Saskatchewan at the very least, which is sizeable. Probably a guy working those underground trains in New York City could say the same, just a different place, just a different name.

Now, of course, they got the same thing in the sky. They call them flyways. Thing is, where else was there to go but up. Made a lot of sense to me though I never flew myself. Couldn't bring myself to hitch a ride on anything didn't have tracks attached to the ground, preferably solid steel ones you couldn't help seeing even supposing you were practically blind. Of course, I always had a car for driving back and forth to town and that. I know you can make better time in the air. I don't dispute that. Probably be a damn sight better when we're all flapping around up there together.

The fact is I wouldn't have been any damn good as a pioneer either. This was my time, on the tracks. I belong on the Livelong Line. One side of the fence or the other would have been just as bad for me, pioneers or flying farmers. No. I belonged where I was.

I mean, I don't suppose I'd have been a hell of a lot of help back then any more than if I was to go and get a job with Air Canada today. The thing is these explorers and pioneers had nothing whatsoever to tell them where they'd been. They had to travel light, you see, coming over on the boat — and even then hardly anything made it through the trip overland, broke or lost, most of it, they say. And those poor buggers, even when they got to where they stopped, it didn't mean nothing but a number. They still didn't know where they were.

It must have been hard, you've got to grant them that. Must have been a bitch back then, not having any tracks. Whereas now, as I say, they got the patterns on the land, they got the patterns on the sea, they got the patterns on the sky, right up to the moon and farther still. The other day they up and gone to Saturn. They got almost all the patterns now. I don't say all, but most. Too many for my liking. In fact the only one they need's the pattern for the head — maybe that'll tell us why there's all this craziness around. And not just here. It's all over the place. I seen it on TV. I seen it on the news. No place left that's not screwed up somehow as far as I can see. Whole thing's crazy as a bag of hammers.

Friend of mine north of town has got himself one of these satellite systems and you wouldn't believe what they got on the dish these days. This friend's got a receiver nearly as big as his barn and, as I say, you wouldn't believe what they show, even to kids, unless you seen it for yourself. When you stop to think of some of the things that are whirling around the world all day and all night long, depending on which side of the earth you happen to be on, you've got to know there's something drastically wrong.

Now they're taking up the tracks. All up and down this country — not just mine, not only the Livelong Line. We're not alone here. Figure they don't need tracks no more, not ones you can see, at least. So they took them up. Even took down the trestles, took up the ties, everything, if you can believe. For what? Little piles of charred old ties marking mile after mile. It's a wonder they didn't send a truck up for the cinders.

Taking down the elevators too. Pool-A anyway. Pool-B burned down in the fall. Somebody set a match to it if you can imagine. They figure it was Indians but I figure it might have been one of those seismic crews out on a tear. There's been a lot of them around here lately. Everywhere you look you see their trucks. Wild buggers too. They don't seem to care. I guess most of them don't live around here. They just don't seem to give a damn what happens to the place. I hear they get good wages, though. The oil sure pays, that's a fact. Which is more than I can say for the railway. Course back in the old days I guess there were some said *they* run roughshod too, didn't give a damn about the land, the real land I mean, not the paper kind you buy and sell blind without ever setting eyes on it. Ship her east. Ship her east. They say there was good money in that too.

I'm not complaining now either. What would be the use. Besides, I had my job to do and I did it. You've got to stand somewhere and do something. My job was on the Line. I got my clock and that's all right. It's what I like. No better way of spending time to me. And it doesn't really matter what you do, you see things go past, clickety-clack, clickety-clack. Even the engineer.

I'm not sorry I did my time on the railroad back in those days. Better than now. No way a man can keep track of anything now, the way things are. What with the speed and everything up in the air and all. I figure the best thing a man can do is sit back and enjoy the sights. You don't even need a ticket to get to Smithereens.

Now, of course, the time has come to get back on the job. I just started back on the line. Only it's not so easy this time round, not so cut and dried.

We used to have a little verse we'd say to the young people up here. It was the easiest way to teach them to remember the towns on the Livelong Line—

> If your HEARTSWELL
> You'll LIVELONG
> In a FAIRHOLME
> In GLASLYN

Sounds so peaceful, so hopeful. You'd have thought they all held tickets to heaven the way they named the towns. You have to admit they must have been bushed by the time they got this far. Maybe found all they ever really wanted in the first place was some holy peace and quiet.

Over the years a lot of people told me this was a stupid way to live, standing beside the tracks, taking my own sweet time, doing whatever I liked, minding my own business, as long as I did my job. But you know, the place was on the map, part of the pattern, you might say. And somebody's got to live here for Christ's sake. If they can do it up south, then why the hell can't we do it down north. There's places in the world done it already. I seen it on TV.

Besides, somebody's got to work for the CNR. Not that it's going to make much difference where in the world you work or which side you're on or what you think or what you are pretty soon. We're all in it together in the end. Goddamn thing's got us all by the throat, every mother's child.

I'm pretty well as close to being a free man as you can get without being altogether dead. Just standing up here in the bush by myself, doing my job, not talking to a soul. Nobody there to listen anyway, nobody there to hear, as far as I know. What's to say? Why talk about nothing. Yackity-yack, yackity-yack. At least I never heard anyone call my name, till just lately, of course, when I was called back on the line. Then up I got and went to work again.

My brother, Owen, moved to the coast years ago now. And he used to say to me when he'd come home, "How can you stand it stuck up in the bush where you can't even see what's going on. What's the point? All your life looking up the line, looking like you could see all the way to Trestle with nothing but a pair of ordinary eyes."

"I'm waiting for the train," I says.

"Waiting for the train," he spit. "Even when it comes Jack Lune, you don't know where it's been."

"I do," I says.

"You only know the names, Jack — and afterward you don't know where it's gone," he says.

"I do."

"You only know the names. You never been. It's nothing but a bloody backwater."

"It's on the map," I says, "and as long as it's on the schedule, the train's got to move through here to get to where it's going. In that respect the Livelong Line's no different from any other line."

When they abandoned the line and took up the tracks and the ties, Mrs. Harrow over at the Post Office wrote and told my brother I'd started back to work. Which is why he came back a couple of weeks ago. This time he just stands and watches me, careful and kind of puzzled. Kind of worried too, I guess. A doctor, he says, could help me some. He figures I should go back to the coast with him. To a place called Riverview. Real peaceful gardens and grounds, lots of roses, he says. And he says, "Look around you, Jack. There's nothing here. You can't tell me you're going to miss that."

I wasn't born yesterday.

Imagine. My own brother. Jumps a plane in Vancouver, then hops a bus in Saskatoon and comes all the way up here to tell *me* they abandoned the line (as if I don't already know) and I should start packing and fly back with him. And I have to tell the son-of-a-gun the whole thing all over again, "Like I told you before, Owen, I got called back." But he won't buy it this time either, just turns away, gazes down the track and whistles "I am calling you-ou-ou-ou," under his breath, into the wind. So I almost give up.

Only before he leaves I tell him a rhyme the little girls here in Livelong use in the spring when they're skipping rope —

> Over the trestles, over the ties
> Everyone's living, everyone dies
> Somebody's telling everybody lies
> Who-ooo-ooo?
>
>> Clickety-clack
>> Clickety-clack
>> Clickety-clack

And then I tell him he might just as well move on down the

line without me. Because this is as good a place as any to do what I'm doing. I says, "You got your ticket and I got mine."

Finally I says to him by way of explanation (because it's pretty clear to me from where I stand), "Look here, Owen, just because you can't see the pattern don't mean there isn't one. Even Air Canada can tell you that. You never heard of flyways or nothing? You just got off the plane.

"And just because they took up the tracks don't mean there's no train. In fact I believe it's right on time, according to my watch. Which is why I came. And why I've been here all along."